A Woman Lost

Mary /
Always follow
Your dreams.

T.B. Markinson

A novel by

T. B. Markinson

This book is dedicated to my partner,
for everything.

Chapter One

"Hello."

"I'm getting married."

"What?"

"I'm getting married."

"Peter, it's"—I rolled over in bed and looked at the clock—"five in the morning, on a Sunday. I'm not in the mood for a prank." My entire body ached; I'd been awake most of the night.

"It's not a prank, Elizabeth. I am getting married."

I sat up in bed.

"We're flying in next week to have dinner with Mom and Dad. She wants you to join us."

"What?" I rubbed my eyes, wondering if I was dreaming. My brother and I were not close in any way. I didn't even know he had my home phone number. Was my number listed? And I was shocked that he'd admitted to his bride-to-be that he had a sister.

"Madeline wants to meet you. Oh, and bring Meg." He sounded upbeat. It was four in the morning in California, an hour later here in Colorado.

"We broke up." I tried to keep my voice calm and quiet.

"Oh, my gosh. When did that happen?"

"Two years ago."

A long, awkward silence followed.

"Oh … wow … that's too bad. Well, is there someone else?"

I wanted to tell him that girls, let alone love, just didn't fall from the sky. Instead, I looked over at the naked woman in my bed and chuckled. Well, maybe girls did fall from the sky. Good grief, she could sleep through anything. She always said her mom was intentionally loud during naptime so she would be a sound sleeper; apparently, it worked.

"I'm not ready for that." I didn't mean I wasn't ready to date. Obviously, there was a woman with me, but he didn't know that on the other end of the phone. I meant I wasn't ready to introduce anyone to my family … again.

"Hopefully you will still join us. Maddie is so excited to have a sister."

I thought to myself *fuck no. No way.* I wasn't going to have dinner with Mom, Dad, Peter, and now a fiancée. *No fucking way. I'd rather gouge out my own eyes and then eat them.*

"Um … sure … where should I meet all of you?"

"At the club."

Of course! The club. I should have known. Why would they go anywhere else?

* * *

I grabbed my chai from the barista in the coffee shop, and announced, "Peter called."

"Who's Peter?" asked Ethan, and poured an insane amount of sugar into his coffee before we sat down at the table. He always ordered the special of the day, never a fancy drink with a shot of this or two squirts of that. He loved coffee with sugar and none of the hoopla.

"My brother, you ass."

"Oh, my god! How is God?" He straightened his

starched shirt. To say he was fastidious would be an understatement.

"He called to tell me he's getting married. Oh, and get this: he wants me to join him, his fiancée, and my parents for dinner." I blew into my steaming cup of chai. The vapors fogged up my contacts, and I had to blink several times to see again.

"You said no, didn't you? Tell him you have a violent case of the clap and if you sneeze they'll get it."

"I'm meeting them Monday night."

"Jesus! You do like your public floggings."

"He asked me to bring Meg."

Ethan giggled as he stirred his coffee. "Talking to you about your family always makes me feel better about my own messed-up situation."

"Yeah. When I told him we broke up, he actually said, 'Oh, my gosh.' Like he gives a crap."

"He did not! He always was such an ass. *C'est la vie.* So bring the new girl."

"Sarah? Are you kidding? She's not ready to meet the family. And besides, I insinuated I wasn't seeing anyone, so I can't bring her now. It will seem desperate."

"Don't you mean *you* aren't ready to introduce her to the family, and other things, I might add?" He gave me a knowing look.

"That could be the case." I smiled and took a huge gulp of my chai.

* * *

Sarah and I woke up before the alarm trilled, but neither of us wanted to crawl out of bed yet. She reached over and ran her fingers through my hair. "What are you doing today?"

I rolled over to face her, gazed into her quizzical brown eyes. "Not too much today. I have to teach." I stroked a strand of hair off her cheek. "Tonight I am having dinner with my family. Oh, and I'm meeting Ethan for coffee today before

I head down to Denver. You?" My finger moved down her face to stroke her breasts.

She stared at me for a moment in disbelief, and then she bolted upright. "We have been dating for almost a year, and you have never had dinner with your family. I didn't think you were even in contact with them."

I ignored the comment that we had been together almost a year; actually, it was closer to six months. And the first three or four months included only a few casual dates. However, it was not the right moment to remind her of that.

"My brother is in town with his fiancée. We're having dinner to welcome the poor girl into the family."

"Oh." She stared at me with sad doe eyes. "I better get ready for work."

I watched her walk into the bathroom and step into the shower. Then I rolled onto my back and placed the pillow over my head. "Shit, shit, shit."

* * *

Normally, Ethan and I met at the coffee shop on Saturdays. But when he couldn't make it, we rescheduled. Meeting him would help take my mind off my impending family dinner.

"My god, Ethan, she looked at me like I had just run over her dog and had then backed up and run it over again." I sipped my chai and stared out the window at College Avenue, the main street of Fort Collins. "I'm so screwed."

He nearly choked on his coffee. "Can you blame the girl? Not only did you plan dinner with your family and not mention it for a whole week, but you are meeting your brother's fiancée. She has to be wondering why you didn't invite her. Hasn't she moved in with you?"

"N-no," I stammered. "Not completely. She's still paying rent at her place. She just stays with me every night … and most of her stuff is at my place, but it isn't official. We have not moved in together." I turned away from his knowing glare and stared at the other patrons in the coffee shop.

"How long are you going to string this girl along?" He shook his head. Not a hair was out of place.

Ethan and I had been *really* good friends at one point. We worked together part-time at the college library. I was just starting my PhD program in history, and he was starting his in English. Since we studied the same time period, we talked a lot about our classes. After working together for two years, Ethan quit the program on completion of his Masters. He opted for teaching at a high school in a neighboring city, and we didn't see much of each other.

But then, out of the blue, we met for coffee. We had so much fun we started to meet for coffee once a week, and continued to for two years. Then both of us hit rough patches in our lives. His marriage was on the rocks. My relationship fell apart completely. We became therapists for each other.

Our weekly meetings switched from discussing our research and learning, to bickering, fighting, and calling the other person on their shit. We had fun doing that, too. No matter how brutal we were to each other, the next week, both of us would be right on time. Dysfunctional: yes. Bizarre: yes. But we needed it. Or at least that was what I told myself.

We would tell each other things we wouldn't dream of telling our loved ones or partners. We knew each other better than our significant others did, indulging in an odd, sometimes intrusive intimacy that never went beyond our coffee dates.

"I don't know what you mean." I eventually answered his earlier question, staring across the table at him, watching his nervous habit of pulling at the corner of his neatly trimmed moustache. *How does he make it so narrow and precise?* I wondered. We sat in the back corner, hiding from a gaggle of college students in the shop. "I'm not stringing her along." Again, I avoided his eyes. Instead, I stared over at the barista, who was making a Frappuccino.

Ethan took off his Coke-bottle-thick glasses and cleaned them on a serviette. "Yes you do. Don't try that shit with me,

Lizzie."

"I don't know what to do, Ethan. I care about her, but when I look at her—sometimes, I don't feel anything. When she's sleeping at night and I've got insomnia and can't sleep, I get annoyed that she is in my bed. The other night, I was on my back and she was up against my left side with her leg draped over me and her arm around my chest."

He frowned impatiently and motioned for me to get to the point.

"Wait, that's not the weird part." I continued. "She was holding my earlobe! The arm she had draped over me—she was holding my earlobe. And I started to think: *why?* Why was she holding onto my ear? Then I couldn't stop focusing on the fact. I mean, who does that? Who holds their girlfriend's ear while she sleeps? Who?" I threw my arms up in the air in exasperation. "She wasn't rubbing it. Not feeling it. Just holding it. I don't think I slept at all until she rolled over. Who holds someone's ear?" I took a nervous sip of my chai, embarrassed by my rant about Sarah. Why did it even bother me so much?

"I'll admit that it's a little weird. But it doesn't seem like something you should obsess about. She probably didn't know she was doing it. Do you think maybe it had something to do with your insomnia? When you can't sleep, you focus on anything and everything you find annoying. You're a freak, and so is she. You two are perfect for each other." He gave his southern smart-ass smile.

"Very funny. You might be right." I took another sip and said, "Oh, have I mentioned that she has started to say 'I heart you' now."

He raised his delicate eyebrows.

I shook my head. I really didn't want to tell him why she had started saying that, but then I caved. "We'd only just started saying 'I love you' and I wasn't very comfortable saying it, and then I saw this hanger in the bedroom, from the drycleaners. Anyway, I noticed that it had an advertisement on it that said 'We love our customers' but instead of the word love, it had a heart. What is up with that?" I detoured again, hoping he'd forget I mentioned it. "How did the heart come to symbolize love? … Really, it's just a muscle."

He motioned for me to stop stalling. "Oh, all right. Right after seeing the hanger, she was getting ready to leave, and I said, 'I heart you.'"

Ethan burst out laughing.

"She thought it was adorable. Now it's kinda our thing … I guess." I rolled my eyes.

"Lizzie, I didn't know you were such a romantic." He batted his eyes at me.

"Yeah right …" I took a deep breath. "Are these feelings and thoughts I have about her ... about us ... are they normal?"

"Not after this long. Maybe after twenty years, but you two should still be in the honeymoon phase. You should be running home from classes so you can rip her clothes off. Staying up all night talking in bed, naked bodies intertwined." He wrapped his gangly arms around himself in a weird contortion.

Ethan was slim, tall, effeminate—the kind of man everyone thought was gay. He adamantly refused he was, but being such a scrawny, open-minded Southern boy did not help his cause.

"Naked bodies intertwined," I mocked. "Tell me something, oh relationship guru, why should I listen to you? You hate your wife."

Ethan had been married for four years. A year ago, he confessed to me that he wanted to leave, but he hadn't told his wife yet. Deep down, I think he's afraid his friends and family will think he is gay for sure.

"Low blow. Very low blow, Lizzie." He pulled his keychain from his pocket. A nail clipper dangled on the chain. Ethan proceeded to clip one of his nails, and then he carefully put the keychain away.

"Do you expect anything else from me? I despise my

own girlfriend. Why would I treat my best friend differently?" I raised my chai in his direction in salute, and said, "Yes, my friend, I am a bitch."

"Oh, I never doubted that. That, my dear, is why we are best friends. You are a bitch, and I am a stuck-up bastard from Mississippi. Neither one of us has any morals or standards."

Despite being a Southerner, when he moved out west, Ethan had soon discovered it was better to lose his southern accent—especially as an English major. His department was full of snooty kids who believed they were elite students. His accent made them look at him like he was a Neanderthal who had married his sister.

I took another sip, and watched the traffic crawl past. "She wants us to go to therapy," I confessed. "Apparently, I don't open up enough. She wants us to learn how to communicate effectively—whatever the hell *that* means." I waved one hand in the air.

Ethan spat out his coffee. "Are you serious?" He wiped his mouth with a napkin and then used it to mop the coffee off the table. "You're just now telling me this. What did you say?" He couldn't stop laughing.

"I said I would think about it. Who do you and Lisa see? Is it working for you two?"

He threw his stir stick at me. "God, you *are* a bitch!"

"And you, my friend, are a wimpy intellectual. Throwing a stir stick at me … Ooooo … I'm scared." I threw it back at him.

My cell phone interrupted. "Speak of the devil," I said, as I looked at the caller ID. "I better get it." I opened the phone, and said in an overly cheery voice, "Hey, baby, how's your day going?"

Ethan whispered, "Don't overdo it."

I quickly covered the mouthpiece and kicked Ethan in the shin.

He yelped louder than necessary to get back at me.

"Yeah, I'll be leaving in a few minutes. I don't want to be late. My mother can be a bitch sometimes."

"That's where you get it from." Ethan giggled. I kicked him again, much harder this time.

"Ok, honey. I won't be very late tonight." I mumbled, "I heart you," and then I closed my phone. "You can be such an ass," I told Ethan. After chugging the rest of my chai, I stood up. "So what's the excuse tonight? A pulled groin muscle so you don't have to screw your wife?"

Ethan stood too. "Nah, I used that one last week. I may have to slip her some sleeping pills."

I stopped in my tracks on the way to the trash can. Turning back to him, I asked in disbelief, "You don't actually do that do you?"

He winked at me and threw his cup away.

"So," Ethan asked, as we walked to our cars, "when was the last time you saw your folks?"

"Christmas, or one of those holidays. I'm not sure if it was last year or the year before."

"It's August. Are you going to be okay tonight?"

I shrugged. "Don't know. My mother can be brutal. She'd have no qualms about ripping the heads off of kittens."

"Well, good luck. Call me if you need to talk. By the way, I dig the pinstripe power suit. You look hot." One hand leaning on the roof of his car, Ethan gestured with the other to my clothes. "I wouldn't worry too much about losing Sarah. You're beautiful, and successful, and I think she loves you. Oh wait ... she hearts you." He snickered.

"Thanks. I think." I shook my head. "Are we on for Saturday?"

"Of course. You know Lisa thinks we are having an affair?"

"So how long are you going to string her along?"

"*Touché.*" He stooped and climbed into his car, turned the engine on, and then rolled down the window. "I heart you." He waved limply and smirked as he drove out of the parking lot.

I watched him pull away. Briefly, I stared at my key in the car door. Was I sure I wanted to do this?

Chapter Two

When pulling into the parking lot, I tried to remember the last time I had been to the country club. I used to eat there all of the time as a child. The food wasn't even that good, but that didn't matter to my folks. All that mattered was that people saw us there several times a month. I always hated it. We lived in Colorado, not on the East Coast, for Christ's sake. Our family didn't come over on the *Mayflower*.

The hostess watched me approach and asked in a snotty voice, "May I help you?"

"Yes I'm meeting the Petrie family for dinner?"

"Oh, are you a friend of the family?"

"I'm the daughter." I smiled wearily and straightened my blazer to look more presentable. I had my hair down, instead of in my normal ponytail, and I had put on eye shadow and mascara. Usually, I only did that when I was out with Sarah, but even then, I preferred the *au naturel* look—or at least that was my excuse.

The hostess tried to soften her bitchy look. "I didn't know they had a daughter."

I'm sure she didn't. My parents didn't really spread the

news about my existence.

"I think I am early, though." I changed the subject.

"You aren't early. Your party is already seated." She tilted her head like a confused puppy.

I looked at my watch and noticed it was a quarter to seven. *Nice, Peter— telling me the wrong time.*

I followed the hostess through the maze of tables surrounded by overdressed, pompous asses. I recognized several of them—women who had been under the knife and hadn't changed in the past ten years. Or maybe I didn't recognize them. Rich women were a dime a dozen here. It was how they made it known they had money. How they made themselves feel superior whenever, in fact, they felt inferior.

"May I ask what time my party arrived?" I quickened my pace to keep up with the lanky hostess.

She turned to me, obviously puzzled. "I think they've been here thirty minutes."

Bravo, Peter. Bravo. Tell me 7:30 p.m. and then show up a little after 6:00 p.m. I should have known.

As the hostess led me to the table, she asked, "Do you live far away?"

"Not really. I live in Fort Collins."

"Oh … you're right. That's not very far." She looked disappointed in me.

"I'm working on my PhD. I don't have a lot of free time to hang out." Why was I justifying myself to this girl?

"That makes sense."

Well, thank goodness the hostess accepted my excuse. As if I needed that haughty girl's approval for my absences from family dinners at the club. We reached the table.

"Here's the last member of your party." The hostess plastered a huge fake smile on her face.

"Right on time, Elizabeth." My brother stood to shake my hand. I'd never understood why he always insisted on shaking my hand, or on using my full name. Everyone else called me Lizzie.

"Hello, Peter. I thought dinner was at 7:30." I stared at him angrily. Then, following a deep breath, I blurted out, "Hello, everyone. I hope you haven't been waiting long."

Mom answered, "Half an hour. That sounds about right for you." She took a sip of her scotch.

"Peter told me dinner was at 7:30 p.m." I threw him another nasty look. Mom's statement had already pissed me off. I was usually the annoying person who showed up early for everything. Whenever I went to a party, I had to wander around the neighborhood so I wouldn't show up too early and annoy the host. Yet, Mom preferred to think of me as a complete and total fuck-up.

Peter smiled at me, his usual backstabbing, shit-eating grin. It was one of those charming smiles that could make most women believe anything. His clean-cut appearance helped. Tonight, my brother was going casual; his tie was loosened. "I remember telling you 6:30 p.m."

I turned to the woman I assumed was my brother's fiancée. My mouth fell open; I think my jaw may have even hit the floor. Oh, my God! She was stunning, easily the most beautiful woman I had ever seen. Finally, I found my voice again. "Hello."

I reached out to shake her hand and she rose graciously and accepted it. Long blonde hair. Stormy, ocean-blue eyes. Flawless skin. Very little make-up. And arched eyebrows that suggested a devious side.

My brother's fiancée flashed me a smile that almost made me wet. "I'm Madeleine," she said. "But my friends call me Maddie."

Madeleine. What a beautiful name.

"Very nice to meet you, Maddie. People close to me call me Lizzie." I shot a look at Peter, hoping he'd get the hint. I despised being called Elizabeth.

"Geez, my bad. I'm sorry I didn't introduce you two. I don't know where my head is." Peter kissed his fiancée before sitting back down and placing his napkin in his lap. Why he had stood that long in the first place baffled me.

"I apologize for my tardiness," I said.

"Always the schoolteacher, Elizabeth." Peter tsked.

I took my seat opposite my father. A man of few words, my father gave me a nod of acknowledgment. I knew he wouldn't talk much, if at all, during dinner. My mother, unfortunately, hadn't learned from him.

"Oh, it doesn't matter," stated Maddie. "I'm just glad that you made it here. I hope the drive went well."

"Yes. Quite pleasant. It's always good to get some time to relax."

"I definitely know what you mean. I love to drive. Whenever I'm stressed out or need time to think, I jump in my car and drive my worries away."

"I hate driving. Too many fucking assholes on the road," said Mom, following her statement with another swallow of scotch.

"Maddie, do I detect a southern accent?"

The blonde flushed and looked over at Peter and then at my mom. "Well, I was born in Alabama, but my family moved to California when I was in high school."

My mother bristled. Not only was she from the South, but she was also from California. My mother always believed herself to be a great woman, ranking herself among the Rockefellers and Carnegies. The idea was preposterous, of course. She was a small town girl from Montana who had married a man who became wealthy. Before that, they lived in a trailer. It was hard not to say anything to ruffle my mother's feathers, but I didn't think that was the best way to get to know my future sister-in-law. Everyone else in the family already hated me. It would be nice to have one ally in the bunch. I wondered why Peter had taken such a risk. He had to know Mom wouldn't approve of a Southerner. I bet her family had connections to his work.

The waiter came over to take my drink order.

"Don't bother offering her alcohol," said Mom. "She can't drink." She raised her scotch glass and took another slug. Then she set the glass down and smoothed her navy suit.

The suit covered the whitest shirt I had ever seen, and a pearl necklace ringed Mom's over-stretched neck at the collar. The pearls and shirt were stark against her olive skin. The combined effect was Mediterranean.

I ordered a Coke. "It's not that I can't drink, Mother. I don't like to drink when I have to drive." Her statement embarrassed me. My mother always referred to my preference for drinking only at home. I was such a lightweight that one drink gave me a buzz and forced me to find a cab. In Fort Collins, there was no cab service; hence, I never drank in public.

After the waiter left, Peter said, "Seriously, though ... a Coke? Come on, Elizabeth. Why don't you try some of this wine? It's one of the best they have to offer."

Peter always pretended to be a wine connoisseur, swirling his glass, sniffing it, and doing all of that annoying rigmarole to show off his knowledge. I hated wine. Every time he offered me wine, I reminded him that I loathed the stuff.

"Peter, you know she shouldn't drink wine," Mom scolded. "She's already been pulled over for a DUI." Another gulp of scotch.

"I was not, Mother!" I looked over at Maddie, horrified of what she would think. "I used to deliver newspapers when I was an undergrad, to help pay the bills. To save time, I rolled the papers while I drove my route. There wasn't much steering going on, so I got pulled over. Once the cops realized I was just working, they let me go. I was never arrested or cited for anything."

"They never gave you a ticket? Not even for reckless driving?"

"Nope. They were very nice about it. It was almost like we had a bond of some sort, since we all worked really crappy hours. The hours were brutal."

I watched my mother raise the scotch glass to her lips again. I had once seen her drive away and lap the house eight times before she was able to get out of our neighborhood. She kept driving by the house as I watched from the front window. She hit the same trash can twice. And I was the fuck-up with alcohol?

Peter asked, "You can't stay the night?"

"No. I have class first thing in the morning. It'll be easier to head home tonight."

"I thought college professors got to pick their own schedules." His smile was truly smeared all across his face.

"Professors do. Doctoral students do not. We have to teach the classes no one else wants to teach." I tried not to bristle. His condescension got under my skin, but I had learned over the years not to show any weakness around my family, or they would pounce.

"What classes do you teach?" asked Maddie, giving me another bedeviling smile.

"I teach Western Civ," I said, gazing into her gorgeous blue eyes.

"I have to admit that history wasn't my best subject." Her smile this time was shy, sexy, but she never took her eyes off my face.

I reciprocated. "I hear that a lot. It surprises me that people aren't fascinated by it. But I think the problem is that too many teachers concentrate on the facts—you know dates, places, and names. I want my students to appreciate that history is the greatest story ever told. It has violence, sex, love, romance, adventure, betrayal, drama, comedy. It has it all."

"You teach your students about sex?" sniggered my mother, The Scotch-lady. The extravagant diamond on her ring finger nearly blinded me as she raised her tumbler to her mouth again.

Out of everything I had just said, *that* was what Mom honed in on.

"I don't get out the dolls or anything." I rolled my eyes.

"But sex is important to history." I swiveled my head in Mom's direction. She took another sip of her drink and looked away.

"What do you do, Maddie?" I turned back to the blonde.

"I'm an interior designer."

"Really? One of my good friends studied interior design at CSU. Her program was tough. She pulled all-nighters all of the time."

The waiter arrived with my Coke and I took a sip. Secretly, I wished I could add a shot of rum, maybe two shots … or three.

"Yeah, a lot of people think all we do is put pretty throw pillows on a couch. They have no idea how complicated it is." She laughed.

"You should see her work; it's beautiful." Peter leaned over and kissed Maddie's cheek. I wasn't sure if he was marking his territory or being affectionate.

Could he be jealous that Maddie and I were hitting it off? I wouldn't say that fireworks shot into the sky for all to see, but there was a connection. Was it apparent to all?

"I'd love to see your work. Any chance you brought your portfolio?"

She laughed and shyly rolled her napkin. "Yes I did. I have an interview here in Denver."

"Maddie and I are moving back home," Peter casually blurted out as he reached for a roll from the middle of the table.

I looked at him, curious. "Oh? I had no idea."

He had been living in California for the past five years. I only saw him for the occasional holiday, and even that seemed excessive. During all those years, I had not visited him; nor did he visit me.

"We want to be closer to family now. We're hoping to start our own family soon." He raised his glass to our mother.

I looked at my mom, then at my laconic father, then back at Peter. Poor girl. Poor kid.

Then a thought crossed my mind. Could I seduce Maddie?

The waiter came over and took our food order. While the others ordered, I took in Maddie's charms. Madeleine. Captivating. A name befitting such a magnificent creature. Her beauty could rival the Greek goddess Circe. How did Homer put it in *The Odyssey*? Circe was the most beautiful of all gods. Yes, Maddie could rival this goddess.

Seducing my brother's fiancée would normally be a repulsive thought to me. Yet, I wasn't repulsed. Did Maddie cast a spell on me? What would my mother say? I bet it would be priceless.

Chapter Three

I held the steering wheel with my left hand and dialed Ethan's phone number with my right. I hoped no cops were around, but it was after ten at night on a Monday, so there wasn't much traffic on the highway.

"She's gorgeous."

"What?"

"She is, without a doubt, the most beautiful woman I've ever seen."

"Lizzie, who in the hell are you talking about?"

"My brother's fiancée. Ethan, she's hot. No, wait. Hot is too vulgar for Maddie. She's a goddess who should be fed grapes while reclining on satin sheets."

"Then why in the hell is she with your brother?"

I could tell I had woken him up; he wasn't coherent yet. Maybe he had taken the sleeping pills by accident. "Beats me. I still think he's a total ass. Are you already in bed? You didn't give your wife sleeping pills, did you?"

"No. I didn't have to. Are we still on for Saturday?"

"Yeah, I'll give you the full report then. Good night, my sissy of a friend who can't tell his wife that it's over."

"Bitch."

I smiled and pressed my foot down on the gas pedal. I wanted as many miles as possible between me and my family.

* * *

Back in my own bedroom, I leaned down and kissed the top of Sarah's head.

"How was dinner?" Her voice sounded like ice that had started to crack but had refrozen instead.

I kissed her crown again. "I survived. Sometimes I forget just how much I despise those people."

"What's she like?" Sarah was in bed, lying on her side with her back to me, flipping through the TV channels.

"She seems nice. Cute, funny, charming—like all of the other women Peter has dated. How was your night?" I stripped down to my underwear and bra and climbed into bed behind her.

"Pretty quiet. I worked on some reports."

She smelled of lavender. "Did you take a bath? You smell good."

"Yeah. I had a stressful day."

"I'm sorry." I kissed her neck, felt her body respond as I worked my way up to her ear. She pressed her body closer to mine. I ran my hand down her body and slid it back up slowly. Sarah's breathing became heavier. Rolling her onto her back, I kissed her lips, slowly at first, then passionately as if our lives depended on it. I climbed on top of her, slowly rubbing one hip between her legs. She arched her back and moaned.

"You're so sexy." I gazed into her chocolate-dark eyes and brushed the hair off her face. Then, I leaned down and kissed her again. Her neck. Her nipples. All the way down her stomach. When I reached her lower stomach, she moved her pelvis urgently, arching her back. I quickly peeled off her pajama pants. When I tasted her, she moaned again. My lips moved over the inside of her right thigh, then her left. The thrusting of her hips told me she wanted more. I wanted her to want it, so I continued to kiss her thighs. Then I found her clit—darted my tongue across it. She dug her nails into my shoulder as I took her in my mouth. I slid my fingers inside her, thrusting them in and out of her slowly, tasting her simultaneously. Sarah's hips thrashed more urgently. There was no holding her in place. It took some work to keep my tongue lapping at the right spot, but I knew she couldn't come unless she was gyrating like mad.

Her hips were moving so fast now, grinding into my face, so that it took everything I had not to stop. I loved that she got so fucking wet, literally pouring into my mouth as my fingers slid in and out of her so easily.

Her nails scored my back again and then she arched completely, her legs shaking. I stopped licking but kept my tongue against her clit to heighten the sensation of her orgasm. Slowly, her body began to relax. I slithered up her body and lay next to her, wrapping my arms around her.

"Feeling a little less stressed?" I whispered into her ear.

She laughed, her sexy bedroom laugh. "Yes, but I'm still mad at you."

I kissed her head. "And you have every right to be. I was an ass, a self-absorbed ass."

"At least you can admit it." She pushed me onto my back and climbed on top of me, leaning in to kiss me. She whispered, "Don't ever do that again."

"I won't."

"How early do you have to get up in the morning?"

"Don't worry about that. I'll skip my bike ride. What else do you have in mind?"

She smiled, but didn't answer with words.

* * *

"Elizabeth?"

The clock read six in the morning. "Yeah, Peter, what's up?"

"Apparently, not you. I thought you had an early class." I

could almost smell his smugness. My brother was the type who wanted others to know he was a very busy man. He would tie his shoelace without stopping, too busy to pause for something so insignificant.

"I think eight o'clock is early. Is everything OK?"

"Yeah. Maddie and I enjoyed having dinner with you. I have to take care of some stuff today and it will take all day. Maddie has never been to Fort Collins, so I was wondering if you would show her the town. How many classes do you have today?"

I rubbed my eyes. "My last class is at eleven. I can meet her after that."

I gave him directions to my office and then hung up. Rolling over, I noticed Sarah was not in the room. I listened, and heard the shower running. When I wandered into the bathroom, there was no sign that she had heard the phone. In an instant, I decided not to tell her about my afternoon plans.

* * *

The classroom door opened and I watched as Maddie slid in and took a seat in the back row. Carefully stepping over the cord to the overhead projector, which displayed my lecture outline, not wanting to stumble in front of her, I asked, "Can anyone tell me what the word *defenestration* means?"

A sea of blank stares.

I chuckled. "Of course no one can! That would mean one of you actually *did* last night's reading. I should give you guys a pop quiz on the material." I paced back and forth in front of the class before settling behind the podium.

"Nah, you don't want to do that. It would be more work than just telling us. You would have to think of questions, then grade them, record them, pass them out," said Joshua, the most talkative student in the class.

"But, Joshua, you forget that teachers love work, especially historians. We love to read, write, grade—you name it. We love tedious stuff." I glanced at my lecture notes to focus my attention on my class, and not on Maddie. "Defenestration means to throw someone, or something, out a window."

"Are you going to throw one of us out a window?" joked Joshua.

"Don't tempt me, especially after last week's tests, which I have graded and will return after class." I saw some looks of panic. Good. "But we are only on the first floor, so it wouldn't be much fun to toss one of you out. Besides, I am not that strong.

"In 1618, some noblemen, upset after King Ferdinand violated their religious beliefs, went to the royal palace and threw two of the king's advisors out of a window. The gentlemen survived by landing in a pile of manure. Yes, manure." I stopped and looked out at the students. Some smiled. Others just looked like they wanted the whole thing to be over. I didn't dare look at her. "This incident started what became known as the Thirty Years' War, which goes to show how some wars came about by really inane incidents. But any one of you who has been in a relationship knows that most fights start over petty things. So, the next time your significant other gets angry when you yawn at the mere mention of his or her parents, and he or she flips out because you think they are dullards and what's going to happen when you have children, etcetera, etcetera, etcetera, just remember wars have started over such trifling matters. And remember what Winston Churchill said: 'Those who fail to learn from history, are doomed to repeat it.'"

I looked at my watch. "All right we'll go into the details about the Thirty Years' War next time. Remember to do the reading. You should have the novel *The Adventures of a Simpleton* read in its entirety. It will behoove all of you to read it. I am not going to say any more on the subject." I walked over to the whiteboard, wrote the words Pop Quiz, and underlined them. "Now, if you want your tests back, come and get them."

After spreading the exam books on the table, I stood back for the feeding frenzy. Maddie sashayed towards the front, and I felt my heart flutter wildly. I had thought she looked amazing last night, but today she was in jeans and a white T-shirt that didn't suggest a good figure—they downright proclaimed it for all to see.

"Lizzie?" One of my students, Jill, interrupted my fantasy. "Can I set up a time to go over the test with you?"

She got a D, I remembered, and I gave her an encouraging smile. "Of course, Jill. I won't be in my office today, but will you be on campus tomorrow? I can meet with you then. What time works for you?"

"I'm done at two tomorrow. Does that work?" Her head drooped in shame.

"Yes, I'll be there. Please bring in your exam so we can go over it together." I gave her a pat on the back.

I turned in Maddie's direction and smiled, but a few more students gathered around, wanting to talk about the test results. I answered their questions patiently, all the while staring at Maddie out of the corner of my eye. If only my students knew what thoughts I was having, they might not think of me as a stuffy historian.

Finally, we were alone.

"I'm so sorry to keep you waiting."

"Gosh, don't apologize. It was fun watching you with your students. They seem to like you."

"The feelings are mutual. I adore all of them, even the smartasses." I gathered the uncollected exams and placed them in my bag.

"Hope you don't mind my barging in on your class."

"Not at all. I hope you weren't bored."

"Did those guys really land in shit?" She chortled.

"Yeah, they did. There are some things that you just can't make up." Realizing I was staring, I said, "Do you mind if we stop by my office before we skedaddle?"

"Lead the way, professor." She motioned for me to walk

in front of her. *God, did she know how sexy she was?* I picked up my bag and slung it over my shoulder. Then I led her outside. It was a little after noon and the campus was packed with students and professors, running to and fro.

Fall had come early, and I could smell it in the air, but it was still seventy degrees outside. Colorado was known for having the most days of sunshine during the year; today was no exception. To the west, the Rocky Mountain foothills were set against a brilliant lapis sky, scattered with clouds. The leaves were beginning to speckle yellow and red.

"Where did you go to school, Maddie?"

"I went to a small college in California. This campus is huge. I'm amazed by the number of students." Maddie gazed around with her mouth slightly agape.

We walked past one of my favorite spots on campus, and she stopped to look. I watched her as she read the quote carved along the top of the bench. "If I have been able to see farther than others, it was because I stood on the shoulders of giants," she said, her tone curious. Her eyes moved to the sculpture adjacent to the quote. It was a pendulum.

"It's about the scientific revolution," I offered.

"What does he mean?" She gawked at the glittering pendulum.

"It's Newton. He's exclaiming he would never have been able to discover gravity if it weren't for all of the other scientists who paved the way for him. He's giving credit to a long line of people who asked questions and who risked their lives by challenging the Catholic Church." I paused and looked up at the pendulum again. "This is one of my favorite places on campus."

"Because of the scientific revolution, or because of pendulums?" She smiled as she spoke.

"The revolution, in a way. You have to admire people who stood up to the leaders and said, 'I think you are full of shit.'" I hesitated for a second, and looked away from her, up at the puffy white clouds. "I have personal reasons as well."

Her eyes returned to my face. I could tell she was expecting me to continue. Commanding me to.

"I'm grateful to those who have advanced science and medicine. I have an illness." I didn't like sharing this weakness with people.

I noticed a flicker of panic in her eyes. "N-no … it's not terminal," I stammered. "But it's an illness nonetheless. Before the medicine was developed, the outcome wouldn't have been fun. Now, all I have to do is take a pill each night. Simple as that."

"I didn't know. Peter never said anything."

"I never told them." I never referred to Peter or anyone in my family as an individual. They were always a "them" for me. I glanced away from her penetrating stare and motioned which direction we should take to my office. "It's not too much further," I said.

She smiled, but a hint of sadness crept into her eyes.

We walked on, to my office.

* * *

"You'll have to excuse the mess," I said as we entered my office. "I can only work when surrounded by chaos." Papers, open books, and journals were spread everywhere, including the floor and all available chairs.

"I can tell you spend a lot of time here." She pointed to all the teacups and dirty plates.

"You could say that. I'm trying desperately to finish my dissertation. I would like to close this chapter of my life. And I work better here than at home." *I would like to close this chapter? Come on, Lizzie! Who in the hell talks like that? Stop being such a pompous ass.*

"Your girlfriend must get jealous?" She gestured to the framed photograph on my desk.

I'd never really considered that the picture made it clear we were in a relationship. Sarah had given the picture, with instructions to put it on my desk. It finally clicked why.

"It has been the source of a few fights. She thinks I'm a workaholic."

"What do you think?" She crossed her arms.

"Oh, I know I am … but I love what I do. Researching makes me happy, even more than teaching, and as you can see"—I waved to all of my crap in the office—"I immerse myself in my work." I paused to set my bag down and put in a couple of books I needed to take home that night. "You know what else makes me happy?"

"What?" She uncrossed her arms.

"Eating. How 'bout grabbing some lunch?"

"You're the boss."

* * *

We sat outside on the patio at Coopersmith's, my favorite restaurant in Old Town, Fort Collins, talking, laughing, and sharing funny childhood memories. It had been a long time since I had laughed this much with one person—and, the whole time, I could not take my eyes off her.

"So, how long have you and your girlfriend been together?"

"Not very long, only six months ... wait ..." I started to count on my fingers. "Maybe it's getting closer to eight months. What about you and Peter?"

"Over a year. You aren't close to your family at all?"

"Was it that obvious?" I chuckled. "Let's just say I'm the black sheep of the family. I keep to my own most of the time."

"Your mother doesn't seem to like you."

I was somewhat taken aback by her bluntness, but I tried not to show it. "We have our differences."

"Do they know you're gay?"

"You don't hold back, do you, Maddie?" I smiled at her. "Yes they know, but we all chose not to discuss it. Let me guess, Peter never brought it up?"

"No. I didn't even know you existed for quite some time.

Then he brought up your existence very casually. I was a little surprised. He dropped hints about you, but never proclaimed he had a sister."

Peter had a way of inserting things into the middle of the conversation, as if he had already mentioned it and the listener just forgot or ignored him. If anyone questioned it, he made them look like an insensitive ass.

"Huh, Peter and I are a lot more alike than I thought." I explained what had happened the previous day.

"Yes, you two are a lot alike. You don't open up much." She punched me lightly on the shoulder. "It can be very frustrating you know."

"Why are you hitting me? I have my own angry woman at home." I rubbed my shoulder.

"Peter isn't here, and I'm sure if you're like him at all, you deserve to be hit—and much harder, I might add. Am I wrong?" She looked at me with those incredible eyes.

I whistled through my teeth a little. "This is a difficult position to be in. If I say yes, I'm an asshole, then you'll always think of me as an asshole. But if I say no, you'll know I'm lying, and you'll always think of me as a liar. If you were me, what would you do?" I flashed my most cunning smile.

She burst into a loud guffaw. "Oh, my God! You two are so much alike it's fucking scary. Did your parents teach you two never to answer a question directly? Are they CIA?" Her head bobbed up and down in excitement as she spoke.

"You met my father ... he could be." I motioned to the waiter that we needed refills. A Coke for me, and a merlot for Maddie. "I can't remember the last time that man and I had a conversation. So who knows? Maybe the vice president of a financial company thing is all a ruse. At least that would make him more exciting."

"I think he hates me."

"He's not the one you have to worry about. Watch out for Mother. And, just a warning, Peter adores her." I wanted to mention that I thought it was sick how he pandered to her, but I didn't.

"I know, but thanks for the tip." A look of worry marred her lovely face.

"So are you ready to join this crazy family?"

She looked away for the first time. "I guess." She shrugged.

I couldn't help but chortle. "You guess? Geez, I hope when I decide to take the plunge with a woman, she doesn't say, 'I guess it's the right thing to do.'"

She hit me again. "Shut up."

Her look was bewitching. No wonder Peter was enraptured with this young creature. My guess was that she was twenty-four years old. Peter was seven years older than me, nearing thirty-five.

"What about you? Have you considered, as you so elegantly put it, taking the plunge?"

"No." I paused. "Not recently."

"Not recently? So, who is the girl who broke your heart and made you so bitter?"

"Bitter? Me? Bitter? What gave you that impression?" I said.

"You know, you and Peter both have that incredible smile. You two flash that smile and you think you can convince anyone of anything. I think that's why I agreed to marry your brother."

I didn't know what to say.

"Well, that and that I love him," she mumbled.

"Here you are. I was beginning to worry."

I looked up to find my girlfriend standing outside the railing of Coopersmith's with her best friend, Haley. "Hey, sweetheart. What are you doing here?" I stood, leaned over the railing, and kissed Sarah's cheek. For an instant, I felt like vomiting.

"Haley and I came for dinner. I tried calling you to see if you wanted to join us, but I kept getting your voice mail. I just assumed you were holed up in your office with your nose buried in some book."

I saw her glance over in Maddie's direction. Then she gave me an accusatory look.

"Shit!" I reached into my left pocket and pulled out my cell phone. It was still turned off. "Honey, I am so sorry. I forgot to turn my phone back on after class." I didn't even try to flash my smile this time. Her eyes told me that wouldn't work. I didn't think even a night of fucking was going to save me from the impending argument, either. I tried a diversionary tactic.

"Maddie, I'd like you to meet Sarah and her friend Haley. Sarah, this is my brother's fiancée." I stepped away from Sarah, in case any punches were thrown in my direction.

"I hope you don't mind me stealing Lizzie for the day," Maddie said. "Peter had some business to take care of, and he thought this would be a great opportunity for me to get to know my future sister-in-law." She stood up and hugged Sarah, and then shook Haley's limp hand. Haley wasn't the hugging type, and her demeanor let everyone know that.

Sister-in-law. The words suddenly made me feel ill. For the past several hours, I had been doing my best to imagine her naked. I was such an ass.

"It's very nice to meet you," Sarah said, as pleasantly as possible, considering she wanted to rip my head off.

"So, you two are having dinner. Do you guys want to join us?" I asked.

"That's a great idea. We've been sitting here so long, I'm famished. You won't believe this, but we came here to have lunch." Maddie paused and then blurted out, "Sarah, Lizzie is quite the storyteller. She must keep you laughing all the time."

Sarah smiled and tried to relax. She and Haley walked through the side gate and then sat down at the table. One thing I really admired about her was that she would never fight with me in public.

"Oh yes, I think that's why I fell in love with her," Sarah said. "She can be quite charming. And there is that smile." She touched my cheek briefly.

For an instant, I thought she was going to sock me. Her eyes told me that was what she really wanted to do.

Instead, Maddie hit me again. "You see, I told you about that smile of yours." She laughed her sexy laugh.

I smiled, and then I looked over at Sarah again. I was in for a very long night. Did she just say she was in love with me? We had barely said I love you to each other. In love? Was that the same thing, or was there a deeper meaning? I made a mental note to discuss it with Ethan.

Chapter Four

"I can't believe you! After yesterday … again? Again, you do it. Do you just not care? Obviously, you don't." Sarah paced back and forth waving her arms in the air while I sat on the couch.

For the past five minutes, she had been ranting and raving, uttering short sentences or fragments, and not making much sense. "And then, last night. I can't believe I fell for that. So what did you think, you could come home, fuck my brains out, and all would be forgotten?" She picked up her pacing. Her arm-flailing reached a manic level. "And I have never known you to have your cell phone off all day. Jesus, on our first date, you kept checking it whenever it rang. Even if you didn't answer, you still checked it. You thought you were so smooth about it, but I knew." She stopped and pinned me with a glare. I noticed she was breathing heavily.

"Sarah, it was such a last minute thing. Peter called this morning to arrange it. It's not like I thought to myself, hey, it was so much fun hurting her the first time, I'll try it again."

She stared right at me and for a second she looked like a puma ready to pounce. Then she said in a somewhat calmer, but still shaky, voice, "So you admit that you hurt me."

I stood up, walked over to her, and looked her right in the eyes. "Yes, I admit that I hurt you yesterday. And I admit that I hurt you again today. I don't know what I was thinking. But I was going to tell you when I got home. I had no idea it would turn into an all-day affair." She winced at the word affair and I instantly regretted my word choice.

"Why are you so mysterious all of the time? Sometimes I feel like I don't even know who you are. Why can't you just let me in? Half the time, I wonder if you even want to be with me."

I remembered what Maddie had said and it took everything I had not to smile when I pictured her punching my shoulder.

"I'm so sorry." I took Sarah into my arms. "I don't try to keep you out of my life. God, Sarah, who knows why I'm so private? It just happens. Can we just agree that I'm a moron?" I held her really tight.

She whispered, "Sometimes, I don't like you."

For the first time in quite some time, I felt something for Sarah. I looked at her and my smile was genuine. "I'm so sorry, sweetheart. I'm so sorry I hurt you."

She looked shocked. At first, I didn't know why. Then I felt her wipe a tear from my cheek. She kissed my forehead and rested her head against my shoulder. "Please, Lizzie," she whispered. "Just let me in every once in a while."

I nodded and kissed her. "I will." At that moment, I meant it. I really meant it.

Sarah's eyes hardened. "Lizzie, I love you, but I won't be with a liar. No more lies."

I promised.

* * *

"I truly meant it, Ethan. When I said it, I meant it." We were sitting in our usual spot, the coffee shop, on our usual day, Saturday. I had just finished explaining the past few days to him.

He stared at me while he sipped his coffee.

I downed a significant amount of my chai and then exclaimed, "Damn! That's hot, hot, hot."

Ethan chuckled. "Man I used to love that song."

"What are you talking about? A song about a girl burning herself while drinking a chai?" I waved my hand in an attempt to cool my burning tongue.

"No, you idiot. The song 'Hot Hot Hot' by The Cure. Check it out. It's a fun song. You can't always listen to audiobooks, you know."

"Why aren't you saying anything about the real topic instead of some stupid song?"

"Lizzie, there's nothing I can say. You have painted yourself into quite the corner." He was staring at the barista.

"What, are we going to talk in code today? The man with the yellow hat owns a monkey."

He chuckled. "I loved *Curious George* when I was little, too." He placed both hands behind his head and leaned back in his chair.

"That's great, Ethan. Let's not talk about my situation. Let's discuss children's literature."

He could tell I was upset. "Don't get mad at me, Lizzie. You should be mad at yourself."

"I … I know. How do I get into these situations?" I banged my hand on the table and almost spilled my chai.

"You do have a knack for it. I don't know what to tell you. It took you forever to let me in, and I know you haven't even let me in completely. It's just how you are. Sarah will have to accept that about you. The question is: do you want to stay with her?" He stared at me intensely.

I stared back into his Coke-bottle glasses. "What do you mean?"

"You convinced her that you love her by squeezing out a few tears. But ask yourself why there were tears. Were you sad? Or were you just so overwhelmed with the situation that you didn't know what to do? I've seen you almost cry here when they were out of chai. You're so wound up all of the time that sometimes you crack. What made you crack that day? Also, you aren't the most honest person. You have a way of telling people what you think they want to hear and not how you feel."

Right then, my cell phone rang. I stared at it for a second before I answered. "Hello."

"Hey, Lizzie. It's Maddie. How are you doing?"

"Hi, Maddie. I'm doing well. What are you up to today?" I looked at Ethan to keep him quiet.

He stared at me in disbelief.

"Hey, we're leaving town on Tuesday," Maddie said. "Would you like to get together for lunch tomorrow?"

"Yeah, sounds great. How about I come down there this time?"

Ethan started to wave his arms frantically in the air and mouthed, "No."

I hushed him. I didn't think Maddie even noticed the commotion.

She continued, "I have a better idea. Why don't we meet in Boulder? Peter tells me that they have good shopping along Pearl Street."

"Sounds good. I know some superb restaurants there."

We quickly arranged where to meet, and I hung up.

Ethan shook his head in bewilderment, "Are you going to tell Sarah?"

"Tell Sarah what, Ethan?" I looked him right in the eye.

He laughed. "You're playing with fire, Lizzie. Be careful. Is Peter going to be there?"

"I didn't ask, but I have a feeling we'll be alone."

"So, what's it like going on a date with your future sister-in-law?" He furrowed his brows.

"I'll let you know."

"Well, it's a good thing you turned your phone on today." He reached for his coffee and started to sip it, but then paused. Holding the cup close to his mouth, he added in a sinister voice, "Or is it?"

I smiled.

"Don't try that with me. I don't think your smile is all that cute."

I pretended to be hurt. Ethan laughed and I turned my attention to the window and watched the cars drive by.

After a minute or two, I said, "Sarah mentioned to Maddie that she was in love with me. What does that mean really?"

Ethan stared at me like I was a dingbat.

"I mean, I know we say I love you, but is 'in love'"—I waved my hand—"oh, I don't know, even stronger?"

"Well, it isn't as deep as saying 'I heart you.'"

"Come on, I'm being serious."

"So am I, Lizzie. Sometimes you sound like a relationship idiot. You analyze everything. People who think there's a difference between love and 'in love' are only fooling themselves. What are you so scared of?"

I stared back at him and watched him tug at the corner of his moustache. I didn't have an answer for him.

Did love scare me? Could I spend my life with just one person? Or would I end up like my parents, hating my partner? I pictured them at the club when I had met Maddie. My father hadn't spoken to any of us. My mother never said a word to my father, but I had felt her hatred seething inside. The thought terrified me. Would I be like my father and Sarah like my mother? I shivered.

* * *

That night, I took Sarah out to dinner. Afterwards, I planned on taking her to a movie she had wanted to see. For the first half of the meal I kept trying to come up with ways to tell her that I was meeting Maddie in Boulder but that I wanted to go alone. Usually, we kept Sundays just to ourselves. I was obviously struggling to find the right words.

Instead, I chattered on and on about my students and the papers I had just graded. She talked about her students. Sarah taught English at one of the local high schools. For the most part, it was a pleasant evening, which made me feel even more like scum. There we were, having a pleasant meal discussing our work, and all I could really think about was how to ditch her on Sunday, our day together, and spend it with Maddie.

"Oh, I almost forgot to tell you. Matt called and he's coming to town tomorrow. I hope you don't mind, but we are going to have lunch with his parents." Matt had been her boyfriend in high school. They had remained close friends throughout college. He was a cool guy, but he always felt slightly uncomfortable around me.

I nearly dropped my fork. Doing my best to regain my composure, I said, "Really … it's supposed to be nice out tomorrow." Slicing off a piece of steak, I continued. "Maybe I'll hook up my bike and go for a ride in the mountains." I placed the chunk of steak in my mouth.

She smiled. "Geez, it will be such a lovely day for a bike ride. I wish I could go."

I didn't want to risk her changing her plans, so I said nothing; instead, I motioned to the waitress for our check.

"What do you want to do now?" Sarah looked, and sounded, relaxed, as though all of the week's earlier events had never occurred. I marveled at her way of compartmentalizing problems in her head.

"I thought we could go see that movie you've been dying to see. It's playing at the Cinemark on Timberline."

"Which one?"

"*Moonrise Kingdom.*"

She squealed and clapped her hands. "I've been dying to see that. It's been out for a while." She smiled. "I thought you'd forgotten that I wanted to see it."

I grinned back at her and led her out of the restaurant and to the car.

Chapter Five

The next day, I stood awkwardly on the corner outside one of the stores on Pearl Street and watched Maddie wait for the crosswalk sign. She stood there smiling, looking radiant, until finally, the light changed and she approached.

"How was your drive?"

"Oh, my gosh, Lizzie, I got so lost on my way here." She was breathing heavily. "Is there always so much construction in Colorado? Every major road has some detour. It's crazy. And the people here do not understand the concept of merging. This one guy actually stopped while trying to get on the highway. Who stops when getting on the highway?" She flipped her hair back. "If he tried that in California, someone would have hit him out of spite, or shot him." She hugged me and kissed my cheek. Her perfume made me giddy.

"Yes, there is always construction here, especially when the weather is nice. And I have to agree that people are idiots behind the wheel. I try to stick to the back roads out here. Not so many blockheads. Plus, you get to look at horses and cows."

Really? Really! Was I this much of a moron all of the time?

Horses and cows! She was a California girl, why would she want to look at horses and cows?

"I better get used to it … I got the job." She jumped in excitement and let out the cutest little squeal.

I hugged her, overcome with excitement, fear, and anger. She would now become a permanent fixture in my life. For the first time in my life, I was jealous of Peter. Everyone had always assumed I was. He had everything: good looks, charm, wit, intelligence, and confidence. But I had never wanted to be like him. At that moment, I wanted to *be* him.

We pulled apart and I looked into her eyes. "That's great, Maddie. Peter must be so happy for you."

"I think he is. He bought me a new car last night. The BMW I wanted." Another squeal.

I laughed and said, "That's so my mom."

I immediately regretted it. She didn't deserve such a callous remark.

But she just laughed at me. "I knew you would say something like that. It's almost like you can't help it. You just say what you think, especially when it comes to your family. Your mouth opens and the words spill out even if they are words others really don't want to hear. I love it. I love your verbal brutality."

"Verbal brutality? That seems a bit harsh. But I like it. It's very to the point. In fact, it's something I would've said."

She did a little curtsy for me and we laughed and started walking along Pearl Street.

* * *

We sat outside a little fondue place. The weather was gorgeous, and when the sun shone at that time of year, Coloradoans flocked to alfresco venues. We sat at one of the tiny tables squeezed onto an even smaller patio. Maddie's bags, squashed under the table, made it hard to get comfortable, but I didn't mind.

She held her wineglass against her cheek, propping her

head up with her other arm, her elbow resting on the table. "Tell me something you haven't told anyone else."

I thought for a moment but didn't question why she was asking. I wanted to find the right answer. "I really enjoy riding my bike—"

"And I really enjoy chocolate chip cookies," she interrupted.

I smiled. "Now hold on and listen to what I have to say before you make a smartass comment."

She nodded in acknowledgement and sipped her wine. "Okay, but you'll have to make it more interesting than 'I like to ride my bicycle.' Or I won't divulge my deep, dark desires." She ran a finger along my arm.

Her suggestive wink made me swallow hard. It was too late to come up with something sexier. *Shit!*

I swallowed again and forged ahead. "For the past few years, I was pretty sick. For a while, the doctors couldn't figure out what was wrong with me. All that time, I didn't work out at all. So, as you can imagine, I got out of shape. Now, I'm doing everything I can to get back into shape.

"Have you ever been told you have an illness that's trying to kill you? Fortunately, mine is treatable. I take a pill each night. But when I first heard the diagnosis, I went online and looked it up. One hundred years ago, this disease was a death sentence. Well, that scared the crap out of me. I know I won't die from it, but I want to get into the best shape of my life, just in case I get something else. I want to be ready."

Maddie's eyes darted towards a couple walking by. She casually asked, "What illness do you have?" She continued watching the man as he pulled out a chair for his wife.

I stifled a laugh. Her smooth way of inserting the question impressed me. She didn't want to seem too eager to learn my secret.

"Oh, I hardly mention its name. When people learn you have an incurable illness, they romanticize it. Why they do this astounds me. Many immediately think of cancer and chemo treatments. My illness isn't glamorous. If you can call cancer glamorous."

"Poor, Lizzie." She laughed. "Stuck with a sub-par ailment. As a Petrie, that has to bug the piss out of you. You all like to excel at everything, even being sick."

Her reply stung, but it intrigued me. Maddie wasn't like other women I flirted with. Her honesty cut to the quick. If I wanted to pursue anything, I had to pick up my game.

"Okay, smartass. I have Graves' Disease."

"Ha!" She slammed her hand down on the table. "I knew that would get you to spill the beans. You are more like your brother than you would like to admit."

My blood boiled, but I smiled. She was playing me. Not that I would admit that to her.

"Seriously" — she put her hand on mine and squeezed— "are you okay? I haven't known you long, but I would like to keep you around. Besides, you can't let me fend for myself. Your family is—"

"Full of assholes." I interrupted.

"Exactly!"

I didn't have the courage to ask if she included Peter in that category. Or me.

Diverting the conversation away from my family, I said, "Once, when I told a woman I had Graves' Disease, she asked if they called it that because I would end up in a grave."

"Is it?" She leaned closer, concerned.

"No. Of course, that would make my illness cooler." I teased.

"Don't you mean more tragic. Then, when you tried to seduce women, you could say, 'I don't have long to live. Before I go, I would like to know the true meaning of love.'" She sighed dramatically and coughed like someone on his or her deathbed.

"Would that work with you?" I perked up in my chair.

"Of course not! I would only sleep with a cancer patient." She winked at me.

I shook my head. "You are terrible. Now I need to come down with cancer."

Smiling, she squirmed in her chair, and asked, "How often do you ride? Your bike, that is." Her face reddened.

"Almost every day." A breeze blew some of my hair into my mouth and I casually pulled the strands off my lips, wishing I had a hair tie to pull it back into a ponytail.

She looked at me like *so what*. "This is your big secret?"

"I've turned it into a challenge. I am determined to ride my bike 3,000 miles during the next six months."

"3,000 miles ... are you insane?"

"Of course! But that isn't the point. I figured if I ride at least 20 miles each day, it would only take me five months to reach 3,000. Some days I go for longer rides. Those days add up to at least two days worth, which gives me some wiggle room for days it snows and stuff." Saying this out loud for the first time made me feel rather silly.

"You've put a lot of thought into this."

"Yes." I fidgeted in my chair. Why did I share this with her? Now she would probably think I was batty. A bike challenge, what, was I five?

"So why haven't you told Sarah?" Her accusing eyes watched my every move.

I shook my head slowly. "I guess I didn't even think of telling her. She knows I go riding almost every day. I don't know why I haven't told her the rest. Most people don't want to hear about illness or be reminded about it. At first, they're sympathetic and want to hear the details, asking how you're feeling, but that fades quickly. People don't want to hear about it. They certainly don't want to be reminded of it. It scares them, even when it isn't cancer."

Again, she changed the subject. "Is there a reward or something for reaching 3,000 miles?"

"A dog named Zeb."

She choked on her wine. "A dog named Zeb ... what are you talking about?"

"I figure that if I can stay focused on the challenge, it'll show reliability and prove I'm responsible enough for a dog. A dog is a lot of responsibility."

She chuckled. "You're very different from how I thought you were going to be."

"What do you mean? What did you think I'd be like?" I slumped down in my chair.

"Don't get me wrong, you and Peter are very alike in some ways. You two are almost identical twins. It's scary sometimes. You are both secretive. And you are both very driven individuals. But something else drives you … not just success." She paused and took a sip of wine. "Challenge. Yes, you love a challenge." Another sip of wine. "However, I haven't figured out if you like to conquer things as well. Or people." She patted my arm, letting her hand linger a few moments.

"Now, your turn." I looked eagerly at her.

"I'm not sure you can handle my secret," she said in a demure voice.

"Oh, come on! Or I'll think you're rodomontade."

She set her wine glass down. "A what?"

"Rodomontade. Someone who's a pretentious braggart." I flashed a cunning smile.

"How long have you been holding onto to that one?" She poured more wine into her glass. "Do you use such impressive words all of the time or just around those you are trying to impress?"

I didn't want to admit that I saved them for those who intimidated me.

"Stop stalling." I dipped a strawberry into the chocolate fondue.

"Okay. I wouldn't want you to think of me as a rodo-thingy."

"Rodomontade."

"You can keep saying it, but it doesn't make it sound any cooler." She took a sip of her wine. "This secret isn't a big secret. I mean many people know about it … but I haven't told your brother. And, I should add, I don't intend to."

I waited anxiously. *What could it be?*

She looked away and blurted out, "I'm bisexual."

I choked on my water. Did I accidentally swallow an ice cube, and was it now lodged in my throat? Beating my chest with one fist, I imagined my face turning a vivid violet.

Maddie started to stand to help me, but I motioned for her to stay seated.

Still gasping for air, I said, "You got me on that one."

"What do you mean?" She looked puzzled.

"You're joking, right?" I sipped my water gingerly to relieve the tickle in my throat.

"Are you against bisexuality?" She looked miffed.

"What? N-no. Of course not. I—" I looked around, searching for the right words. "I only thought you were trying to one-up my 'I like my bike' secret."

She laughed angrily. "A child could top that one without even trying."

"You're serious, aren't you?" Peter would not take this news well. Oh, and my mother. Maddie was playing with fire.

"Yes. I thought I could share it with you. Obviously, I was wrong. Dead wrong." She crossed her arms.

"Oh, Maddie. I'm so sorry. I never meant to imply anything. I'm just shocked, that's all … not that you are, but you're with Peter …" I hesitated. "Really, you can never tell him. Or my mother. Never my mother."

She looked terrified. "I know. That's why I wanted to talk about it. It's killing me, this secret."

"Shit, Maddie. I'm so sorry." I reached across the table and patted her hand.

"Shit. What? You don't have some fancy word for that." She pouted.

"Excrement, but that doesn't quite suit the conversation. And it's not that fancy." I picked up my fork and tapped it against the table.

I sensed she regretted telling me. Let's face it; I did a horrendous job of handling the situation. Really, I don't think I could have bungled it more.

"Listen. I'm here for you. If you ever need to talk, I'm here."

Her eyes softened. "Thanks, Lizzie."

"Ah, Peter hasn't mentioned a prenup or anything has he." I put up my palms. "I know it's none of my business, but I was just thinking out loud."

"Ha! No. Trust me, Peter won't ever mention a prenup. Let's just say my father can make or break Peter's career."

I knew there had to have been a reason Peter risked marrying a southerner.

"That's good. That's perfect, actually." I smiled weakly at her.

She looked more confident. "I warned you."

"Warned me about what?"

"That you wouldn't be able to handle my secret," she teased.

It was a real corker. One to keep—in my family.

Chapter Six

"How was your day?"

It was Monday night and I had just walked into my apartment. The front room was right at the entrance, and Sarah was sitting on one of the chairs in front of the television. She picked up the remote and muted the show. Glancing at the screen, I saw that she was watching a favorite of hers, *The Bridges of Madison County*.

"Very long," I answered. "How was yours?"

Sarah stared at me. She had this weird look in her eye. Was it fear or anger? "Have you been working all day and night?"

"Yes. I guess I lost ..."

"Track of time?"

"I'm sorry, Sarah. I probably use that excuse a lot."

"About three or four times a week."

I sighed, dropped my bag, and slumped down on the couch next to her. Rubbing my eyes, I asked, "Why do you stay?" I wasn't trying to be mean or cold.

"That's the stupidest question you could possibly ask me at this moment." She watched me, intent on what I would say.

I sat up and leaned closer. She kissed me before I had a chance to say anything. Before I knew it, we were both naked on the floor.

Afterwards, she rolled over and looked me in the eyes. "You've never been like that before."

"Like what?"

"It's hard to describe. It's like you wanted to possess me. Not only were you in control, but it was like you were dictating all of it."

"I'm sorry, baby."

"It wasn't bad, Lizzie. In fact, it was fucking hot. But you have never been like that before."

The next morning, I rolled out of bed at five and hopped on my bike. I rode as hard and as fast as I could. It was like my legs became part of the machine, pistons pushing me further and further on the trail. The pain of exerting myself beyond my normal speed and distance disappeared. All I saw and felt was the path in front of me. After carrying the bike upstairs, I checked the odometer—341 miles so far.

When I walked into the bathroom for a shower, Sarah said, "Is it that hot outside already? You're dripping with sweat."

I pulled my shirt off and looked down. Sweat poured down my stomach. Even with all of the riding I had been doing, my stomach was still a little paunchy. I suppose I am almost thirty, but it still bothered me.

"Don't get too close to me." Sarah backed away. "I just got out of the shower and you, Lizzie, need to get in."

I stepped closer and pulled her to me. She tried pushing me away, but when I kissed her, she gave in. Her towel fell to the ground. I moved us both toward the shower and turned on the water. She did not fight me when I pulled her in with me and fucked her up against the wall.

Afterwards, while Sarah was getting dressed for work, she said, "I don't know what has gotten into you these past couple of days, but I really like it."

Maddie and Peter left later that afternoon. I didn't call to say goodbye. Neither did Maddie.

* * *

"I can't even tell you how much our sex life has improved. It's like we can't get enough of each other."

Ethan stirred more sugar into his coffee. "You can't have the one woman you want, so you're trying to possess the other."

I stared at him, giving that a thought. "Sarah told me that one night—that I fucked her like I wanted to possess her. Is that what I am doing?"

He wiped some crumbs off the table with a napkin. "What do you think?"

I shook my head. "The other day, Maddie commented that I love a challenge, but she wasn't sure yet if I liked to conquer things as well. I don't really know what she meant by that."

Ethan laughed. "Yeah, right."

I looked at him. "What does that mean?"

"Let's just say that you are an extremely driven individual."

"Well, what's wrong with that?" I pushed up my shirtsleeves.

"Nothing. As long as you don't hurt the ones you love while striving for perfection."

"I don't strive for perfection." I scoffed.

"No ... really? When's the last time you received a grade lower than an 'A?' Have you ever received an A minus? I doubt it. How many honor societies do you belong to? I know you're Phi Beta Kappa. I'm surprised you haven't joined some bike-racing challenges yet."

"Listen, smarty pants, I got a 'B' once." I pointed my stir stick at him.

Ethan chuckled and shook his head. "Once. Wow, I stand corrected." He put his palms up mockingly.

"I'm not that uptight, you know."

"Oh, I know. Like you would never cry if this place ran out of chai and you didn't get your way." He laughed.

"Whatever, Ethan. You know you're more uptight than me. Have you driven home lately during work so you can take a crap in your own home?"

When Ethan was in high school, he would drive home to take a shit. He was never very comfortable with his bodily functions, or anyone else's. Sex was a big issue for him, since it involved fluids that grossed him out—even his own. I wondered if he ever masturbated.

"I live across the street from the school. I can walk there."

We both laughed. "So we both have our issues."

"Fair enough. I'm going to grab another coffee. You want another?"

"Sure. But doesn't coffee make you want to poop? I'll understand if you have to make a mad dash for your car."

"Knock it off, wise guy, or I won't get you a chai."

"All right. Let's call a truce, for the day at least."

"Sounds like a plan, Miss Perfect. What class did you get a 'B' in?"

"Astronomy. All I wanted to do was look at the stars, but the professor wanted me to do mathematical equations."

"Are you saying there's a field you haven't conquered?"

"Oh, shut up. Go get our drinks, and I hope your coffee gives you the shits. I would love to see you run out of here holding it in and then drive twenty minutes to Loveland."

"My car is souped-up for those types of emergencies."

"Maybe I'll get you a police siren for Christmas."

"That would be awesome."

He wandered over to the counter to get our second round of drinks.

Chapter Seven

"I see that you're still riding your bike. How's the great bike challenge going for you?"

I didn't have to turn around to know it was Maddie. I knew it by her voice, and besides, she was the only one who knew my bike challenge secret.

"Really well, actually. How's the new job?" I slowly turned around and gazed into those beautiful blue eyes. It had been weeks since we had seen or spoken to each other.

"I love the job. They're starting to trust me with my own projects." She paused. "How far did you ride? You're dripping in sweat."

Neither of us mentioned how odd it was that she'd showed up outside of my apartment. She'd never been here before. How did she find out where I lived? I wasn't sure she had forgiven me yet for the conversation we had at our last meetings. I hoped both of us could forget the incident.

"I had a lot of energy, so I went longer than normal. I rode to LaPorte and back." I tugged at my T-shirt, which was sticking to my skin. "Geez, look at me—I'm a mess! Do you want to come in? I'm dying for a hot shower. You can hang out while I get cleaned up."

"That sounds nice. Hope you don't mind, but I won't hug you until you shower." She waved her hand in front of her nose. "Stinky."

"Smelly McGee, that's me."

As soon as the words left my mouth, I froze. What had compelled me to make such a nincompoop out of myself?

Maddie snapped her head up to eyeball me. "Oh, wow. That's pretty dorky, even for you. I wouldn't suggest trying that one on the ladies." She snickered.

"Come on, smartass." I led her up the flight of stairs to my apartment, searching for my pride with each step.

"Is Sarah home?" Maddie asked.

Had she sensed my embarrassment and wanted to divert the conversation away from my gaffe?

I laughed, feeling more at ease. "She doesn't officially live with me. But no, she isn't here right now. She and her mom are bonding today. They're having breakfast, and then they'll shop till they drop. They are definitely shoppers. When I go with them, I have to take energy shots just to keep up."

"Two women after my own heart. You don't like to shop?"

"I prefer to have someone else do it for me."

"So you always have a girlfriend to take care of you?"

"You're spunky today."

We walked into my apartment. She looked around and said, "Not what I was expecting."

"Really? What did you think my apartment would look like?"

"I wasn't expecting a feminine touch." She gestured to the fresh flowers and candles on the table.

"Thanks—I think." I fiddled with my hoop earring.

"I mean you aren't a bull dyke or anything." She laughed. "But you aren't super fem either." Color flooded her cheeks. "I'm sorry. I tend to put my foot in it. To be honest, when I met you, I wasn't sure what to expect. Peter doesn't have any photos of you and you don't come up during family gatherings. I thought you were a raving feminist and all of them were embarrassed by you. I was taken aback when you walked up to the table, looking normal, like a female version of Peter. But you were wearing makeup. I had envisioned a woman with a shaved head and covered in tattoos." She stepped from side to side nervously.

I watched her eyes wander over every crevice.

"Don't tell Peter that we look alike," I warned.

"Oh, I won't!"

She turned back to me. "I thought you would have a very sterile apartment. No unnecessary items. No personal touches." She motioned to photos of Sarah and I on the mantle.

It was my turn to blush. "I can't take the credit for the personal touches or for the flowers. Sarah loves to decorate. She has a fetish for fresh flowers and Yankee Candles. I can't even guess how much she spends each week on them." I chuckled. "I swear, as soon as she started staying the night, she began putting her mark on my place. And maybe she didn't like the smell. I have to admit, I do like the smell of the clean cotton candle."

We stared at each other, awkwardly.

"Make yourself comfortable. It won't take me long to clean up." I went straight to my bathroom, turned the water to hot, and stripped down. Before stepping into the shower, I frowned at myself in the mirror and said, "Behave, Lizzie. This is Peter's fiancée." But I didn't want to follow my own advice. I felt compelled to pursue Maddie.

I usually take an extravagant amount of time in the shower, but that day I rushed through the routine. It wasn't that I didn't trust Maddie in the apartment—actually, I didn't care what she got into—but I didn't want to waste any time. I didn't see her that much.

She was perched on the couch, reading one of the history books I had been perusing for my research.

"What did you get yourself into while I was in the shower?" I said, towel drying my hair.

"Your sex toys, of course," she quipped. She winked and flashed an arch smile. Then she gestured to the book. "The Hitler Youth, from the excerpts I have read, they don't sound like a fun bunch to hang out with." She sat up. "I mean, I assumed they wouldn't sit around the campfire singing 'Kumbaya' and shit. But from what I read, some of them were monsters." The color drained from her face. "And at such a young age."

"I think a lot of people don't like to think that children can be evil. It's cool in a horror story, but in real life, it makes many people tremble. You have to remember, though, these kids were indoctrinated at an early age.

"And not all of them were like that, of course. There are stereotypes. Actually, membership in the Hitler Youth was mandatory." I walked over to my bookshelf and grabbed a book. "Here's a memoir of a boy who had to join the Hitler Youth in childhood. He was a weakling, and he didn't fare too well. In fact—" I stopped mid-sentence. "I'm sorry, but sometimes it's hard for me to turn off the historian in me. Do forgive my transgression." I bowed slightly.

"Your transgression? You and Peter are the only two people I know who talk like that."

I felt slightly uncomfortable about the mention of my brother's name, and about yet another comparison to Peter.

"Well, Mom beat us if we didn't ace our vocabulary tests. By the way, how is the old biddy?" I sat down on a chair, heavily.

"She seems like her old self." She looked out the patio door.

"So, still demanding, demeaning, and full of debauchery, but not the fun kind?"

"I guess you could say that. How is it that I know how your mother is and you don't?" She turned to me, staring hard.

"I haven't spoken to her since we all had dinner together. We aren't, shall I say, a close-knit family." I intertwined my fingers and then pulled them apart to enhance my point.

"I'm not so sure about that." Maddie sighed. I could only guess that Peter and Mom were pushing family and duty crap on her. I had no idea why Peter agreed with such antiquated notions of what the wife of a well-to-do businessman should be like.

"Anyway, I have something for you." She jumped up and went to the counter, where she had set her purse.

I was extremely curious about what that "something" was.

She pulled out a small box and handed it to me.

"What on earth are you up to, Miss Maddie?" I opened the box. A bracelet. It was silver, and it reminded me of those chain-links we used to make in school to decorate the Christmas tree, except the links were much smaller and were not made of colored construction paper.

"When I saw this, I immediately thought of you. In your office, I noticed you had a copy of *Atlas Shrugged* on your desk. The bracelet isn't a blue-green, but it symbolized something else for me."

I gazed into her eyes and replied, "This I am dying to know. Do tell."

"Seeing you in your domain, aka your office, I saw how you're chained, in a way, to your studies. I've never seen so many books and articles piled on top of each other in such a tiny office. Really, Lizzie, you need a designer." She laughed and added, "And a candle, or some incense or something. It's very stale in there. Maybe your fave: clean cotton."

I started to laugh.

She looked at me, unsure whether she had offended me.

"Bravo! Bravo. No one has pegged me so quickly. Not only that, but no one has realized I don't mind being chained to my studies. I love that I am. Would you help me put it on my wrist, please?"

She smiled and looked relieved.

"But shouldn't I be the one getting you gifts … to help you celebrate your upcoming nuptials?"

"Oh, you aren't getting out of buying me a gift or two. Trust me. I'm a girl who likes gifts."

"I don't doubt it. Well, since you drove all the way up here to give me this." I rattled the silver chain. "Can I take you to lunch, madame?"

"Why, yes, of course you can."

We both laughed together. It was so easy to be around her. I couldn't explain it, except that it was easy. Usually, I didn't get along with people all that well. I preferred books. Give me Dickens any day. But maybe not today.

* * *

Sitting at Coopersmith's, both bundled up in sweaters this time, we chatted.

"Does your dad ever talk?" Maddie asked.

I wiped a smudge off my water glass. "No. Not much. And when he does, it's more like barking orders. He usually starts every sentence with a verb. Not a statement—a command."

"I feel like I can't make a connection with the man—see, I just called him 'the man,' not my future father-in-law, or by his name, Charles."

"Don't take it too personally. 'The man,' as you say, doesn't communicate all that well. He doesn't communicate with anyone, unless it's a computer.

"I remember a time when my father tried to throw away a trash can. It was an old one, so it was pretty beat up, with holes and a stench that would kill a rat—maybe a rat had died in it—anyhoos, he placed it in a much larger trash can. When the trash guys came, they carefully pulled the beat-up can out of the other trash can and set it on the curb with the remaining cans. 'The man' was furious. His face was beet-red and a vein in his forehead was popping out. I could tell he was having a temper tantrum, even if he didn't say anything. The next trash day, he hid it inside one of the larger trash cans under a lot of wet, stinky garbage. But when he came home from work, there it was again, sitting on the curb with the other trash cans.

"The following week, he set it next to all of the others with a note that read: 'This is trash, please take it.' When he came home, he saw they'd removed the note, and presumably threw it away, but left the can. It outraged Dad beyond belief. He doesn't speak much, but when he does, and when he's angry, it is a sight to behold. The next week, he was determined to be rid of the can.

"That next trash day was a little windy. When it was like that, sometimes one of the trash cans would wind up in a ravine in the hogback. One of us would have to traipse down there and retrieve it. When I left for school, I didn't remember seeing the old trash can. But when my father came home that night, he was ecstatic it had finally gone, but so had another one. My father walked down to the ravine and retrieved one.

"For some reason, I decided to walk down there, too. I just had this feeling. And, of course, I saw the old trash can down there. He must have seen it too, but decided this was his only way of getting rid of the damn thing."

Maddie laughed while I told the story. I didn't realize right away, but that was the most I had ever said to her at one time. It was the most I had said to anyone in a long time actually, unless it was a lecture, or to Ethan.

"I can't believe they threw the note away but left the can. That's one of the oddest things I've heard in a while."

"Wow, you must be hard-up for stories right now."

"Well, I hang out with your father. I'm in a drought."

"*Touché.*"

"Actually, I'm surprised your father sets out his own trash. Peter would never do that."

"Mom always wanted servants, but my father has always refused. He grew up poor. He's cognizant of his upbringing.

Of course, he did concede to having a nanny, but I always wondered whether he just wanted to ensure we would survive our childhood. Mom wasn't the nurturing kind, if you know what I mean."

We sat in silence for some moments. Then Maddie asked, "Is that why you hate your family so much?"

I set down my knife and fork and watched the light drizzle outside slide down the window. "You know, Maddie, at one point I could give you a whole laundry list of why. But all of the memories are fading. To be honest, I can't pinpoint the reason I decided to go my own way. At one point, I had a reason, or reasons. Now it's just more of a feeling. Whenever I'm around them, I don't like them."

"Is that why you never told them you're sick?" She took one of the flowers out of the vase on the table and smelled it.

"I never even thought about telling them. No one likes to hear about other people's troubles. Even Sarah tunes out when I mention feeling ill. I figured that they would care even less. At least Sarah loves me."

Maddie sipped her wine, her eyes on the busboy who was clearing the table next to us.

We sat in silence again. Maddie seemed to be mulling something over.

"That settles it. Peter is picking up this check." She pulled out a credit card and set it on the edge of the table.

"What are you talking about?"

"I'm tired of the bastard not caring."

I could tell the wine was kicking in. Although I wanted to push her on her declaration, I was torn about doing so. Were my intentions to help a friend? Or were they to drive a wedge between my brother and his incredibly gorgeous fiancée? I sat silently while she, or Peter rather, settled the tab.

Before we left, Maddie handed me the flower she had confiscated earlier and patted my cheek tenderly.

* * *

Later that night, I was on the couch with Sarah, watching one of her stupid comedies. I had never been an Adam Sandler fan, or a fan of movies like that, but Sarah loved them, so I agreed to watch one with her. She was stretched out in front of me, my arm wrapped around her stomach. I felt her touch my wrist.

"What's that?"

I looked down at what she was touching—the bracelet Maddie had given me.

"Oh, I was cleaning out a box in my closet and I found this bracelet I used to wear during high school."

She fidgeted with it a little, and then said, "It looks weird. Is it a chain of some sort?"

"I'm not sure, but I've always liked it, so I put it on." I shrugged and turned my attention back to the movie.

That was that. I didn't know that lying to my girlfriend would come so easily, and without regret. I reached for a handful of popcorn and ate it. Sarah didn't suspect anything odd. She snuggled even closer. I squeezed her waist and kissed the back of her head.

Chapter Eight

"She gave you what?" Ethan choked on his coffee.

"Ethan, don't be so dramatic. You can see with your own eyes."

He reached out and stroked the bracelet, as if he thought it would disappear at his touch. "I can't believe it. Why would she give you a piece of jewelry? You don't give jewelry to someone you barely know. What do you think it means?"

"Come on, Ethan. Focus here. I'm telling you that I lied to my girlfriend. That's the issue right now. I lied, and I didn't feel bad about it. Right after I lied, I held her tight and kissed her head, as if I felt closer to her. *That* is the issue; not that Maddie gave me this." I shook my wrist.

"But what does it mean that you're wearing it, and *you lied*! You lied to Sarah!" His eyes grew big behind his glasses. He waggled his finger in my face. "You lied to her *and* you are wearing it."

"Thank you, Captain Obvious." I saluted him.

He stared at me; I mean he *really stared* at me. Then he looked down at his coffee cup. Speaking more to his cup than me, he said, "She bought you a bracelet. You not only accepted it, but you continue to wear it. And you lied to Sarah about it." He turned his eyes back to me. "Have you taken the bracelet off since she gave it to you?" He arched one eyebrow.

"Um ... no. No, I haven't. Why?" It had been too much trouble taking it off to shower, so I had showered with it on. Laziness was the reason I hadn't removed it, I told myself. "I have clumsy fingers that can't work the tiny clasp, and I don't want to ask Sarah each day; that would seem wrong."

"That's it! You don't have a crush on her." He looked back at his cup. "Crushes are innocent. We all know they won't go anywhere. But you ... you actually like her."

Sunlight streamed in through the window. "What are you talking about, you crazy little man?" I snatched my sunglasses from where they were perched on top of my head and put them on.

"Yep! I'm right. You only call me 'little man' when you feel threatened or on guard and you want to knock me down." He rubbed the whiskers on his chin triumphantly. I could picture him as a child in the playground, outwitting one of his bullies in front of the prettiest girl in school. When did he decide to grow a beard? I had never seen him unshaven.

I sipped my chai. "She's my brother's fiancée, Ethan."

"And you are wearing her bracelet."

"Do you know her? Do you know her pattern of giving gifts? She's probably trying to get one of the family members, one who isn't crazy, on her side. We can't assume that just because she gave me this"—I touched the bracelet and tried not to smile—"she likes me."

"Interesting. I wasn't talking about her just now. I said that *you* like *her*. But you just hinted that she likes you as well."

I shook my head in frustration. "Oh, you are twisting everything so it will turn out like a Jerry Springer show. Why do you like drama so much?"

He smiled and sipped his coffee. For once, he didn't say anything. He just kept smiling at me. I sat silently and drank my chai. Every once in a while, I caught him glancing at the bracelet. He tapped his fingers on the table, causing me to grimace. His nails were cut too short for my taste.

Finally, I said, "She's Peter's fiancée. There is no hidden meaning behind the bracelet."

"I disagree."

"And what evidence do you have?"

"The proof is in the bracelet."

I laughed.

Ethan beamed at his own cleverness, or what he believed was cleverness.

"What's it like in your little world?" I queried.

"So you are threatened, or is it confusion?" Puzzlement spread across his face.

I shook my head, frustrated.

Ethan said in a grave voice, "Be careful, Lizzie."

"What do you mean? I'm sure Sarah won't ask about the bracelet again."

His face plainly showed that I missed his point. "I'm not talking about that. I've seen you sabotage your life on more than one occasion. All I'm going to say is look before you leap."

"I have no idea what you're talking about." I fiddled with a pen that sat on top of my leather-bound journal.

"You run away instead of dealing with your issues."

"Issues ... issues ... I don't have issues!" I bounded out of my chair and hotfooted to the bathroom.

"You see!" he bellowed.

Chapter Nine

I sat in my office, behind my messy desk, grinning woozily at Maddie, who had stopped by to fill me in on her latest misadventure.

"Oh, my God, Lizzie! The most embarrassing thing happened to me the other day. For lunch, I had sushi. And let's just say it didn't settle well." She winked at me. "So there I was, in this meeting with a prospective client in their home. They wanted to redo their bedroom." Maddie paused and waved her hand in the air. "But that's beside the point. I was sitting there in their home, discussing their needs, when all of a sudden I felt something. You know when you start to get diarrhea you get a sharp pain in your stomach. Well, I got this cramp. I tried to push it out of my head and focus on the conversation. I started to fidget in my chair.

"So there I am, trying to wrap the meeting up as soon as possible. But the husband kept going on and on about how he doesn't want a really feminine room. The entire time, I'm trying to hold it in.

"Then, I just couldn't hold it in anymore. I had to ask them if I could use their bathroom. I walked as fast as I could down the hallway—without looking like I was about to shit myself. When I sat on the toilet, I exploded. Seriously, I couldn't believe how fast it shot out of my ass. And I'm sitting there hoping they couldn't hear me. But I could feel I wasn't done, so I flushed the toilet, so I wouldn't clog it. And then I braced myself for round two.

"That's when I noticed the toilet didn't flush completely. I started to panic. *How in the world can I go out there and tell them that I had the shits and I clogged their toilet?* I thought. So, I jumped up and saw that there was a plunger. Picture this: I'm standing there with my pants around my ankles, plunging like a mad woman, squeezing my ass cheeks so I wouldn't shit myself.

"And then I sensed I wasn't alone. I looked over my shoulder and saw that the blind was up and the window was open. Their neighbor was watching me with his mouth open. You better order a coffin."

"What?"

"I'm gonna die from embarrassment."

I smiled, "Could he hear you?"

"Oh, Lizzie, I don't even want to think about that." She shook her head and laughed. "I was completely mortified."

She laughed so hard she squeezed out a fart.

"Did you just break wind?" I asked, floored.

"Break wind!" She roared with laughter.

Trying to recover my composure, I said, "Careful. You might do it again."

Maddie had started to pop in more and more at my office. I was only too eager to set aside my work to be entertained by her. Afterward, we wandered over to the Lory Student Center and grabbed a bite to eat.

I couldn't help but think that she was coming up with reasons to see me. I would never tell that story to anyone. Maybe I would tell Ethan. Maddie's carefree attitude drew me in. No one in my family would admit to that story. I was learning how much she trusted me with her secrets.

* * *

I let out a sigh when I heard the phone ring. There was only one person I knew who would call at this hour. I rolled over in bed and picked up the phone. "You are aware of the time?"

"Good morning to you, little sis." He sounded cheerful, but in a condescending way. "It must be nice to be a student. I've been up for hours working."

I looked at the clock. It was six in the morning. Peter had always been a liar.

"To what do I owe this wake-up call?"

"Maddie and I would like to invite you and—I'm sorry, I don't know your girlfriend's name—to dinner tonight. What do you say, can you make it?"

"Well, I can. I'll have to ask Sarah."

"Put her on the phone. I know I can convince her."

I could almost see his sleazy smile. "She's in the shower. Don't worry, I'll ask her."

"All right, my address is 1648 Quentin Road. Mapquest it. Be here at 7 p.m., Elizabeth. I gotta go. I'm getting another call."

I didn't bother saying goodbye, since I knew he had already hung up. I stared at the bathroom door. Should I invite Sarah? The last two times I hadn't, she'd flipped out. If I got caught again, it would be over for sure. But did I want her to go?

She walked into the bedroom, drying her hair with a towel. "Did I hear the phone?"

I laughed. Sometimes I thought she had special powers. "Yes, you did. Peter called to invite us to dinner tonight. Would you like to go?"

"What?" She stopped in her tracks and dropped her towel on the floor.

"Do you want to go to Peter's for dinner tonight? You know, my brother," I teased.

She ran over to the bed, straddled me, and leaned down, holding my arms above my head.

"Are you asking me to a family function?"

I smiled. "Well, he invited you, and it would be rude if I didn't extend the invitation. And I remember you telling me that you wanted me to let you in more. I'm warning you, though, it's like stepping into a viper's den."

"Don't be a jerk right now. This is groundbreaking for you. The mysterious Lizzie is letting me into a part of her secret world." She leaned down and kissed me.

I brushed her hair out of her face. "It's not a secret world. I don't like them much, and I'm surprised that anyone would want to subject themselves to my family." I shrugged to the best of my ability, since she was still holding down one of my arms.

A puzzled look crossed her face. "Why did you laugh when I asked if I heard the phone?"

"What?" I ran my free hand over her breasts and down her torso.

"You laughed when I asked the question. Why?"

"I don't know. I just did." I laughed again. "Come here." I pulled her closer and kissed her. Then I asked, "Can you be ready by five? I know you'll have to leave practice early, but we have to be there early." Volleyball season had started, and Sarah was the girl's JV coach.

"What time is dinner?"

"Seven."

"We'll be really early." She looked perplexed.

"Trust me."

She smiled. "Of course, I trust you, and I'll be ready at five."

Chapter Ten

We arrived at Peter's house a little after 6 p.m. Part of me was surprised when I saw his house. The other part thought, *Typical Peter.* Simply put, it was ostentatious. He had a four-car garage. Floodlights pierced the sky near every tree. And from the looks of the neighborhood, it was newly built. The house was reminiscent of a plantation home.

"What does your brother do?" Sarah gasped.

"Investments of some sort. And he kisses Dad's ass."

"It seems to work for him." Sarah leaned closer to the windshield to get a better view.

I parked the car on the street and we trekked to the front door. We had to climb a winding stone staircase to ring the bell. Where in the hell did my brother think he lived, the old south?

Before I rang the bell, I gave Sarah my are-you-sure-you-are-ready-for-this smile. She smiled back at me, but her expression lacked confidence. For a brief moment, I felt bad for her. Then again, she had been asking for this, so here she was. I turned to the door and pressed the bell. I could hear church bells chiming. *Oh God, Peter. Do you think you're Jesus?*

Maddie opened the door and immediately threw her arms around me. "I'm so glad you are here." She let me go, and then threw her arms around Sarah just as enthusiastically. "Sarah, I'm glad you could make it."

She whisked us past the foyer and into the kitchen. Peter was standing at the bar, preparing a scotch. That was when I knew my parents were in attendance. *Nice, Peter. Real nice not to give me all of the information.* I should have suspected. His nose was so far up their asses it would require surgery, and massive amounts of therapy, for Peter to stand on his own two feet.

"Hey sis, you made it. And you must be Sarah. Maddie told me you were quite lovely. Well, that figures. Elizabeth is of the same stock, and boy do we catch fine-looking women in our family." He nudged me with his elbow, winked, and lifted his glass to toast Maddie.

Sarah obviously didn't know what to do after this little performance. She chose to go with a deer-in-headlights look. It was the best choice, considering.

"Don't mind him, Sarah. He just pretends to be crude. Deep down somewhere, there's a nice guy … or I keep hoping there is." Maddie patted Sarah's arm.

"*Touché*, Maddie." Peter took a swig of bourbon and then left the kitchen, carrying the drinks. I turned to Maddie and asked if my parents were present.

"Your mother is. Your father hasn't arrived yet. Something at the office held him up." She fluttered to the other side of the kitchen. "Really, Lizzie, what does he do? There is always some emergency. And now Peter is always held up as well. This is the first night in weeks that I've seen him before ten." Anger flashed in her eyes.

"You got me. We don't talk much." I shrugged.

"Yes, that's right, the mysterious family. Sarah, have you noticed that about Lizzie? Like she tells you just enough about herself, but deep down there's so much more." Maddie laughed and continued preparing a salad.

To my surprise, Sarah came to my defense. "She does

have a mysterious side, but when she comes home late, I know what she has been up to. It's usually because she's had her nose buried in some book and has lost track of time." She leaned over to kiss my cheek. Right then, both my mother and brother entered the kitchen. It took a trained eye, but I could see my mother flinch when she saw the kiss.

Peter smiled. I could practically see him counting the extra money he would inherit.

"Look, Mother, for once Elizabeth is on time for dinner." Peter helped Mom to a barstool.

Sarah glanced at her watch. I looked at the clock on the microwave. It was six-thirty. Sarah looked at me and chuckled. I think she was starting to see why I did certain things, like show up so early for everything.

"Maddie, is there anything I can do to help with dinner?" asked Sarah.

"You are a dear, but to be honest, most of it is done. I picked up dinner from this darling restaurant down the street." She smiled at Sarah. "I hope neither one of you is vegetarian or I'm afraid all you will be eating is this salad." She tossed it some more and then set it aside.

I could tell she was nervous. Why? Because of Sarah, perhaps?

"Fear not, we are both carnivores." I smiled at Maddie and she reciprocated.

As she reached for a serving platter on top of the fridge, I saw a large hole in her sweater. It looked like it had been well worn and the hole was testimony to that.

"Maddie, why do you insist on wearing that sweater? That hole is the size of the Grand Canyon. We are not paupers, my dear." Peter waved his arm to point out the luxury of their lifestyle.

"I love this sweater. It's the most comfortable one I own, so I'm sorry but you'll just have to endure seeing me in it." She flashed a stubborn smile at Peter, who turned away to say something to our mother.

The Scotch-lady did not look impressed by Maddie's determination to be comfortable. I couldn't remember the last time I saw Mom in a pair of jeans or shorts. She would always tell me, "It is better to always dress nice, because that one time you wear sweats, the whole world will stop by to see you."

Of course, I never lived by that mantra, but Peter did. On the rare occasion he wore jeans, they were guaranteed to be of the nicest quality and the most expensive. Even then, they looked starched. What was the point of wearing formal jeans? Especially when they resembled "mom jeans."

"How's your job going, Maddie?" Sarah asked, an obvious attempt to divert attention from the sweater.

I looked at Sarah. Usually, she was so quiet she would hardly ever engage in conversation with a group of people she did not know. I stopped to wonder whether she was trying to impress me or support me, or whether she just felt comfortable with Maddie's southern, carefree attitude. It was like they were old friends.

"Well, should we sit down and start dinner?" said The Scotch-lady before Maddie could even answer Sarah's question.

"It's all ready. I was waiting for Charles," Maddie explained.

"Oh, he can eat the leftovers." Mom looked at her watch. "Serves him right for being late again."

"Mom, I'm sure something important held him up at the office." Peter looked troubled.

Was he upset that he would have to choose a side? He was never good at that when it came to our parents.

"How 'bout I get you another drink?" he told her.

"I would never turn that down, but I'm famished. And I have to leave soon."

I was sure that was a lie. I examined her thin, persnickety face. Yes, she was fibbing.

Peter's face was priceless. He looked as if he might cry. I

reveled in the moment, wondering whose side he would take: Mother's or Father's. *Come on, Peter. Make a choice for once in your life.*

"Hello all."

Goddamnit! Why did he have to show up right then? I turned to find my father standing there, his expertly tailored three-piece suit hiding his belly.

"Dad, you made it!"

For a second, I thought Peter was going to wet himself with excitement. He reminded me of my neighbor's cocker spaniel, who peed whenever he was excited.

The Scotch-lady took another sip of her drink, but she didn't even look in her husband's direction. Was this why I was so screwed up about relationships? I glanced over at Sarah. To my astonishment, she showed no reaction to the scene at all. Was she just overwhelmed by it all?

"Sorry I'm late ... got held up, you know," he said in a deep voice.

Maddie's jaw almost hit the floor. She looked at me, and I could tell she wanted to shout, "Oh my God! That's the most your father has ever said."

Peter must have seen the expression on her face too, because he said, "Maddie, do you think we can get some food on the table and feed all these hungry people?"

I wanted to hit him.

She retorted, "I could if you would get your lazy buttocks out of my way."

To his credit, he didn't rebuff her. Did he know he would lose the battle? Her southern charm didn't quite take the sting out of it, but gave her words the illusion of being heartfelt.

I could tell my father was impressed. He loved a woman with a spark. That explained why he hated my mother: her spark went out years ago.

"If you'll take a seat, I'll bring out the salads?"

I followed my father into the dining room. He was the

man to follow. His girth announced that he never missed a meal.

The dining room, considering the size of the house, was quite modest. The table could seat eight comfortably. In the middle was a beautiful yellow rose centerpiece in what I assumed was a Waterford vase. No paintings graced the wall; instead, an elegant candelabrum hung on the wall behind the table. And, of course, all of the votives were lit.

Sarah and I took a seat together on one side, and my parents sat at the ends of the table. I found that surprising, but maybe they figured they paid for the house so they might as well have that honor. I was pleased. At least I didn't have to stare at them across from me all night.

Maddie walked in with the salad and seemed to wince a little when she saw the seating arrangement. Peter gave her his not-right-now smile. She shook her head and said, "I'm happy that all of you could join us this evening."

After placing the bowl by the man of the house, Charles, she sat down. "Peter and I have an announcement." She placed her hand on Peter's.

Panic overcame me. I stopped breathing.

"That's right. After much finagling we have finally got our schedules squared away, and we have set a date for the wedding."

What a relief! I thought for sure she was going to say she was pregnant. I didn't think I could handle that.

"That's great news. When's the big day?" asked the romantic, Sarah.

"July fourteenth," replied Peter.

I started to panic. *Please Sarah, don't say anything.*

"Did you say July fourteenth? That's Lizzie's birthday." Sarah sounded baffled by Peter's oversight.

I wasn't shocked at all.

"Peter, you didn't tell me your sister's birthday was the fourteenth." Maddie genuinely seemed upset. I hoped she'd throw the salad bowl at his head.

"What? I thought ... that's right it is. I got so caught up on scheduling I totally spaced it. It's not easy you know, coordinating mine, yours, Mom's and Dad's schedule." He threw his fork down on top of his salad defensively. Coordinating with my schedule obviously wasn't important to him.

"Well, I guess we'll have to come up with a different date," Maddie said, scowling at him.

I was glad we had come to dinner; the drama was pure entertainment.

I stammered, "A-are you kidding ... keep it on my birthday. That way I won't forget it. I'm horrible at remembering things like that. You have to keep it."

"Doesn't say much about you as a historian, if you can't remember dates." Maddie laughed and took a sip of wine. I could tell she was seething but was trying to regain control.

"I told you history is the greatest story ever told, remember ... not just dates."

She nodded, but the anger was still present.

"You wouldn't mind?" Peter seemed relieved. "Because we already started reserving everything and making initial plans."

"Nah. I don't really celebrate my birthday anyway."

Sarah squeezed my leg under the table. I could feel her nails digging in. We had planned a trip to the Tetons that week. I glanced at her again, but didn't know what to say. What could I do? Say, "No way, Jose, that's my birthday?" Wouldn't that be childish?

"Good. It's settled then. The date is July fourteenth," declared Peter. "And we won't have to buy Elizabeth a cake, since there will be wedding cake."

What a nice thought, Peter. I tried to remember if I had ever had a cake on my birthday.

Maddie looked at me, but I couldn't tell what she was thinking. I smiled and raised my water glass in her direction. A weak attempt, I know, but it was all I could do at the time.

She smiled and turned to Sarah. "How are your classes going?" she asked.

"What? Another student?" cackled The Scotch-lady.

"No, Mother. Sarah teaches high school English."

"My classes are good. They're always good this time of the year … wait and ask me in December and my answer will be quite different." She giggled.

"High school, huh?" Peter looked at me. "They don't pay you guys much. Would you consider yourself more of a volunteer?" He chuckled.

"Peter, what an awful thing to say." Maddie's beautiful face scrunched into a frown.

"All that I'm saying is that teachers don't make much." He paused, looked briefly at Mom and Dad, and then said, "It's a good thing Elizabeth has a trust fund, since she didn't go into the family business."

Family business. What were we—gangsters?

My mother bristled. I often wondered if she had tried to cut off my trust fund. My father just looked bored, but that was normal, so I wasn't sure how he felt. He would be great at Texas Hold 'em.

"Peter, thanks for your concern. But I have my own trust fund." Sarah's expression was one of triumph.

Maddie glowered at Peter.

"What? I was just making a joke. She gets so touchy about these topics. You know, Maddie, I'm starting to think you aren't a Democrat at all, but a hard-core liberal." Again he chuckled, but it sounded nervous this time.

"How can you be a Democrat? You're from the south? Aren't all Democrats supposed to be from the northeast?" asked my mother.

"I thought Arkansas was a southern state?" I quipped.

"You know, I'm not from there, but I think you are right, Lizzie," Maddie replied, a huge grin on her face.

"Wasn't one of their governors … oh, what is his name … a Democrat?" I went further. "And didn't he become president?"

"And didn't he marry a lesbian?" My mother pronounced it Les-Bi-An. Some words she liked to enunciate for dramatic purposes. Lesbian had always been one of them, for obvious reasons. However, she only did it in certain settings; in public, she ignored me completely. Even when I was a child she acted like I was a stranger. One time, when I was small, I accidentally knocked over a display in a store. I turned my beet-red face to her. She looked me up and down and said, "You better go find your mother to clean up this mess." I was devastated.

I squeezed Sarah's leg to give her some support. She placed her hand on my knee. Peter, technically the host of the meal, stayed out of it and refused to make eye contact. Maybe he felt that, since he was denied the host position at the head of the table, he wasn't the host after all. Father, seated at the table head, didn't really accept me anyway, but he appreciated anyone who could ruffle my mother's feathers so he looked on with a smirk.

"Jesus, Mother! She isn't a Les-Bi-An. Just because a woman is powerful, doesn't mean she is gay."

"That's obvious." Mom raised her drink in my direction.

Bravo, Mother. Bravo.

Maddie caught my eye. "Maybe we should start on the entrée? Anyone else hungry?" She stood and started for the kitchen.

"You know me, Maddie. I'm always hungry." Peter nearly shouted after her as she rushed away. He patted his stomach to emphasize the point. I noticed that, for the first time, it was starting to bulge a little, which made me smile. The only one who didn't have a belly in our family was The Scotch-lady, but only because she kept to a strict liquid diet.

Chapter Eleven

"Les-Bi-An!" Ethan laughed while saying it. "I can't believe she said that ... and at the dinner table. How rude! No one in my family would say it during dinner." He continued to giggle.

"Well, we aren't from the polite south, my friend." I stared at the hot barista while she made our coffees. *Was I a pig? Or did I just appreciate beauty?*

"What did Sarah say about it?" He flipped the pages of a book that sat on the table. It was *The Da Vinci Code*.

"You know that book is riddled with historical inaccuracies." I gestured to the novel.

"Oh, I know, professor." He raised one palm in the air. "But somehow I'm persevering. Have you ever looked up the word 'stodgy'?"

"Hmph!"

"Oh, don't get your panties in a bunch. Loosen up, Lizzie! Now tell me how Sarah reacted to your mom." He placated me with a smile.

"To be honest, she was really quiet on the ride home. And when she was getting ready to go shopping with her mom this morning, she barely talked to me."

"Does she go shopping with her mom every Saturday?" He looked at his phone, its insistent beeping telling him he had a text. "Dammit, I've only been here ten minutes and she's already getting on my case." He slammed the phone down on the table.

His wife hated that we spent so much time together.

"What do you think her silence means?" he asked while he fired off a text to his wife.

"Got me? Maybe she realized I'm a much bigger challenge than she thought."

"Or she felt bad for you." He paused to read his wife's return text. "Her family is accepting, right? Maybe Sarah doesn't know what to say to you. She's been pushing you to let her into your family, and now she sees how they treat you."

"Maybe. It's a possibility. But she should know me. I don't care what they think." I leaned on the table and propped my chin in my right hand.

"Not at all? Come on, Lizzie, deep down most of us want acceptance, especially from our families."

I tilted my head in my hand and leered at the barista, ignoring Ethan. Seconds passed and I noticed he followed my gaze.

Ethan casually said, "She looks like your ex."

Holy shit! I thought to myself, bolting upright. *He's right.* She had long blonde hair, deep green eyes, and a beguiling smile. "I thought she looked familiar."

He laughed. "Maybe Maddie is good for you. Before, you would have made the connection right away and gone on and on about it." He made limp-wristed circular movements in the air.

"Don't you mean Sarah?"

"Nope. I mean Maddie. You have been so different these past few weeks—more relaxed, happier, and easier to talk to. You've always opened up after some coaxing, but now you don't need any prodding."

"I don't know what you're talking about."

My phone beeped. A message flashed up on the screen. "Oh great, Sarah wants me to have dinner with her mom tonight." I paused before sending a text back.

"Are you going?"

"Don't see how I can say no. She had to put up with my family last night. Besides, her mom is nice." I shook my head. "You know me, I just hate family dinners … I'm not good at things like that. Geez, Sarah and I hardly go to dinner, let alone with other people."

"And you say my marriage is bad."

I chuckled. "I guess people who live in glass houses shouldn't throw stones."

"Especially you! You wouldn't hit a thing. How is it you never played softball as a kid? Don't all dykes play in college? Sorry, I mean *Les-Bi-Ans.*"

His joke caught me by surprise, and chai almost streamed out my nose. It burned like hell.

"Have you been drinking long?" He smirked.

After coffee with Ethan, I decided to hit the Poudre River bike trail. One thing I love about Colorado is that even in late October the weather can be gorgeous. I looked at the mountains to see if any clouds were rolling in, but all I saw was clear blue sky.

For the first ten miles, the vibrancy of the red, orange, and yellow leaves contrasting the lazy river awed me. I had always loved being surrounded by nature. Since it was late in the season, there weren't too many people out on the trail.

I pulled off the trail at my favorite spot and sat by the river. Sunlight glittered on the ripples of the slow, meandering stream. This time of year, before the winter snow melt, it was more like a dribble. In the spring, it gushed.

Picking up a smooth stone, I tried my best to skim it all the way across. It jumped twice and then sank to the bottom. Infuriated, I tried again. Skip. Skip. Then nothing. I had seen countless fools skip stones here. Why couldn't I?

"Lizzie, stop it." My words floated through the thin air.

I picked up another stone, lined it up carefully, and released. Jump. Jump. Then I saw it no more. I laughed mirthlessly at my ineptitude.

Giving up, I sat there, contemplating life, love, and the kind of stuff one thinks about when sitting next to a river, until I noticed the weather beginning to change. A strong gust of wind sent my bike clattering to the ground. My metal water bottled popped out of its holder and clinked as it rolled over the rocks to stop at the river's edge. The weather could change fast in Colorado at this time of year. Clouds had already started to roll in over the foothills.

Righting my bike, I then jumped on and started the trek home. The wind came in gusts, and when it did, I had to use all of my strength to stay on the bike. At points, the wind picked up my front tire and turned it perpendicular to the rest of the bike. Colorado weather—you never knew what was going to happen. The saying was, "If you don't like the weather, wait ten minutes and it will change."

After struggling for over an hour, I finally made it back to my apartment. As I lifted my bike up onto my shoulders to carry it up the flight of stairs to my apartment, a familiar voice behind me said, "Only you would be crazy enough to go for a ride in this wind."

I turned my head. "It was beautiful when I left … no wind at all."

"Oh my gosh, Lizzie, you're bleeding." Maddie sounded concerned.

I looked down. Blood dripped from my shin down into my sock. "Yeah, a tree branch hit me. I tried avoiding it, but as you can see"—I gestured to my shin—"I wasn't successful." I laughed.

She shook her head. "And what about your arm?"

"What?" I looked at my left arm and then my right. Sure enough, my right arm had a gash as well. "I don't know what happened." I paused to think. "But that does explain why my arm started to hurt. I just thought my arms were tired from struggling to stay on the bike."

"You're a mess. Let's get you upstairs and get you cleaned up." She took the bike, lifted it onto her shoulder, and started up the stairs. Her manner told me not to mess with her. When we reached the landing outside my door, she noticed the computer on my bike. "792 miles. Not bad." She flashed her sexy smile.

At my front door, she put her hand out for my keys. I sighed and handed them to her. She opened the door, hung my bike up, and then turned to me. "All right, I hope you have a first aid kit."

"I do. You look like you would ream me if I didn't." I walked into my bedroom. Maddie followed. It felt weird for a brief moment. Then she followed me into the bathroom.

"Wow! This bathroom is spotless. Who cleans it, you or Sarah?" She eyed me.

"Uh ... we have a cleaner. I wipe down the sinks and counter each morning, but the sparkle is Miranda's doing." I opened the cabinet under the sink, searching for my first aid kit.

"Peter wants me to hire a cleaner, but, oh, I don't know ... it feels weird to have a stranger in my home." She fidgeted with some flowers on the counter.

I stood awkwardly, not knowing what to say. Did she think I was a snob?

She smiled. "Maybe I should. I hate sticking my hand in the toilet."

I crinkled my nose in disgust.

Wanting desperately to change the subject, since I didn't want her to think of me as a prig, I handed her my first aid kit.

"Good." She laughed. "I don't have to beat you now."

"You wouldn't pick on the injured, would you?"

"Yes! If they're stupid enough to go out in this wind." She gently whacked the back of my head.

"Ouch!" I stepped back in case she struck again. "It wasn't windy when I left." I pouted.

"Didn't you look at the weather channel? I thought for sure you would be the type to check that out."

"What do you mean 'the type to check that out'? Just because I study history doesn't make me a dork."

"I'm finding it doesn't make you smart, either. It's a good thing you weren't seriously injured. The wind is gusting up to 60mph. And there you were, out there riding, you moron." She laughed as she dabbed hydrogen peroxide on the cut on my shin.

I tried not to react, but my leg jerked away.

"You and your brother are such babies." She started to dab my elbow. "The cuts aren't bad at all. All you need is a couple of Band-Aids. I'll put them on after you shower. How can you sweat so much in the cold? I can't believe you are in shorts and a tee when it is only 50 degrees outside."

"I'm not impressing you at all today, am I?"

"Are you trying to impress me?" I wondered what arcane thoughts her smile concealed.

I ignored the question. Or was I scared to answer it? "Is Peter working today?" I asked instead.

"Of course. Saturday is just another workday. Is Sarah shopping with her mom?"

"Yes. Our partners are quite predictable."

"Well, then, get in the shower and then take me to lunch. I'm famished. And I will tell you about this crazy appointment I had this morning."

I gave her a look.

"I know … I know." She put her palms up in the air. "I bust Peter's balls for working on a Saturday, when I made an appointment as well. But wait until I tell you about it. It was so worth it. Now, get into the shower." She turned and left the bathroom.

I turned on the water—hot, since I needed to warm my bones. The wind had chilled me all the way through. My cuts stung when the water hit them. Rushing through my routine, I pulled on a shirt and some jeans.

When I walked into the front room, Maddie shook her head. "Did you put a bandage on your shin?"

"Um … sure."

"You're such a liar. Come on, back into the bathroom."

I felt like I was being scolded.

"Wow, you do like a hot shower." The mirror was still steamed. "How am I supposed to put the Band-Aid on with your jeans on?" She smiled.

I fidgeted.

"Would it make you feel better if I closed my eyes?"

"Yes, it would. But I don't think you'll actually do it." I started to undo my jeans, feeling relieved that I had shaved recently and had put on clean underwear that didn't have any holes. That could have been extremely embarrassing. Standing there with my jeans around my ankles, I prayed that Sarah wouldn't walk in. Normally, I wasn't religious, but at that moment, I was.

"Okey dokey." She patted my leg. "Let's see your elbow."

I pulled my jeans up so fast I almost ripped the bandage right off.

"Easy, tiger. You are injured enough. Don't rip off more skin."

"But I'm receiving such top-notch care, so why not?"

She didn't respond right away, just took care of my elbow. Then she looked me in the eyes. "Someone has to take care of you."

She smelled of orange blossoms. No words came to me. I just stared back. The look only lasted a few seconds, but it seemed much longer.

"Are you going to take me to lunch now? I'm starving. And I am dying to tell you about my appointment." She looked at her reflection in the mirror and messed with her hair.

"All right. All right. I guess it's the least I can do after you played nurse today."

"I still can't believe you went riding in this wind. Do you hear it now, you ding-dong?" She hit my shoulder. "Good thing it isn't trash day or your dad would have to go to the ravine to retrieve his trash cans."

She was right: the wind was howling.

* * *

"Oh, my God." After we were seated at Coopersmith's, Maddie grabbed my arm. It was obvious she could no longer keep the story bottled up inside. "So I went to this client's house. At first, everything seemed normal. I sat down with a man and his wife and they started to tell me what they envisioned and stuff. Then the husband cleared his throat and said they had one challenge. His sister, who is mentally challenged, lives with them and has a habit of breaking things, so they wanted stuff that couldn't be thrown or easily broken.

"At first I thought, *Wow, what a great couple. I don't think I could do that* … yada, yada." She waved her arm in the air. "Anyway, we started taking a tour through the house. They want to re-do the entire house. And they are quite well off, so it'd be a large project, which I was stoked about. Ka-ching!"

She paused to take a drink.

All I could think was: *Wow! She might be up here a lot more.* This was fantastic news! I tried to hide my excitement by taking a sip of Coke.

"When they started to show me the sister's bedroom, the wife mentioned that the sister wasn't there. At the time, I didn't notice any apprehension, but now, looking back, it was there." Maddie paused, her eyes glowing. "Yeah, it was definitely there."

She wiggled in her chair and waved her arms again. "But I'm jumping ahead of myself. The couple told me the sister is almost completely non-verbal. She only says a handful of words, such as big wheel, peanuts, and her own name.

"We were almost done with the tour when we went down into the basement. I finally met the sister"—Maddie took a deep breath—"Lizzie, I kid you not. She was sitting in a recliner completely naked, with her legs up in the air, masturbating." Maddie started to laugh uncontrollably. She took more deep breaths and said, "And she kept saying the words 'big wheel' and 'peanuts.'

"I didn't know what to say or do. All of us just stood there dumbfounded. Finally, the husband ushered us up the stairs.

"I know it's not the PC thing to ... to"—she paused for a second to laugh again and then sucked in some air so she could talk—"to laugh at that. But when I got into my car ..." Maddie was gasping for breath. "I couldn't stop laughing. I laughed so hard I almost peed myself."

I laughed too, not just at the story, but at Maddie. Her face was scarlet but she looked so beautiful and serene, even while struggling for air and laughing so hard.

After she settled down a little, I asked, "How in the heck did you end that meeting? I mean, what did you say, 'Nice meeting you, but I'm sorry this didn't work out'?"

She was still laughing as she said, "Oh, I took the job."

Fuck yeah. She took the job. Oh my god, this was the best news ever. "You did? That's great. A job like that must pay a fortune ... not to mention how great it will look for your portfolio."

She smiled. I could tell she was proud of herself, and she deserved it. "What did Peter say when you told him?"

Maddie muttered, "Oh, I haven't told him. We're supposed to have dinner tonight, so I'll probably tell him then." Her tone turned serious. "Are you mad at me?"

I almost choked on my Coke. "What? Because you laughed at a person with a disability? No ... no, not at all."

"No, you idiot." She lightly slapped my arm. "Not because of that. Are you mad at me for the other night?"

I racked my brain. "Maddie, I have no clue what you are talking about ... unless you mean wearing a sweater with a hole in it."

She swatted my arm again. "Not that, you moron. You

know, the other night when your mom was so rude to you. I didn't say anything. It's been bothering me since."

"Really? Why?" My voice cracked a little.

"Because she is such a bitch. I'm sorry, Lizzie, I know she's your mother, but God, what a cunt."

I laughed. "Don't worry. You can say whatever you want about my mom and you won't hurt my feelings or make me mad. I've never called her that, though. I call her The Scotch-lady."

It was her turn to chuckle, covering her mouth with her hand so she wouldn't spit out her food. "You're right. She always has a scotch in her hand … Scotch-lady … I like that. Who else calls her that?"

I paused and thought. "To be honest, I've never told anyone I call her that."

She put her hand on my arm and whispered, "Your secret is safe with me." Her wink gave me goosebumps.

For the rest of the meal, all I could think about was that Maddie had taken the job. I didn't know much about interior design, but I believed she would have to be up here quite a bit until it was done. Maybe I should start expecting more pop-ins … wait, was that an oxymoron? How did one expect pop-ins? Oh well … who cared. This was the best day ever.

Chapter Twelve

I tarried as long as I could with Maddie, but I had promised to have dinner with Sarah and her mom, and Maddie had to drive back to Denver. We said our farewells and I sped home to arrive before Sarah returned from shopping.

By the time Sarah entered the apartment, I was sitting on the couch with a book and a pen. I had read a few pages, but the thought of Maddie working in the same town preoccupied my mind. I glanced back at the pages I had read and saw I hadn't marked any up at all. I knew it wasn't sinking in.

"My, you are engrossed in your book."

I smiled. "It looks as though shopping was a success today."

Sarah stood in the doorway, five large shopping bags garlanding her arms. I noticed there were smaller bags tucked inside the larger ones. "You could say that. One of these days, you'll have to join us again. I'll pack you some energy drinks." Sarah set the bags down and came to the couch. I lifted my legs so she could sit and then placed my legs on top of her.

"I got us the coolest blender. Now we can have bona fide margaritas." She stroked my leg, running her hand up my shin beneath my baggy jeans. Of course, she felt the bandage. "What did you do to your leg?" She started to lift my pant leg up so she could look.

"Oh, it's nothing. I was riding my bike and I was struck by a blowing tree branch."

She stared at me. "You rode your bike in *this* wind? Are you crazy or something? Let me take a look, God knows you wouldn't have taken the time to bandage it properly."

Before I could protest, she ripped the bandage off. Sarah paused. "This one must have hurt you. You actually put Neosporin or something on it." She secured the bandage again and leaned down and kissed it. "Do you need Tylenol or anything? Does it hurt?"

"Nah, I'm good. Thanks, though." I didn't want to talk about it, so I quickly changed the subject. "So, what amazing treasures did you find today?"

"Oh, the usual—some clothes. And mom and I found some of the cutest things for you. I found some jeans that will show off your ass." She pinched my butt. "Might as well show it off. You work so hard having a nice one, with all of that bike riding and hiking. I still can't believe you went riding in this wind." She shook her head.

I mentioned once, early on in our relationship, that I abhorred shopping and that I'd love to have someone do it for me. Ever since then, whenever she went shopping with her mom, Sarah picked out clothes for me if she saw something she liked. It was sweet really, that she and her mom took the time to help a fashion-impaired person. And, to be honest, I had started dressing better.

"I should have known. Honey, I'm going to have to give up this teaching thing and work with my brother so I can build a closet the size of a house for all of your clothes."

She smiled a huge smile. "Well, maybe we should stop paying rent for two places and pool our resources for a larger place together."

Holy fucking shit, I walked right into that one. No way. No how.

I was not ready for that. I looked into her eyes and saw anticipation, hope, and fear. I couldn't do it. "Uh … we can talk about that. But if I'm not mistaken, we have to meet your mom for dinner. What outfit did you buy for me tonight? And by the way, how much do I owe you?"

She slapped my leg and then said, "Oh, my gosh, did I hurt your shin?"

"No, you're good." It did sting a little. "Geez, I get injured and then my girlfriend hits me." I sat up and kissed her cheek.

* * *

"You look fabulous." Sarah's mom gave me a hug and eyed my black pinstripe pants and shiny purple shirt. "I have to admit that we did a great job picking out that outfit."

"Thanks, Rose." I stepped back from her and my hand flew to the fabric. The shirt was very soft, silky almost. If I knew anything about clothes, I might know the fabric, but I didn't. I made a mental note to look at the tag to see what it was made of.

Rose said, "I checked in with the hostess and our table is almost ready."

Fort Collins was one of the largest cities in Colorado. But since it was a college town, there weren't many nice restaurants. On most occasions when we dined with Rose, we went to Jay's Bistro, one of the classier joints.

Sarah and Rose chatted while I looked around. Mother and daughter looked so much alike: short dark hair in a fashionable cut, penetrating brown eyes, beautiful skin, and large smiles. And both always dressed impeccably; family money paid off for both of them.

Rosalind Cavanaugh, who hates her full name and prefers Rose, married young. Sarah told me her father had swept her mother off her feet and they married right after Rose graduated from high school. He was a year older. James Cavanaugh was the only child of a wealthy couple and he had never worked. Instead, Sarah's parents traveled all over the world. After six years of marriage, they had Sarah. James's health started to fail soon after her birth. He died before Sarah was three. Rose and Sarah grew really close. Consequently, when Sarah moved to Colorado to attend the University of Colorado in Boulder, Rose followed. They acted more like sisters.

While they gossiped about one of their distant relatives, I scanned the restaurant and noticed a professor who had taught me during my undergrad days. For a brief moment, I panicked. I hated socializing and kissing ass just to aid my career, and I was so awkward and shy in those situations that it made both parties uncomfortable. He obviously didn't recognize or remember me. Thank goodness.

After we were seated, Rose looked me directly in the eyes. "So, Lizzie, I heard you are a Les-Bi-An."

I looked at Sarah, her expression mortified.

Then I started to laugh. I laughed so hard my cheeks hurt. Finally, I said, "I take it Sarah told you about her first, and maybe last, meeting with my family."

"It better not be my last." Sarah crossed her arms and glowered at me.

"Well, I can't see why you would want to endure them again."

"They are your family, Lizzie ... unfortunately," she mumbled the last word. Around her mom, Sarah let her guard down completely.

"You're telling me. You know what they say: you can't choose your relatives." I shrugged.

"That's a bunch of hogwash. Family is what you make it. And as far as I am concerned, you're more part of our family than your own. How often do we all see each other? Once, maybe twice a week." Rose winked.

Of course, we met only briefly on Saturdays before their shopping excursions. From my first introduction, Rose had always accepted me as one of her daughters.

"I'm glad you feel that way, Mom, because Lizzie and I have something to tell you." Sarah took a deep breath and turned to me. "We are moving in together."

We are what? Oh no, she didn't. She did not just put me in this situation! I looked at Rose and then at Sarah. Their faces were glowing. Did they plan this?

The waitress came by and announced the dinner specials. She departed quickly, giving us more time to think over our choices. Maybe she sensed the awkwardness. I'm sure my face was a brilliant scarlet, and I was gasping for air.

Rose was the first to speak. "Well, it's about time. It's no secret Sarah spends every night at your house. You two are going to buy a house, right? There's no sense throwing away your money on rent."

Sarah took a sip of her wine and left me to respond.

"I guess so … we really haven't talked about the details yet … but I guess you're right … only making someone else rich by paying rent." *Oh shut up, Lizzie.* I knew I was digging an even bigger hole for myself. I swayed in my seat, dizzy from the oppressive air.

"And Sarah, didn't you tell me Lizzie's brother is marrying an interior designer? If you ask me, all of the signs are pointing to home ownership."

Someone please throw me a fucking rope.

Chapter Thirteen

After dinner, I texted Ethan and begged him to meet me the following day. Both of us arrived at the same time. Distraught, I couldn't wait to sit down and tell him the news. While we waited in line, I explained what had happened.

"You're buying a house together?" blurted Ethan.

I put my fingers to my lips to shush him. As I guided us towards the back of the store, away from the crowd, I said, "I don't know what happened. When you think about it, Sarah played a masterful hand to do it in front of her mother. She knew I wouldn't have the gumption to say anything. And now it's too late. They practically have an interior designer hired." I collapsed into a seat.

Ethan sat down too, and whispered, "Did they call her?"

"No, but it's only a matter of time. These people don't mess around, Ethan." I looked nervously around the store. Why? I don't know. Was I expecting Sarah and her mom to pop out with brochures advertising homes for sale? "Once they have an idea, they strike like a king cobra."

He started to laugh. "Like a king cobra?"

"I don't know. I saw a show the other night about this

crazy guy who tracked down a king cobra in some jungle so he could touch its head … it was on one of those nature channels."

"Was it Animal Planet? I love that channel." He rubbed the top of his head and I noticed that he needed a haircut, and that he had a few gray hairs.

"Focus, Ethan. I'm about to make the worst mistake of my life. How do I get out of this?"

"I should have known something was wrong when you texted me. We've never had coffee two days in a row. My wife was pretty upset."

I banged my head on the table and almost spilled my chai. "You are not helping me."

"All right. All right." He laughed. "I've never seen you like this. Sorry, I was just having fun."

"I guess it isn't so bad. At least she didn't say we were getting married. I hate those gay commitment ceremonies; what a joke." I scoffed.

"Yeah, Lizzie, you're right. It's much better to sign a thirty-year mortgage together."

I groaned.

"Geez, Louise, you are easy pickings this morning. You're a mess, Miss Lizzie." His eyes sparkled.

"Listen, southern boy, you better help me."

"That's better. I was starting to miss the threats. All right, you want me to give it to you straight? Just tell Sarah you aren't ready to buy a house."

"You're right." I straightened up in my chair. "That's all I have to say: 'Sarah, I love you, but this is too much, too fast.'"

"Do you love her?"

I kicked him in the shins and he squealed.

"It's a simple question, either yes or no." Rubbing his shin, he inched his chair away from me.

I glared at him. "What's wrong if I want to take things slow?"

"Slow, huh? How long have you been dating?" He

tugged on his frayed collar.

"Almost a year." I paused. "Oh, shit! I think our anniversary is this week."

"Oh, how romantic, Lizzie! You're buying your girlfriend a house for your first year anniversary. What will you buy her on your tenth? A small island or something?"

"Hardy har har, Ethan." I slurped angrily at my chai.

"Seriously, though. It would behoove you to go the whole nine yards for the anniversary. Trust me, women hate to be blown off, and your track record has been horrible lately." He shook his head and tsked.

"Thanks for the tip."

"I'm always here to help." He raised his cup in cheers.

"Any suggestions?"

"How 'bout a ring? You're heading down that path, little miss homemaker." Ethan placed both elbows on the table, rested his chin on his hands, and batted his eyelashes at me.

I would have kicked him in the shins, but he was right. Sarah was playing her cards well. I needed to pick up my game. At least I could learn how to bluff better. Why did she feel the need to trap me?

"One good thing about this whole house business is that Sarah has stopped mentioning we should go to couple's therapy."

"Oh, that's right. I forgot she thought you weren't opening up enough. Well, buying a house is opening your wallet, so maybe she just wanted more gifts the entire time."

"Oh, shut up."

"Good one. I'll have to remember that comeback."

I shook my head and then laughed.

* * *

After coffee with Ethan, I took his advice about going all out for our anniversary. I didn't buy a ring, but I decided to head home for my car so I could visit the grocery store. I hardly ever cooked for Sarah. Boiling water was a challenge for me.

The one meal I'd made her before hadn't gone over well. But I wanted to try again. Problem was, I had no idea what to cook.

I hoped I would find some inspiration while wandering aimlessly around the aisles in Whole Foods. I didn't.

After thirty minutes, I was still clueless. I didn't want to make something simple, like spaghetti. I wanted to show a little more effort than boiling some noodles and warming up sauce. And there was no way in hell I was going to try to make my own sauce. I didn't think Ragu was anniversary dinner material. Yet I knew I couldn't veer too much away from a simple meal. Before Sarah started staying over every night, I didn't even own any spices other than salt and pepper. And cinnamon—I love cinnamon toast. She was the one who bought us a fancy spice rack with spices I had never heard of. Why did I think this was a good idea?

I wandered over to the butcher and peered down into the glass case. Veal seemed too hard. Finally, I spied some steaks. That was when the idea hit me. I asked the butcher to pick out his two best fillet mignons. Sarah loved asparagus, so I picked some up, along with potatoes. I thought about buying a cake, but then I thought she might think it was cute if I made cupcakes. I added some sprinkles, to decorate the cupcakes, to my basket. On the way home, I stopped at a hardware store to buy a small grill to cook the steaks.

As I drove by the mall, I heard Ethan's voice telling me I should go all out for this anniversary, so I ran into a jewelry store and picked out a necklace. It was nothing too fancy, but I had a feeling she would love it. Sarah loved amethysts.

It wasn't until I got home and set up the grill that I realized I had never cooked on a grill before. For the life of me, I could not light the darn thing.

Before I knew it, Sarah was standing behind me on the balcony, chuckling. "What's the matter: you never took a class on how to light a grill?"

I spun around and smiled bashfully. "They actually teach

that in college?"

"No, you nerd! Weren't you in the Brownies or Girl Scouts or something when you were a kid?"

"Nope."

"Have you ever been camping?"

"Camping? You mean that thing that involves tents and washing in the river."

"Yeah, that thing."

"Nope."

"Do you want to tell me what you're up to out here then?" She cocked one eyebrow.

"Would you believe I wanted to burn my dissertation?"

She crossed her arms.

"Oh, all right. I was trying to surprise you. I know our anniversary isn't until Wednesday, but I thought I would make you dinner and I got this grill to cook the steaks and asparagus. I wasn't expecting you this early. Why are you so early?" My voice squeaked.

"Don't interrogate me. You're the one sneaking around," she teased.

Panic seized me, but then I realized she meant buying the grill and making her dinner.

Hiding my crimson face, I lit another match and dropped it onto the stone-cold coals. Nothing.

Sarah snickered at my ineptitude. "You were going to cook me dinner. Wow ... you've never cooked me dinner before." She seemed touched.

"That's not true. I made you dinner once, but you laughed at me." I pointed a useless match in her direction.

"You made me Frito pie! You heated up refried beans and mixed it in Fritos, cheese, and salsa. That isn't cooking, my dear."

"You have to admit it was delicious."

She laughed. "Yes, as a great snack, but not a meal."

"Okay, wise guy. Help me light this grill so I can throw the steaks on."

As she walked to the grill, Sarah said, "By the way, I'm pretty impressed you remembered our anniversary. And all of this is sweet." Her delicate lips brushed my cheek, and I got a whiff of her perfume. I loved the smell of jasmine.

"Ah ... wait until you see the cupcakes."

"You bought cupcakes? I love cupcakes."

"No, I bought cupcake mix and things for us to decorate them with."

I watched her lean over the grill. Her skirt hitched up and I caught a glimpse of her pink satin underwear. Excitement coursed through me and I felt like I was seeing her the first time. Sarah always wore sexy lingerie.

"Are you looking up my skirt?"

I beamed. "Ab-So-Lute-Ly."

Casually, she glanced at me over her shoulder, teasing me with her eyes. "I felt your leer."

"Leer!" I scoffed. "You make me sound like a dirty old man ... or like one of your students. If you bent over like that in class I bet all of the boys would *leer* at you."

"And a couple of the girls." She winked at me. "Does it make you jealous? Thinking that some of my students might have the hots for me."

"*Moi!* Jealous!" I acted hurt. "What about you ... do you ever get jealous ... that ... er ... some of my students might have the hots for me?"

Sarah stood up and walked slowly towards me. Her confident stride turned me on, and she knew it. She leaned in to kiss me and I felt her hot breath. Suddenly, she pulled back. I stumbled forward causing her to laugh.

"Elizabeth Petrie, I know what I want. And no, I don't get jealous." She placed a finger on my mouth. When I tried to lick her finger, she pulled that away as well.

Feeling foolish, I asked, "And what do you want?"

"Oh that's for me to know and for you to find out." She kissed me, deep and passionately. My fingers slid up her skirt, but she didn't let me explore. "The coals should be hot now."

Gently, she pushed me away.

That isn't the only thing.

"Okay … I see how you want to play it today," I teased.

"That's another thing, Lizzie, I don't play with people."

Did she know about Maddie?

Regaining my composure, I changed the subject. "Come on, let's get this failure of a dinner on."

"Trust me, this is not a failure. This is perfect, and nicely timed, I might add." She gave me a devilish grin.

I pulled her necklace out of my pocket and dangled it in front of her. "I might as well give you your gift as well."

"Lizzie! It's beautiful!" Her eyes glistened.

"Turn around so I can put it on."

She obeyed. I clumsily got the necklace on, and then wrapped my arms around her petite waist.

Sarah touched the amethyst gingerly. "I have to admit that you're getting warmer."

I cocked my head. "What do you mean?"

"You're starting to figure out what I want."

I thought I had a pretty good idea—a house with a white picket fence. *Would it be so bad?* I peeked down her shirt. God she had a sexy figure.

"You're leering again."

I blushed. "I can't help it. You look stunning today."

All of her muscles relaxed and she melted against my body. "I really do love you, Lizzie."

"And I heart you."

Chapter Fourteen

After a day of classes and working on my own research, I called it a night around eight. All I wanted to do was to take a hot shower and crawl into bed. These long days were starting to kick my ass, and I was regularly avoiding going home at all.

The crisp night air cleared my head and invigorated my muscles as I rushed home. The bike computer inched past 1,000 miles. Smiling, I peddled harder.

As I put the key into my door, I heard giggling inside the apartment. Was Sarah on the phone? I panicked. Maybe she was talking to Maddie about decorating the new place.

I entered to find Sarah and Haley sitting on the couch, a pizza box, two wineglasses, and an empty bottle of wine on the table before them. It took a second for this to sink in. We hadn't even moved in together yet, but she was already inviting friends over for pizza and drinks.

"About time! What do you do all day and night without calling?" inquired Haley.

Second shock of the night: here she was, a guest in my house, and she acted like this.

"Be nice, Haley. Lizzie has to work hard so she can get a

good teaching position once she finishes her dissertation. It's not easy you know." She slapped Haley playfully on the leg.

"Ouch. I was only kidding." Haley sniggered. It was obvious she was inebriated.

Sarah's hand lingered on Haley's leg. I stared at her hand, trying to fathom what it meant. Sarah observed me and stood up quickly, but there was a faint smile on her face. Why?

"Are you hungry, baby? I saved some pizza for you. It's your favorite."

"Actually, I'm famished," I said, pushing my thoughts aside.

"I'll get you a drink." Haley started to get up.

Sarah must have noticed my look of 'Did your friend just offer me a drink in my own home?' and pushed Haley back onto the couch. "Haley, you're drunk. Sit down," she said. Turning to me, she smiled. "Lizzie, what would you like to drink?"

"Do we have any Coke?"

"Yes, we do. One rum and Coke coming up. And, from the looks of it, heavy on the rum." She kissed my cheek on her way to the kitchen.

I sat on the loveseat next to the couch. "So, Haley, what's new with you?"

"Men fucking suck. You're so lucky you are gay. Women would be so much easier. I fucking hate men." She grabbed her wineglass and dramatically gulped the rest of her wine. "Sarah, we need more wine," she shouted.

Haley was never happy. She always had drama in her life, and when there wasn't any, she stirred it up. Her verbally abusive boyfriend had a temper like a clap of thunder. Haley knew he was an asshole, but still she stayed with him. Two or three times a week I would get an update from Sarah. Michael did this; Michael did that. Each time, Haley would swear it was over, but all of us knew she wouldn't end it. Michael had no reason to end it; he treated her like shit, and then he got to fuck a hot woman when they inevitably had make-up sex.

Haley stared at me. I focused on the bookshelves. I could tell she was waiting for my prompt so she could divulge her woes. Instead, I yawned and stretched out my arms.

She sighed dramatically. I continued to ignore her.

"Honey, how was your day?" Sarah returned with my rum and Coke and sat next to me on the loveseat.

"Thanks, baby." I took the drink and pecked her on the cheek. "I really need this tonight."

"I thought you didn't drink." Haley's tone was accusatory.

"Not usually. Only when I'm in my own home."

"Oh. You are one of *those*. Never drink in front of your friends, but when you're at home, you tie one on in the dark. That's cool. I get it."

Neither Sarah nor I responded. Instead, I turned to Sarah and asked her about her day.

"Lizzie, I tell you, I am so ready for winter vacation. Today, one boy burned another boy with a lighter right in my classroom. The burned boy didn't even tell me. Another student told me what happened."

"Are you fucking serious? What the fuck is going on with kids today?" Haley waved her empty wineglass in the air and nearly dropped it. She overcorrected and almost fell off the couch.

I wasn't surprised that Sarah hadn't already told Haley the story; I knew better. When you talk to Haley, you talk only about Haley. She didn't care to know the details of anyone else's life.

I turned back to Sarah. "Are you okay?

"I guess so. College doesn't prepare you for these types of situations, you
know."

"What did you do?"

"The security guys took him to the SRO."

"What the fuck is an SRO? He should go to jail," Haley muttered.

"An SRO is a cop. School Resource Officer. And the boy was arrested," retorted Sarah.

"I'm so sorry, honey. Can I get you a drink?"

"Oh shit, I forgot to bring the wine." Sarah jumped up off the couch and rushed into the kitchen.

Haley set her empty wineglass down on the coffee table. "Jesus! After hearing about that, I wasn't going to mention that she forgot the wine," proclaimed Haley-the-Wonderful. Then she hiccupped.

Sometimes, I really wanted to slap some sense into her. How could Sarah be such good friends with Haley? What a selfish ass! Surely, Sarah wasn't attracted to her. Yes, Haley was beautiful, but would Sarah be so blindsided by that? *No. No, Sarah wouldn't be taken in by such a twit. A puerile twit.*

Sarah returned and filled Haley's wineglass, but not her own. Turning away from Haley, she sat next to me on the loveseat. I offered her my drink and she took a generous gulp.

I spied a copy of the novel *Fifty Shades of Grey* on the coffee table. "Haley, are you seriously reading that crap?" I gestured to the book with my glass.

Sarah blanched. "Actually, I am. Haley said she loved it and gave it to me to try. I thought I'd find it funny, but for some reason, I can't seem to put it down." Color rushed back into her face—too much color.

Why had Haley given my girlfriend a sex book? And why did Sarah accept such a contemptible gift? What reprehensible plans did Haley have? Now, if she had given Sarah a copy of *Lady Chatterley's Lover*, I might have considered her a worthy adversary. But *Fifty Shades*? It was rubbish for the masses. Pedestrian. No, worse! Imbecilic.

I put my arms around Sarah, marking my territory. It didn't go unnoticed.

"Ah, isn't that nice. You two look like lovebirds," muttered Haley.

I resisted my urge to hurl my glass at her head.

Sarah stood up. "Haley, I think it's time I drove you

home."

I darted out of my seat. "Sarah, wait! You've been drinking. I'll drive her home."

If Haley had any nefarious scheme, I planned on thwarting it.

There wasn't an argument, but Haley looked disappointed.

She didn't live too far away, so I was home within ten minutes. I found Sarah in the bathroom brushing her teeth.

Pulling the toothbrush out of her mouth, she said, "I'm sorry about Haley. She isn't normally that bad."

I shrugged and grabbed my toothbrush.

Sarah spat out a glob of toothpaste. "She doesn't understand how hard you work." She rubbed my back. "I know how stressed you are about finding a teaching position."

My mind latched onto her last sentence. I wondered … *That might work!* I might have found my bluff.

Chapter Fifteen

I decided to run my plan by Ethan at our next coffee "date."

"What do you mean?" Ethan plucked a cat hair off his shirt and peered over his glasses at me.

"What if I tell her it's not a good time to buy a house because we don't know where I'll get a job. When she told Haley I have to work long hours so I can get a good teaching job, it struck me that, more than likely, I will be moving in the next year or two."

Ethan stirred his coffee. "I don't know, Lizzie. Maybe you should just be honest with her."

"Does honesty work in your marriage?"

Ethan's nostril's flared slightly and he shot me a nasty look.

"Listen, it would be great to be honest, but you know how much I hate hurting people's feeling. Let's be 'honest'"— I made quote marks with my fingers—"I'm a wimp. Sometimes, it is just easier to lie."

"You don't have a problem hurting my feelings," he said, snarkily. "And you don't have any problems kicking me in the shins either," he added.

"That's the beauty of our friendship. Neither one of us can tell the truth to anyone else. It's like therapy for us. But once we leave this coffee shop, the honesty stops."

"And we're both trapped somewhere we don't want to be." Ethan let out an audible sigh.

"That's not entirely true." I corrected him. "I'm not sure what I want."

"Oh, I forgot, you are only honest with me here, and not even with yourself."

I went to kick him again but hit his chair leg instead.

"Ha! I knew you were going to kick." He looked smug.

"Seriously, though. I'm not sure what I want." I rubbed my toes. "Sarah is a great catch. She's cute, funny, and sweet. I don't mind spending time with her. I'm sure I can get used to the idea. There are worse relationships I could end up in. Hell, I've been in worse relationships."

Ethan set his coffee cup down and looked me in the eyes. "Lizzie, do you hear yourself? 'I don't mind spending time with her,'" he mimicked. "How can you do that to yourself? And most importantly, how can you do that to her? You are dealing with another life here. Fine, screw up your own, but don't screw hers up as well."

I didn't know what to say. I could say the same about him, but we weren't talking about him. Trying to change the subject was pointless.

* * *

Afterwards, I drove down Drake Road towards the foothills. I didn't want to go home; I knew Sarah would be waiting for me. Instead, I headed to one of my favorite hiking spots. At one point on the trail, I could veer off and head up a steep rocky climb. I knew I would be huffing and puffing by the time I reached the top, but I loved the climb. At the top I could sit on a bench overlooking the city and be alone with my thoughts. I made most of my important decisions there.

Am I not only ruining my life, but Sarah's as well? I wondered.

Am I even ruining my life? Aren't relationships built on mad love? Can't two people who get along fine be happy for the rest of their lives? And, the sex is fantastic. Am I just experiencing cold feet? I evaluated the questions from several angles. Even employing the logic I used in my studies when attempting to unravel contradictory historical research findings, I came up with a blank. I just didn't know.

I didn't know. Wasn't that awful? Here I was, considering buying a house with my girlfriend, and I didn't know if I wanted to. I cared about her—that was true. But did I care enough to make such a commitment? Did I care enough to consider spending the rest of my life with her?

The sun started to sink below the mountains, and I realized I better get my butt off the hill or I would have to hike down in the dark. Winter was coming, and it was getting darker earlier. Besides, Sarah might begin to wonder where the fuck I was, and I didn't want to have that conversation again.

* * *

"Wow, that was the longest coffee ever." Sarah's smirk marred her beautiful face. I hated that my actions caused her grief. She deserved better, and I wanted to be worthy of her.

"I'm sorry, honey. I stopped by the office and got caught up on some research." I didn't want to explain that I had gone hiking without her. The look on her face already told me I was in trouble. "Can I take you to dinner to make up for being a jackass?"

"That depends. Where are you taking me?" She set Haley's book down on the couch.

"How about Phoy Doy?"

It was Sarah's favorite restaurant. She loved Vietnamese food. And right then, I needed to get back into her good graces.

She smiled. "At least you know you're in trouble. Good. I've been waiting all day for you to come home." She hit my shoulder. "Serves me right … you told me on our first date that you were a workaholic."

"Tell you what, no more work this weekend. You have me all day tomorrow. I won't leave your sight."

She looked suspicious.

I held up my hand. "Scout's honor."

"You must feel guilty about something. All right, let me go change."

"I have a better idea." I pulled her close. "Let's take a shower together, and then we can both get ready for dinner."

She laughed. "Maybe you should blow me off more, Lizzie. I like it when you feel bad." She kissed me.

I laughed. "Come on, smartass. I want to get you naked, and all wet."

She pulled her shirt off. I took her hand and led her into the bathroom.

Chapter Sixteen

"God, I love it when we shower together," Sarah whispered an hour later, as the hostess sat us at our table. "You have an incredible way of lathering me up."

"Is that what you call it?" I raised an eyebrow.

"In public places, yes." She placed her napkin in her lap.

I suddenly felt uncomfortable. "Have I ever told you I used to be afraid of using too much soap?" I desperately wanted to change the subject.

She cocked her head and looked puzzled. "What do you mean?"

"When I was little. I used to be scared of using too much soap. One time, in the tub, I told Annie I was going to use heaps of soap so I wouldn't have to bathe for a month. Annie laughed and said if I did that I'd get hideous sores all over my body and I'd smell wretched.

"I misunderstood. I thought she meant that if I used too much soap I'd get sores. It wasn't until years later I figured out what she meant. For years, I used only the smallest amount of soap. I was obsessive about it. Every day, I'd spread a very fine layer of soap all over me and then I'd rinse it off as fast as I could. I didn't want any sores."

"Oh, my gosh!" Sarah covered her mouth and laughed. "I can't believe you! You must have been an adorable kid." She paused, crinkling her forehead. "Who's Annie?"

"She was my nanny."

"You had a nanny? I didn't know you had a nanny."

I fidgeted with my napkin. "It's not something you go around telling everyone. I'm not my brother."

I could feel her eyes on me, and I could tell something was brewing.

Our waitress approached to take our drink order. Sarah ordered a chardonnay and I asked for a Thai tea. It tickled me that a Vietnamese place served Thai tea. I suspected that the owners weren't even Vietnamese, since I overheard them speaking Korean to each other.

As soon as the waitress departed, Sarah pounced. "Do you feel like we are getting closer?" she asked, all trace of humor gone from her voice. "I mean, these past couple of weeks I've felt an even stronger bond with you. Have you noticed?"

Why play that game? I wondered. Of course, I couldn't say, 'Why, no, I haven't noticed that.' I'd come off as a bitch. I swear sometimes she phrased things to hear exactly what she wanted to hear.

I had no choice. I cleared my throat and responded, "Now that you mention it, I see what you're saying." I nodded my head slowly in confirmation.

Sarah reached across the table for my hand and began to lightly rub her fingers along my arm. "Lately, I feel like we are closer than ever. I mean, you never would have told me the story about the soap. But now, you just tell me these stories openly." Her voice dropped to a whisper again. "And earlier, in the shower, you have never touched me like that before."

I racked my brain, trying to remember what she was talking about. Yes, we'd had sex in the shower, but it was just a fuck. At least, that was how I thought of it. Obviously, Sarah felt differently. How was that possible? How could two people do something together and have two completely different experiences? I had told her the soap story because I wanted to change the subject. It was a diversionary tactic, not a "let me tell you a childhood memory story" moment.

I smiled and squeezed her hand, unable to think of anything to say. Staying quiet was the best course of action for this particular pickle, I decided.

"What would you two like to order?" The waitress tapped her pen nervously against her notepad. Was she uncomfortable around lesbians?

"Ah ..." Sarah glanced at the menu. "I think I'll try the noodle bowl with salmon."

"And you?" The waitress looked at me, expressionless.

"The noodle bowl with steak and shrimp, please."

I handed my menu to the woman and turned my attention back to Sarah. Her expression confused me. She was smiling, but there was an air of sadness about it. After a few moments, she said, "So, when will you have time to start looking at houses with me?"

"Um, shouldn't we talk to a mortgage guy first? No real estate agent is going to take us seriously without proof we can qualify to buy." I took a sip of my water. "By the way, have you been reading the papers? They all say this is a horrible time to buy a home. The rate of foreclosures is skyrocketing due to variable interest rates. And banks don't want to give mortgages to new homebuyers. So much for the American dream." I shook my head and tsked about the sad fact, all the while wondering: *Am I laying it on too thick?* I knew we would actually be a wet dream for a mortgage broker—two lesbians with trust funds, and both with steady work histories. But I didn't want to point that out.

"I really haven't been following the news. Do you think we should wait for the market to improve?" Sarah squinted a little and looked up from her placemat, which had a map of Vietnam on it.

Holy shit ... I didn't expect this. My spirits started to rise. "Honestly, I don't know much about the situation. However, I do have one major reservation about buying a house right now ..."

Sarah grabbed her wine and took a swig. It was obvious that words failed her. She nodded, clearly urging me to continue.

"W-we both know I won't be working at CSU for much longer," I stammered. "As scary as it seems, I'll have to start looking for a teaching position at a different university. If we buy a house now, what if we have to turn around in less than a year and sell it."

I could immediately tell by her expression that she had already thought of a way around this. "Oh, Mom and I talked about that. We think it would be best to find something inexpensive now, and when you find a teaching job at a different university, we can rent out the house. It would be a great start to diversifying our portfolio."

"Our portfolio ..." I mumbled. *Our portfolio.* The words rolled around in my head like a pinball. *Portfolio ... our. Our portfolio.* I had certainly never considered that phrase before. She really wanted to settle down together. Co-mingle our finances. What was next? A child?

I realized Ethan was right. Here we were talking about buying a house together, yet we hadn't even discussed our future. I was becoming one of those people I hated: the ones who get involved with someone and then have a nasty separation after a few years because they didn't talk about what they both wanted out of life. One of the two always seemed so surprised that the other didn't want everything they wanted—the house, the kids, the picket fence, etcetera.

I had always lectured Ethan for not communicating that, and here I was—a steel trap. How could I do this to her? How could I do this to me? *Nothing good will come of this,* I thought, and looked up into her eyes. They twinkled with happiness.

I smiled back. I did love the way she looked at me with those eyes. No one had ever looked at me like that before.

* * *

Over the next few days, Sarah and I didn't talk much about the house situation. I spent most of my waking hours at the office, working on my dissertation. That was when I received my first email from Maddie. Late one night, my computer dinged, letting me know I had received a new email. At first, I thought it was either a student sending a last-minute request for an extension on a paper due the next day, or a professor burning the midnight oil.

To my surprise, it was from Maddie. It read: *Hey, I found your email address online. Hope you don't mind that I'm writing you. We haven't talked in forever. Are you free tomorrow night for dinner? I have a late afternoon appointment with that family. Maybe I'll have some new stories for you.*

I stared at the computer. One line in particular piqued my curiosity: "We haven't talked in forever." Earlier that evening, I had stopped working and pondered when Maddie and I had last spoken. I was starting to miss her. I wondered if it could be possible she felt the same way?

It took me a few minutes to craft the perfect response: *Hey, stranger. It has been way too long since I saw you. Dinner tomorrow sounds great. What time?*

I hit the send button before I could over-think it. Email was one of the best inventions ever for someone who hated to talk on the phone. It was perfect. I was always much braver via email. I could tell people exactly what I thought and not have to see how they took the news. It worked well with my students and colleagues, and that was what I usually reserved it for. I didn't even have the Internet on at home. I had never bothered, since I had it at work.

A few minutes later, my computer dinged again. I glanced up from my book. Sure enough, it was Maddie again. I opened the email immediately.

Does 6 p.m. work for you? Let's meet at our usual place. Why are you still at the office?

Our usual place, huh? That had a nice ring to it. I quickly dashed off another email:

Six at Coops is perfect. I'm just wrapping up at the office. Why are you up so late?

Her response came faster this time.

10 p.m. isn't that late for me. I'm a night owl. Are you working or avoiding home? ☺

No matter what she said or wrote, Maddie always had a way to make me smile. I responded: *I guess you could say that. Sarah and I have been having a lot of deep discussions about the future and things. I need a break from all of that. So, can I assume the same about you? Are you on the Internet to avoid things at home?*

I instantly regretted sending it. What was I thinking? I hadn't even included a happy face. *Lizzie, get a hold of yourself,* I told myself. *What happened to the serious intellectual who didn't have time for such trifling things?* That was the problem with email: words could be taken the wrong way.

My computer dinged again. Cautiously, I opened her email, as if the process might affect her response. I knew right away that I was okay.

It read: *Very funny, wise guy ... or should I say 'touché.' But you are wrong, I'm not ignoring Peter, since he isn't even home yet ... wait, does that make you right? Am I ignoring the fact that Peter isn't home? God damn you, Lizzie! Why do you have to make me think? It makes my head hurt.* ☺

Again, the happy face at the end of the email. This time, I wasn't going to blow it. I made a happy face first, and then inserted my text before it, so I wouldn't forget.

I wrote: *Hey, I'll trade you. I know Sarah is home waiting for me so we can discuss where we see the relationship going. How am I supposed to see where the relationship is going? I'm not clairvoyant. I don't even know what I am doing tomorrow, so how do I know where I'll be next year?*

Her response made me smile again:

Um ... excuse me, but I thought we established we were having dinner tomorrow night. So, you do know what you are doing tomorrow! Does that mean you are also lying about where you will be next year? I have to wonder. Besides, I thought you people knew your history so you would have a better idea of where you were heading ...

No happy face this time, only the dot dot dot of ellipsis instead. What did that mean? Fuck. I needed to be more email savvy to interpret this shit.

I wrote back: *Very funny. Are you insulting my skills?* ☺

Maddie's response was teasing: *You'll never know.*

I decided to wing it: *Yes, Maddie, you are correct. I do know what I am doing tomorrow, and therefore, I do know what I am doing next year. I have decided to create a portal enabling me to travel throughout different time periods. Just think of it—time travel for a historian. No one will be able to question my theories because I will see how things happened firsthand.*

Maddie didn't respond for at least ten minutes, during which time I tried reading my book, but it was hopeless. I kept looking up at the computer. Maybe I had missed the ding, or maybe I silenced it accidentally.

Then I heard it. I pounced on the mouse and opened up the email.

LOL ... time travel for a historian. You are such a dork sometimes. I love it. Can I travel with you? I would love to see the world throughout history. Oh dang, I hear Peter downstairs. Off to greet the busy worker bee. See you tomorrow. ☺

I did know that LOL meant "Laugh Out Loud." Did she really think I was funny? And why did she call me a dork? I decided to write her back, knowing she wouldn't respond right away but might respond before tomorrow night. I wished her sweet dreams and told her I couldn't wait to catch up with her tomorrow. After I sent the email, I shut down my computer and called it a night.

Chapter Seventeen

The next morning, I popped out of bed before the birds had a chance to announce the arrival of a new day. Even though I hadn't slept well, I was full of energy and ready to get rolling.

"Wow ... you look great. Why are you all dressed up?" Sarah wrapped her arms around me and kissed the back of my neck.

"The history chair is sitting in on my class today. I figured I better try to look like a professor. What's on your agenda today?" I ran my fingers through my hair.

Of course, the history chair was not sitting in on my class. But I didn't want to tell her I was having dinner with Maddie; I couldn't. I hadn't been home the last few nights; I couldn't say I was taking the night off to hang out with my brother's fiancée. It didn't seem right.

"I'm sure you'll do fine. We should go to dinner tonight to celebrate."

"Um ... I can't. Didn't I tell you we have a late meeting today? Gosh, I tell you there is so much drama in the history department. These meetings take forever. So many professors are long-winded." I paused for a moment. "Can I take you to dinner tomorrow night, baby? Or maybe we can meet today for lunch." I hoped I didn't sound desperate.

"Really, you would take me to lunch? You've never done that before. That sounds great … but shoot … we are on assembly schedule today, so all of the periods are shortened. Let's do dinner tomorrow night. How about some place romantic."

"I'll see what I can come up with." I kissed her on the cheek and left for the office.

When I logged onto my computer, I checked my email immediately. No emails from Maddie. I didn't open the emails from my students, preferring to surf the net to find a romantic restaurant for tomorrow night—until I heard my computer ding.

As quickly as I could, I opened my email. Sure enough, it was Maddie.

You are so sweet. I hope you had sweet dreams as well … geez, how many times can I write sweet in one email? I'm going to hit the road. See you tonight, sweet Lizzie.

Her email elicited a smile.

* * *

I floated through the rest of the day, anticipating dinner with Maddie. Not once did I think how wrong it was for me to have butterflies. The closer the hour came, the more fluttering I felt in the pit of my stomach.

Finally, it was time for me to leave my office and head to Coopersmith's. I arrived thirty minutes early and decided to camp out at the bar. Briefly, I considered ordering a stiff drink, but there was no way in hell I could call Sarah to come and pick me up, so I settled for the house ginger ale. I was living on the edge.

"Holy moly, you guys are two peas in the pod. Peter showed up early for every date for the first six months." Maddie set her purse down on the bar next to me and took a swig of my ginger ale. "Except, he would be drinking bourbon or something." She held up one finger to get the bartender's attention and ordered a merlot.

"How was your day?" I asked, noticing she looked gorgeous in a black pantsuit with a shiny silver belt that looped around and hung down like jewelry.

"Just glorious," she answered, but her voice and aura told me all was not well.

It was the first time I had seen Maddie visibly upset. "Oh no, did the woman do more than masturbate this time?"

"What?" Maddie took a sip of wine. "Oh that." She smiled for the first time. "No, the appointment went well. There were no masturbating mishaps."

I stared at her for a few moments while she took a seat at the bar next to me. "So are you going to tell me what's bugging you?"

She waved dismissively. "Oh, I just got off the phone with your charming brother. He can be such an ass sometimes." She laughed.

I squirmed in my chair. I was treading uncharted water. How could I push my brother's fiancée to tell me the juicy details about their relationship? Words started to form in my throat, but I pushed them back down and then forced my own silence with a gulp of ginger ale.

"Easy there, tiger. Are you riding your bike home tonight?" She winked at me.

I was relieved to see the old Maddie, which bolstered my courage to ask what Peter had done.

"He stopped showing up early for dates for one thing. Oh, where should I begin?" Her voice trailed off.

Her demeanor told me I wasn't going to get the information I craved, so I dropped the matter.

"Shall we get a table? I'm starving." I patted my belly and then immediately felt ashamed. Ever since I started treatment for my illness, I could not get rid of my belly. I missed my flat stomach, even if it was an indication my thyroid was trying to kill me.

"Of course you are."

Again, I could not tell if she was cross with me because I reminded her of Peter, or if she was just in a bad mood. I examined her face—not a trace of malice. In fact, she seemed somewhat concerned, which confused me.

The hostess seated us in a secluded corner in the back of the restaurant. Of all the first dates I'd had at Coopersmith's, I'd never had such a romantic set-up. It was even snowing outside. A candle flickered on the table, and the lights were dimmed. Why did I get *that* set-up on *that* night? It was like the hook-up gods were reveling in the fact that I could never have her. Or could I?

Neither of us looked at the menu, both ordering our usual favorites. The only difference was that Maddie ordered a bottle of wine instead of a glass.

When the waitress left, I asked, "Does the bottle of wine mean you'll be sleeping on my couch?"

"What? Do you mean you wouldn't let me sleep in your bed?" she said, and I thought her voice even sounded sultry.

It took everything I had not to blush like a beet. "Of course you can sleep in my bed. I'm sure you and Sarah will be quite cozy."

"I have no doubt." Maddie laughed. "She seems like a cuddler. But sorry to disappoint, I'm checked into a hotel around the corner."

"Oh … that's nice. Do you get to write it off as a business expense?"

"I could, but Peter is paying for this place. He's hardly ever home, so why should I be." She looked out the window and then she straightened up in her chair and set the wineglass down. "Besides, I have an appointment in town first thing in the morning."

"With the people you met with today?"

"Nope. I'm meeting a potential client."

"Another one in Fort Collins? That's great." I was so excited for her that I wanted to order champagne, and I didn't even like the crap.

Our meals arrived. I picked up my fork and wiped it with my napkin before plunging it into my mashed potatoes. I had a feeling she wanted to talk about Peter, but I didn't know how to broach the subject. It wasn't like there was a *Dummies Guide to Stealing Your Brother's Fiancée*. Not knowing what to do, I started to shovel bangers and mash into my mouth.

Maddie looked at me with an odd expression as she sipped her wine and picked at her food.

I was having a horrible time reading her mind.

Then she finally looked right at me. "Can I ask you a question?"

I gave her my most confident smile and said, "Of course." Inside, I was bracing for the worst.

"How come you still haven't told your family about your illness?"

It was not the question I had been expecting. I started to laugh, which felt like the wrong response. "Um … well, at first, when I found out, the thought never occurred to me. After I had time to let it sink in, I didn't want to bother with it."

"You didn't want to bother with it … what in the fuck does that mean?" It was clear the wine was going straight to her head.

"Ah … I'm not sure what I meant. I didn't feel like telling them. I knew it wouldn't change a thing." I paused and then said, "I was already dealing with the illness. I didn't want to deal with them not caring."

She nodded and gazed out the window. The snow was really coming down now. Most of the other customers were packing up and heading home.

"It really bothers you that I haven't told them. That's the second time you've asked me. Do you want me to tell them?"

She smiled at me. "Oh no. Unless you want to. I'm just baffled by your family, Lizzie. I'm so close with my parents and aunts and uncles, and you guys are all strangers." She laughed. "Then there are all of those secrets all of you keep."

I smiled at her. I wondered what secrets Peter kept. I knew hers.

She started to speak, but then stopped abruptly. A strange expression crossed her face. "Would you ever cheat on Sarah?"

I froze. My hand hung in the air, my fork overloaded with mashed potato, which dripped onto the table. Flustered, I set the fork down.

"Ah ... I have to admit, I wasn't expecting *that* question." Why did I say that?

She reddened. "Oh, of course ... I wasn't insinuating you were ... I know you love Sarah."

Fuck!

There was my opportunity, and I blew it. *I fucking blew it!*

Someone opened the front door and a frigid breeze blew out the candle on our table.

"Y-yeah, of course I love Sarah," I stuttered.

Shut up, Lizzie. Shut up! I felt my face turn crimson, and I wanted to throw ice water on my face to temper the burn. I had never felt so awkward and utterly ridiculous. Foolishly, I asked, "Do you want any dessert?"

Maddie's face brightened. "You know, Lizzie, I just might. Screw looking good for Peter." She perked up in her chair and seemed content once again, and then she changed the subject to a concert she was planning on seeing over the weekend. I appreciated the diversion. While she prattled on, I took off my blazer, unbuttoned my shirtsleeves, and rolled them up.

When we left the restaurant, I didn't bother putting my jacket on. I was impervious to the cold.

Chapter Eighteen

All of the pressure from my dissertation, buying a home, and my brother's wedding was starting to get to me. I had been in a horrible mood for days.

"It's not so easy you know!" I laid into Ethan when he asked me if I had told Sarah I didn't want to buy a house.

"Really? Then why have you been riding my ass for years?" Ethan looked frustrated as hell.

I turned away, rubbing my eyes.

He continued. "We have a mortgage, financial accounts, cars, loans, the cat …" Ethan counted their commitments on his fingers before trailing off.

"And I fart in my sleep."

His hand dropped swiftly from the air and into his lap, like a bird shot out of the sky. "What?"

"What?" I shook my head. Had I said that aloud?

"You just said that you fart in your sleep."

"Oh yeah, that." It had just popped out. I never meant to say it.

"You fart in your sleep?"

"I guess so. I'm asleep. But Sarah told me I do."

"That's why you're staying with Sarah, because you fart in your sleep?"

"She loves me. How could I stay the night with someone else? I wouldn't be able to sleep for fear of farting. And you know I already have problems sleeping."

"Are you fucking serious?" He slammed his cup down on the table.

"What are you so angry about?"

"You want to ruin this girl's life because you fart in your sleep?"

"What do you mean ruin her life?" I raised an eyebrow.

"You can't stay with someone you don't love for such a stupid reason."

"Why do you stay with your wife? Because you are too lazy to figure out the financial issues or to decide who gets the cat?"

"Because we've been best friends since elementary school. We respect each other, which is the basis for a good relationship."

"I respect her."

"Really …? Then why don't you start acting like it?" he hissed.

I wanted to get up and leave, but I had already acted like a child earlier. Besides, two of my students were in the back of the coffee shop. Our conversation was already heated. I didn't want to draw even more unwanted attention.

We both sat silently, sipping our drinks.

After several minutes, I broke the silence. "So tell me really, why do you and your wife stay together?"

"Because we love to hate each other … I don't know how to explain it, Lizzie. We are used to each other, and we respect each other. We both love to fight. But in the end, we still respect each other. Are you even friends with Sarah?"

"But what about the sex part?" I asked, avoiding his question.

"We've worked that part out." He looked uncomfortable

in his own skin.

"What do you mean?"

"I don't want to go into particulars, since it really isn't your business." He flashed his southern-boy smile. "But we both know I don't like sex. We've come to some agreement."

"Are you all right with the deal?"

"It's not the most ideal situation, but we are both living with it. That's where you are wrong. Sarah deserves to have some say in the decisions made about your relationship. Stop keeping her in the dark. She's not a mushroom."

"What?" I crinkled my face.

"A mushroom. You keep it in the dark and feed it shit. Stop treating her like that."

I sighed. "She's going to hate me." And I didn't want to hurt her. She was the last person I wanted to disappoint.

"Yes. She'll hate you at first. But, over time, she will appreciate your honesty. If you keep stringing her along, she'll resent you even more. That won't be good. She'll be mean to you, but most importantly, it will tear her up inside. Resentful women are not happy people, and once they reach a certain stage, they never get over the bitterness. Don't be the cause of that."

"I'm not good at this honesty thing."

"No shit? Really?" He chuckled and shook his head. "No one is, Lizzie. But it's part of being an adult. It's time to grow up."

The next day, there was a package in my mailbox at work. I didn't see a return address. Undeterred, I took it to my office and opened it.

Inside, I found a plaster statue of a mouse under a large mushroom. I looked in the box for a note, but there wasn't one. None was needed.

I set the mushroom on my desk and stared at it for several minutes.

* * *

A few days after my dinner with Maddie, guilt was still eating at me. I had been avoiding Sarah and working late almost every night, including nights I didn't have to be on campus. By Thursday, I sat in my office wondering what to do. I decided to shut down my computer at a decent time and head home before Sarah was due to arrive at the apartment. I couldn't remember the last time I had been there to greet her after her long workday.

On the way home, I stopped at a florist and picked up a beautiful bouquet. I didn't feel like going out to dinner, so I decided to order food from her favorite Chinese restaurant. Fortunately, it arrived before Sarah.

I busied myself with setting the table, getting the drinks ready, lighting candles, and putting the flowers in a vase—things to make me feel better about myself. If Haley were trying to steal her away, well I wasn't going to let that happen. I would not lose to Haley.

Sarah entered the apartment as I entertained the last thought.

"Hello?" she called out, obviously surprised to find anyone home.

"In the kitchen," I shouted back. I poured a glass of wine and handed it to her as she walked in.

"Oh, my God." She looked at all of the food and then over at the table. "You got me flowers ... you even lit the candles." She looked flabbergasted.

At first, I smiled. Then I saw Haley standing right behind her. Goddammit. I tried not to flinch. Casually, I grabbed another wineglass and poured some for Haley.

"Someone's feeling pretty guilty."

"Shut up, Haley! Lizzie ... " Sarah's voice trailed off and her eyes glistened. "This is perfect," she continued. "Haley and I were just talking about ordering in."

"Good thing I ordered enough for an army." I smiled my best fake smile and indicated all of the food.

Sarah looked radiant as the two of us carried the takeout

to the table.

Haley couldn't contain herself. "So, what is it? An anniversary or something?"

I took a deep breath. "No, I just thought it would be nice to have a quiet dinner with my girlfriend. I've been working too much, and I've missed our time together."

Haley either didn't take the hint or chose to ignore it completely. She sat down and began heaping fried rice onto her plate.

Sarah grabbed some silverware while I took a seat across from Haley. I knew I should have gone for the silverware, but I was seething over Haley's behavior. She was quickly ruining my happy feeling.

The three of us ate in silence for a few minutes. Sarah and I ate with chopsticks, while Haley-the-Barbarian used a knife and fork.

"Where did you get the food from? It's really good." Haley broke the ice, mumbling through her mouthful of sesame chicken.

I directed my answer to my girlfriend. "I ordered from that cute little place you introduced me to," I told Sarah. "You mentioned it was your favorite Chinese place."

She smiled. *It really doesn't take much effort to impress her*, I thought to myself. *So why don't I do it more often?* I made a mental note to pick up a card to send to her at work. After all, I couldn't mail it to her home, since she was never there. And I didn't want to mail it here. No, definitely not here. That would have given her the wrong idea.

"Wherever you got it from, it's got my stamp of approval." Haley stood up to snatch some of the egg rolls from across the table.

Sarah quickly thanked me, as if she were trying to distract me so I wouldn't hit Haley. *They were just best friends*, I told myself.

"Hey, I set up an appointment this weekend to get wireless Internet." I changed the subject. "They should be here between 11 a.m. and 1 p.m., hopefully."

Sarah set down her chopsticks and stared intently at me. "But I thought we were serious about finding a new place together."

I panicked. "Oh, I thought of that ... I made sure they could easily transfer our service. Besides, I thought it would be nice to be able to work from home more. And you could check your email and stuff ..." I had no idea what I was talking about. I never found out about transferring service. I saw an ad on TV that had mentioned it, but I wasn't sure if that was the company I had signed up with.

Sarah thought about it for a minute. Then she said, "So you will be home more?"

Jackpot. Somehow, I hit the right chord. "Yeah ... and you can too. Can you access your work from your laptop? We can both work at the same time."

Maybe that way she would spend less time with Haley.

"That is a thought. And you said it was easy to transfer the service ... hey we can look at homes online as well." Her face lit up again.

Well, Lizzie, you can't win them all. "That's a good idea," I said, unconvinced. I didn't even want to think about that."

Haley gave me a weird look. Did she know something? With any luck, she was just choking on an egg roll.

Chapter Nineteen

It was 7:30 in the morning and I was already in my office preparing a lecture for the following week. Usually, I tried to stay two weeks ahead, but lately my life had become so chaotic that I couldn't get ahead. Since I wasn't teaching and I only had office hours from one to three, I decided to hole up in my office and put my nose to the grindstone.

I briefly considered not checking my email. If Maddie emailed, would I be strong enough to resist chatting online with her all day? I checked it. *Obviously not*. No emails from her. I was simultaneously relieved and disappointed. No matter, I had work to do.

Half an hour later, I heard the familiar chime that heralded a new email. My eyes darted to the screen and then quickly back to my mound of work. *Screw it*. I read the email.

Maddie wanted to know if I could play hooky today. Of course, she knew I wouldn't be teaching today, and that I had no classes of my own. Maddie was quick to learn my schedule.

I replied that it depended on what she had in mind. Several minutes passed before there was a knock on my office door. Irritated that a student couldn't wait until my appointed office hours, I gruffly answered, "Come in."

Maddie's gorgeous face popped around my door.

I was flabbergasted. "I-I-I just got an email from you," I stammered.

"I know. I got your reply." She held up her phone and laughed. "You're like a grandma sometimes. Cell phones are amazing these days. I can email from it."

That explained why she could always email me on the fly. I was glued to my work computer or my laptop all day and night. I briefly considered upgrading my cell phone, but I had made a big deal to Sarah that people had survived hundreds of years without twenty-four hour access to email. She would smell a rat right away if I suddenly bought a fancy phone to replace the cheap phone that came with my plan.

"So what do you say, professor, do you want to play hooky today?"

I smiled. "I was planning on getting a lot of work done today." I gestured to all of my books and journals.

Maddie was undeterred. "Bring it along, if you must. You can do it where we are going."

Instead of asking questions, I packed up my things. Maddie wasn't one to divulge all of her information at once. She was a strictly need-to-know basis type of gal. Telling me the plan was superfluous. On leaving my office, I stuck a post-it note on my door, canceling my office hours for the day.

Maddie led me to her car. I knew it was going to be a long day when she turned the car onto the highway and we passed a sign for Estes Park. Estes was forty-five minutes away, so people didn't drive there just to run errands for a minute or two. It was one of the many tourist traps in the Rocky Mountains and sat at the base of the Rocky Mountain National Park.

Neither of us spoke much on the drive there. I watched the scenery flash by—horses, cows, and fields reeling past like an old-fashioned movie, all surrounded by an immensity of space.

When Maddie pulled into Estes, it was obvious she knew where she was going. We would be hanging out at a bookstore, and one I had gone to on several occasions.

We camped out at a large table to accommodate all of my books and notes. After ordering a chai, I sat down while Maddie wandered through the store. She returned with several interior design books and flipped through them quietly.

From the way she was thumbing through them, I knew her mind was elsewhere. But where? I had no idea. She jumped out of her chair and wandered back to the bookshelves.

Half an hour later, she came back to the table with a copy of *The Thorn Birds*, another coffee, and a pastry.

There she sat for hours, reading the book, only getting up to go to the bathroom or to get something else to snack on.

That was how we spent the entire day. It was heavenly. Not only did I catch up on my work, but I also got a little ahead. The only dark cloud was Maddie. She seemed out of sorts. I couldn't tell whether she wanted to talk, or whether she wanted to stew in company. I figured she would talk if she wanted to.

She wandered around some more, this time returning with a CD. "Look what I found."

It was an Aerosmith CD, one of their greatest hits compilations. I glanced at the song titles but said nothing. I couldn't think of a song of theirs that I knew. Smiling, I handed it back to her and then took a sip of my chai.

Maddie started to laugh. "Oh goodness, don't tell me you are another one. All your brother listens to is the news, and market updates."

"I don't give a crap about the stock market," I said.

"Then what type of music do you listen to?" she asked.

"You know … whatever is on the radio." I couldn't think of any of the music Sarah liked.

"Wow! What a cop-out answer. Can you name some

songs?" She crossed her arms and stared at me.

I paused. There was no way I could bullshit my way out of this situation. We were sitting too far away from the music section for me to see any titles. "I don't listen to the radio much." I gestured to the books spread around me.

"Do you listen to anything? Or do you just read?"

Why did she have to put it that way?

"Hey, now! No reason to be snotty ... I listen to things. But they happen to be books." I tried my cute smile.

"You listen to audiobooks?" She tried not to laugh.

"Yes ... yes, I do. You were reading *The Thorn Birds* earlier," I said meekly.

"I didn't find it on CD, so I had to resort to the old-fashioned method," she retorted. "When do you listen to them?"

"When I go for walks, or hikes, or sometimes on my bike."

"Not in the car."

"Rarely. Sarah is usually with me in the car."

"What? Are you saying Sarah isn't as hip as you?" That time she couldn't help it; she started laughing. "I thought only grandparents listened to books on tape."

"Watch it, missy. They now come on CD."

"So, do you download them onto your iPod?"

"No. Not exactly." I fidgeted in my chair. The last ounce of my feigned coolness melted.

"You still have a discman? Get out!"

"It still works, you know. And most of the books come on CD. Why download them?"

She laughed again and then stopped. "Hey, wait, most of the books. Do you still listen to books on *tape?*"

I took another sip of my chai. "Well, the library does have some audiobooks on tape."

"Wow. Well, that's a whole different ball game, now isn't it, grandma? You even have a sweater vest on today."

I stared at her and she chuckled. Then she wandered

away from the table again. Looking down at the vest Sarah had purchased for me, I wondered if my girlfriend intentionally dressed me like a stodgy old fusspot. At first, I had loved the vest. My office was so cold and drafty, and sometimes I found sweaters too confining. The vest was the best of both worlds: warm and freeing. Now, I wanted to tear the vest apart.

At around four, we packed up our things. Maddie purchased *The Thorn Birds* and the Aerosmith CD, and we headed back to Fort Collins. Again, she was silent, except for one instance when she asked if it were possible to have a happy marriage if one person was never around.

Alarm bells jangled in my head. How was I supposed to answer a question like that?

I uttered a few ums and ahs. Then I asked if everything was okay with Peter. I didn't want to know, truly. The less I talked or thought about Peter, the better, but I couldn't just ignore her mood.

"Yeah, everything is good. You know, he just works a lot." Then she said cynically, "Just like your father." She gripped the steering wheel as if she wanted to strangle it.

After several minutes, she said, "Lizzie, you really don't listen to music? Can you name one song that you like?"

"The 'Monster Mash.'"

She looked at me out of the corner of her eye as she navigated around a pothole in the road. "Really? The 'Monster Mash'?"

"It's a graveyard smash."

"Can you sing any of the lyrics? Come on, bust it out Ms. Crypt-Kicker-Five." She smiled to encourage me.

"Sorry to disappoint, but I can never remember the words to songs." I shrugged.

"Recite the Gettysburg Address."

"Four score and seven years ago our fathers brought forth on this continent, a new nation, conceived in liberty and dedicated to the proposition that all men are created equal." I continued the speech in its entirety, even though I knew she was making fun of me. It was better than the awkward silence.

"Wow. That was impressive. Do you know any others?"

"Just the usual."

"The usual?"

"You know, the Preamble to the Constitution and the Pledge of Allegiance, and stuff."

"Oh ... of course."

She paused. "So what do you do in your office all night by yourself?"

"You can't expect me to reveal my dark side to you. Besides, what do you think I do all night?"

"To be honest, I picture you in front of a microfiche machine browsing through World War II newspapers."

"Wow ... that was harsh." I tried to smile.

Maddie slapped my leg. "Chin up, tiger, now I know you listen to the 'Monster Mash' while you do it."

"What does Peter do all night?"

Her face clouded over. "Ah, that is a very good question."

I asked if Maddie wanted to grab some dinner, but she said she had to get home to Peter. I was sure Maddie was lying, but I didn't say anything. The rest of the ride home was silent. When I wanted to be alone to think, I wanted to be alone. I figured she felt the same way. And I didn't feel comfortable pushing her on anything.

Chapter Twenty

I beat Ethan to the coffee shop, so by the time he arrived I already had my chai. I watched him walk in the door, all the while pounding away on his phone. He walked up to the counter and ordered his coffee and I peered over my book and noticed the back of his neck was a vivid purple.

He sat down, looking as if he wanted to explode.

"Trouble with the missus?" I closed my book and set it on the table.

Calm gradually washed over his face as he sipped his coffee, which, as always, he had spiked with a ludicrous amount of sugar. "What gives you that idea?"

"Well, your face looks like an eggplant."

"It's just hot in here." He tugged at his collar.

"Uh-huh, keep telling yourself that."

I stared at him but he turned away, looking towards the back of the store.

"What have you been doing?" I asked.

Ethan stared at me long and hard. Then he shook his head. "You know, I don't know. And to be honest, I don't care anymore."

His apathy troubled me. I missed the young grad student who once bubbled with energy and enthusiasm; there was just an empty shell left.

"Alrighty, then. You are coming with me to shop for CDs."

"Really, Lizzie, I'm not in the mood to pick out audiobooks." He removed his glasses and rubbed his bloodshot eyes.

"Why does everyone associate me with audiobooks?"

"What's on your iPod right now?"

"I don't have one." I stuck out my tongue.

"Oh good lord! You still have a discman, don't you?" At least this image got a smile out of him.

"That isn't important right now." I flipped some of the pages of my book. "I want you to come with me to pick out some music. I printed some stuff off, but I thought you could help me round out my selection."

I handed over my list.

"So, Maddie likes music and you want to impress her." Ethan continued to stare at my notes of must-have albums.

"Oh whatever, Ethan." I waved the idea away.

"You should get tickets to Iron Maiden."

"What? Maddie bought an Aerosmith CD. Do I need to add Iron Maiden?"

Ethan sniggered. "So it is about Maddie. I figured." He shuffled through the papers. "What did you do? Google 'must-have albums' or something?" He looked over the names. "Do you even recognize half of these bands?"

I nudged his foot under the table. "No, that's why I need you. So drink your coffee ... we have some shopping to do."

* * *

"What are you listening to?" Sarah shouted from the front room. I hurried out of the kitchen to greet her, carrying a cup of hot chocolate. Steam danced around me.

"Hey, I thought you would be shopping all day." I kissed

her on the cheek. Then I grabbed the stereo remote and turned down the music.

"Are you listening to Pink Floyd?" Doubt and surprise were both evident in her tone.

"Yeah … at least I think that's the CD I put in." I picked up the CD case. "Yep, it's Pink Floyd."

"Since when did you start listening to Pink Floyd?"

"Ethan and I went to the music store today."

She burst into laughter. "Music store? Who still says music store?"

I shrugged and sipped my hot chocolate. "I guess I do." Then I smiled. "Can I get you a drink or something? Here"— I handed her the cup—"you must be cold."

The wind had been howling all day. I went into the kitchen to make another cup. A few seconds later, as I was filling the kettle again, Sarah bounded in. "You bought twenty-something CDs?"

"I think the number is twenty-seven."

"And not one of them on this receipt is an audiobook." She stared at me in disbelief.

"Do you want marshmallows in your hot chocolate?"

She nodded.

I put the kettle on the stove and lit the burner. "We have large and small ones." I stuck my head out of the pantry. "Which would you prefer?"

"What?" She scrutinized the receipt.

"Large or small marshmallows?"

"Oh, I'm trying to process this information." She looked confused.

I stared at her in bewilderment. *Who can't figure out which size marshmallows they want in their hot chocolate?* "I think the small ones would be best," I say, grabbing the bag and smiling at her. "Do you want to pick out the next CD?" I shouted as I walked back into the front room.

Sarah followed me and handed me a Pearl Jam CD from the stack. I looked at the title: *Vitology*. I slipped it in and we both sat on the couch, sipping our hot chocolates, listening to the music.

Several songs later, Sarah paused the music.

"So you didn't buy any audiobooks?"

I shook my head and sipped up a sweet swirl of marshmallow. She stared at me with an addled look and then hit play again on the remote. She looked shell-shocked. I rather enjoyed that.

Chapter Twenty-One

It was the day before Thanksgiving and somehow I had let Maddie talk me into staying with her and Peter for several days. Sarah was with me, too. We arrived Wednesday morning and were soon preparing to watch a marathon of Christmas movies. Sarah and Maddie were feverishly setting out an array of snacks, Peter was upstairs working, and I sat on a barstool, reading a book.

"Oh, shit! I forgot to grab the peppers for the nachos," Maddie said, frowning.

Sarah started to fossick around under bags, plates, dishtowels, and God knows what else on the counter. "Are you sure they're not under something?"

"No. I plumb forgot them. I would remember." She patted her pockets.

We had been to the store a few hours earlier. *Why would they be in her pockets?* I thought. "Can you make them without the peppers?" I asked, glancing at her over my book.

Maddie shook her head adamantly. "Nope. I want those peppers."

"Okay." I grabbed my car keys. "Tell me what kind and I

can go get some."

Maddie's eyes sparkled and then she turned to Sarah. "Sarah, would you mind if I went with Lizzie? She can bore us both, reciting historical facts or the Gettysburg address"—she batted an eye at me—"but a cook she's not. Besides, I don't know the names of the peppers, I only recognize them." Maddie grabbed her jacket and purse.

Sarah laughed. Surprisingly, she seemed happy that Maddie was going with me. She never showed any signs of jealousy, and that bothered me. For days, she had been so excited to be included in my family time over the holidays. When Peter invited her mother, too, I thought she was going to piss herself. I wondered if Maddie had convinced Peter to invite Sarah's mom. Rose had already been booked on a cruise with friends, so she couldn't make it, although she was relieved Sarah and I had some place to go. The past couple of weeks at home had been completely stress-free and enjoyable. And there was no chatter about buying a house. Gotta love the holidays. Cheer was everywhere.

Maddie climbed into the passenger seat. "Sarah seems so different this visit."

"I think she's really enjoying being included in my family." I checked the rearview mirror and pulled out of the driveway. "For so long I think she thought I was an orphan or something."

"And I'm sure you didn't fill her in or anything. I wish I could get Peter excited about something … anything." Her voice trembled a little.

Not knowing what to do, I gripped the steering wheel tighter and concentrated on the icy road ahead. It had been snowing lightly for most of the day.

Maddie rescued me. "I think it's great you drive an old Toyota Camry … and the missing hubcap is so you." She chuckled.

I knew she wasn't being rude; she had a knack for saying what she thought.

"Hey, this baby is paid off, and it has gone all over the country with me." I patted the steering wheel. "This is the best road-trippin' car around."

"I didn't know you liked road-trips. Peter wants us to fly everywhere—first class, of course. But I love to hit the road—see the country for myself." She pretended to drive, turning an imaginary wheel and making a vroom-vroom sound. Sometimes, I wished I had an ounce of her charisma.

She hit the eject button on the CD player and I noticed her manicured nails. Then she laughed. "Just checking to see if it was an audiobook."

"I told you, I don't listen to them when Sarah is with me."

It was Sarah's Kings of Leon CD.

"Any good?" Maddie asked.

"Sarah really likes it. They aren't too bad."

"Do you think she would mind if I ripped it?"

I turned to her. "What?"

Maddie giggled at my innocence. "Not literally. I mean if I made a copy of it."

"Oh … yeah. That shouldn't be a problem at all. Isn't that stealing?" I peeked at her out of the corner of my eyes.

She patted my knee. "You're so adorable sometimes."

I felt color flood my face.

We pulled into the parking lot. Not being much of a shopper, I stopped to look at books while Maddie headed for the produce section. As I rifled through the latest book on Lincoln, she rushed up behind me, grabbed my shoulders, and whispered, "We need to leave. *Now.*"

"But what about the pepp—" I started to ask, but she shushed me. I put the book down when she started pushing me out of the store.

Both of us slipped and slid across the ice and over to the car. Finally, when we had both taken our seats, I asked what was going on.

She smiled and pulled a bag out of her jacket pocket.

Inside it were two small peppers.

"You *stole* the peppers?" My voice cracked. I felt so uncool.

That made her giggle. "Yeppers! I stole the peppers."

"Why did you steal the peppers? Did you forget your wallet?"

She waved that idea away. "Nah, I never pay for these peppers." She held the bag up in my face.

"What do you mean you never pay for peppers?" I looked at her, amazed.

"I usually only need one. Why pay for such a small pepper?"

"But there are two peppers in the bag."

"I plan on making a lot of nachos. Come on and start the car. Let's get out of Dodge."

I did as she said. "What other things do you steal besides peppers and music?"

"Nothing. Just peppers. And copying a CD isn't stealing. Everyone does it." She opened my glove box and grabbed some Kleenex. "Ha! I knew you would have tissues, grandma."

I didn't let her off the hook. "How in the hell did you come to that? Why peppers?"

"I don't know. They are so tiny. I don't want to pay for something so tiny." She blew her nose.

Her logic was so flawed that I didn't know where to begin. Why didn't she steal diamonds? They were small and they were worth more. "Does Peter know that you steal peppers?" I asked.

"Are you crazy? That guy is so uptight."

I was still struggling with my sense of ethics, so I barely had time to consider the notion that Maddie didn't think I was as uptight as Peter.

"I would love to get you high. I mean, Lizzie, your mind would be like ... holy shit."

I stared at her. *How did we move from hot peppers to pot?* I shook my head.

Before I knew it, we were walking back into the kitchen. Peter was standing over the stove, tasting the chili for the nachos.

"Did you get the peppers?" Sarah looked up.

Maddie held up her stolen booty. I watched my brother. *How did these two people end up together? Does either of them know the other?* So many secrets.

"That's great." Peter placed one hand on Sarah's shoulder and said, "Maddie makes the most extraordinary nachos. You will never eat anyone else's nachos ever again." He looked adoringly at Maddie, who patted him on the cheek as she walked past.

"Hey, mind if I rip your Kings of Leon CD?" Maddie asked Sarah, as she waved the CD in the air. I hadn't even noticed her taking it.

I was about to explain what she meant when Sarah readily agreed. I felt somewhat deflated, but I did enjoy the look of confusion on Peter's face.

* * *

My mouth was on fire. The four of us sat on the floor, watching *A Christmas Story* and devouring nachos. After each bite, I took a swig of water and then another bite. Swig. Bite. Swig. Bite. Maddie had placed a box of tissues on the table, and Peter had to keep dabbing at his nose.

"Maddie, what kind of peppers did you get? These are hot." He licked his lips.

The two of us burst out laughing. Maddie was in mid-swallow and her laugh turned to a cough as a wedge of corn chip lodged in her throat. She continued laughing, pounding her fist on her chest to dislodge the offending nacho and swallowing the food down.

Peter and Sarah looked at each other quizzically, neither willing to hazard a guess as to why we were laughing so hard.

"Do you smoke?" my brother asked her. "I know these

two goodie-goodies don't." He nodded in the direction of Maddie and me.

"Sometimes I enjoy a cigarette. Let's ditch the giggle twins." Sarah hopped up to go get her sweater.

"Don't worry, I'll pause the movie so you won't miss anything while you relish your cancer sticks," Maddie shouted, as Peter and Sarah stepped out on the back deck.

"Do you think they went for a walk?" Maddie asked once several minutes had passed.

I couldn't imagine Peter exercising in the fresh air. He was a gym kind of guy. What was the point of working out unless people saw him doing it? I rose and looked out the window. Sarah was walking towards the door, holding something in her arms. Peter was right next to her.

As soon as she entered, I saw that she was cuddling a black kitten.

"Oh, my gosh!" Maddie hightailed over to Sarah. "Where in the hell did you find this guy?" She petted its head.

"Damndest thing. Sarah heard this weird noise in the open space. We went out to investigate. Neither of us could see anything, but we heard this quacking sound around our feet. No wonder we couldn't see it; it's as black as midnight." Peter paused and pointed to the kitten. "Sarah scooped it up, the mangy-looking thing." He looked disgusted.

He was right. The kitten did look like it had mange, and its hair was matted and filthy.

"Well, what do you think, Lizzie?" Sarah put him in my arms. I knew that, somehow, I had just adopted the kitten.

I held it up, gazed into its face. The kitten batted at my bracelet. "I think we should call it Hank."

"What if it's a girl?"

"Won't matter much after we get it fixed."

Sarah took it back and hugged it close to her chest.

I turned to Maddie. "I guess we're off to the store again. We need to buy Hank a bathroom, and some food."

Sarah seemed stunned that I had given in so quickly, but

I had to admit that the tiny black ball of fur was adorable, in a tossed-out orphan kinda way.

Plus, I was on a mission to be nice to Sarah. I wanted her to be happy. If she was happy, I was happy. How much trouble could a cat be?

* * *

The next morning, I woke up early and rolled over to look out the window. It was still dark outside. I stayed in bed, unsure what to do. Sarah was snoring next to me. Should I get up and wander around in Peter's house? I had my bike in the garage, but the roads were icy. I was contemplating risking it when the kitten pounced on my head. Oh well, I was on track to finish the 3,000 miles by the end of January anyway.

I pulled the scrawny thing off me and sat up in bed. Sarah, the cat lover, didn't even move. I rolled my eyes and whispered, "Come on, Hank. Let's get you some breakfast."

Cuddling the kitten close to me, I made my way downstairs to the kitchen. Hank purred in my arms. I noticed one of his ears was torn, an injury that looked to have happened a couple of days ago. After his breakfast, I would do my best to clean up the wound.

"Uh-oh, is Mr. Reardon hungry?" Maddie was in her pajamas, already pulling stuff out of the oven.

I hadn't told her I'd named the kitten after Hank Reardon from *Atlas Shrugged*. As usual, her instincts were dead on.

"I guess so," I said. "He tried to eat my face a minute ago. How long have you been up?"

"Not long."

I poured some kibble into his food bowl. "Liar. Did you even sleep last night?" I looked around the kitchen.

"Why? Do I look awful?" Maddie patted her hair.

Actually, I had never seen her look more lovely, but I didn't say that. As I watched Hank chomp his breakfast, I said, "No, you don't. But from the aroma in here, you've been cooking for quite some time."

She flashed a guilty smile. "I don't know why, but your mother, I mean The Scotch-lady, scares the fucking crap out of me."

Her laugh only made me sadder. *Damn Peter for not caring.* "Well, don't fret. Hank and I are here to help."

"You're a doll. Both of you." She smiled at Hank.

I hoped I looked better than the kitten did. It would take several weeks of food and care to get him in good shape. Not that he noticed; he acted like a prince. I wondered how he ended up on the streets.

Chapter Twenty-Two

"What in the hell is that thing?" hissed The Scotch-lady later that afternoon.

"Oh that?" Peter glared at me. "That's Lizzie's new kitten."

Funny, last night Peter was much kinder to the little furball. Now, Hank was sitting in the chair my mother wanted to occupy.

As I walked over to pick Hank up, I heard an ice cube chink against the side of Mom's first scotch of the day. She would rather take a drink than pet a kitten.

Hank jumped out of my arms and scampered upstairs. Maddie, Sarah, and I watched. More than likely, all of us wished we could have hidden upstairs, too—and the parents had only just arrived.

My father hadn't said a word on entering the room. In fact, he hadn't even said hello, just nodded to acknowledge Sarah and Maddie. Charles Petrie didn't deign to greet his progeny. Peter and I didn't matter. *Did we ever?* Then he waddled over to the chair farthest from the group. I was baffled that he hadn't just wandered straight up to Peter's office. Maybe this was his way of spending quality family time with us—sitting in a leather chair drinking whiskey and reading the *Financial Times*.

I never understood why that paper had pink newsprint.

There they sat: my father reading his paper, my mother sucking down her scotch. No one spoke. Maddie and Sarah slipped into the kitchen to put the final touches on dinner. Peter stood by the fireplace. I leaned against a bookcase. Uncomfortable with the silence, I pulled a book off the shelf and started to flip through it. The clock suggested only five minutes had passed since their arrival.

Several minutes later, Maddie's head appeared around the door. "Dinner is ready," she announced. Even Peter looked relieved. Mister charisma could not get a conversation going.

All of us took our seats and started to dish out the food. The girls had all the fixings for a gourmet Thanksgiving dinner: glazed carrots, mashed potatoes, gravy, asparagus, sausage and bread stuffing, sweet potatoes, turkey, ham, and homemade rolls.

"What are these?" My mother held a pair of tongs over the parsnip tray.

"Those are parsnips," Maddie casually responded.

I thought I detected some fear in her voice.

Mom poked them with the tongs. "Like I said, what are these … stringy things?"

"What? You've never had parsnips, Mother?" I forked one, a little viciously, from off my plate. "They're related to the carrot."

"Oh please, do go on," Mom said condescendingly.

I smiled. "Certainly. They were quite popular in ancient times. Until the potato entered the scene, they used to be a staple. In fact, the Romans believed parsnips were an aphrodisiac." I chewed my parsnip and stabbed another with my fork.

Mother set the tongs down and passed the plate to Maddie. "Fantastic. Not only do I get served these disgusting weeds, I get a history lecture as well."

Maddie picked up the tongs and heaped a pile of parsnips onto her plate before passing the tray to Peter.

My brother peeked out of the corner of his eye to see if The Scotch-lady was watching. She was picking through the slices of turkey to find the best ones. He quickly put some parsnips on his plate and then set the platter down next to our father. To my surprise, Dad loaded some onto his plate.

"So, Sarah, how are your classes going?" Peter looked desperate to bury the parsnip controversy.

Sarah smiled and continued serving herself some asparagus. "Oh, they're okay. I think the kids and I are ready for winter break. Each year, the semester seems to get longer."

"You teach math right?" asked my mother.

Peter burst out laughing. Then he stopped abruptly.

Sarah, surprised by the question since The Scotch-lady didn't really speak to non-family members, quietly answered, "Uh, no. I teach English."

Maddie turned to Peter. Her tone confrontational, she asked, "Peter, why did you laugh?"

"Come on, Maddie! It's well known that boys are better at math. I've never had a female math teacher."

"God, you're such a sexist pig sometimes. And for your information, I've had several female math teachers."

"Grade school doesn't count, Maddie." He winked at her as he buttered a piece of his roll. He popped it into his mouth, and smiled as he chewed.

"Excuse me, I took math classes after grade school."

"You're an interior designer." His voice was too high.

Maddie visibly blanched. "I double-majored. My second major was business."

Peter paused and took a sip of wine. "I didn't know you studied business."

"I thought it might be wise, in case I wanted to start my own design business."

"Oh." He pushed mashed potatoes around his plate.

"Please, tell us, oh history sage, who was the first female math teacher?" My mother stared at me.

"Allegra Calculari Abacai."

Maddie and Sarah laughed while I scooped more parsnips into my mouth. My mother snorted and took another nip of scotch.

I wasn't positive, but I thought I saw a slight smile play on my father's face.

Peter went out of his way to avoid eye contact with everyone.

Then The Scotch-lady stared at me and blurted out, "So are you into bondage now?"

Maddie snorted and nearly choked to death on her wine as she tried to stop herself from laughing. Peter, in the act of cutting his turkey, froze, his knife and fork skewed in midair. And Sarah, poor Sarah, I didn't have the heart to look in her direction.

"How does liking parsnips equate to being into bondage? I'm curious about your definition." I stared at my mother.

She motioned to my arm.

I raised my left arm.

"Not that one. The other one."

Sarah, Peter, Maddie and I all stared at my arm. No one said a word.

"All right, I give in," I said eventually. "What about my arm suggests bondage to you?"

"The bracelet." The Scotch-lady gestured to the bracelet Maddie had given me.

Even Peter couldn't help himself. "What's wrong with it?"

"It's hideous." She sighed and took a long swig of scotch. "For her to even wear it I thought it must be for something else."

The mute man who was my father motioned for someone to pass him the parsnips.

The rest of the meal was eaten in silence.

Chapter Twenty-Three

I started to skip going to campus a few days after we returned from Thanksgiving. Since I now had high-speed Internet at home, I sat on the couch with my feet on the coffee table, my laptop on my knees and the TV tuned in to CNN. I was addicted to news updates.

I felt a newfound freedom, released from slaving away in my cramped office. The entire day, I kept telling myself how much I loved working from home, but as I gazed around my apartment, I started to wonder whether I could still call it "my apartment." Should I start thinking of it as "our apartment?" Should I just accept the inevitable? My eyes wandered over all of the changes in the front room: candles, flowers, framed photos, books, DVDs, and so on. Yes, my place looked better. But was that the point.

The debate raged in my head for several minutes until Hank jumped onto the table, skidding on books and knocking over a cup of tea. All of my papers slid off the table and reshuffled themselves on the floor. Startled, Hank hissed and ran out onto the deck.

I chased after him and scooped him up before he

realized he could jump off the second-story deck and explore a whole new city. Cuddling him tight, I took him back to the couch. I loved how my cat purred when I held him, but he only let me hold him briefly before he skittered off on another adventure. I started to wonder if Hank was "my cat" or "our cat?" Sarah found him, so maybe he was "her cat," even though he was living at my place and I was the one who took care of him.

I decided to head to Petco and get Hank a nametag, just in case he did escape. I picked out a bright purple collar and a nametag and had it engraved with his name and my phone number.

By the time Sarah returned from work, Hank was "my cat." He hated the little bell that jingled every time he moved, so he had hid himself in the bathroom.

Sarah and I fixed some drinks and sat on the couch to watch a rerun of *The Office*. Hank stepped tentatively out of the bathroom. He had developed a habit of sleeping on the rug in front of the heat vent, but this time he immediately jumped in Sarah's lap.

She absentmindedly scratched his head. Then she felt the collar. For an instant, I thought she might get angry I didn't let her help pick out the collar. Plus, her phone number was not on the nametag.

"Oh, my God. Did you pick this out?"

I nodded and hid behind my glass, waiting to see how it would play out.

"It's adorable ... and he has a nametag." She scrutinized the tag.

Hank dashed off her lap, launched off of the back of the couch, and scurried out of the room.

I looked back at Sarah. Tears sparkled in her eyes. Not knowing what to do, I kissed her cheek.

"You make me so happy sometimes. I love the collar you picked out for our boy."

I guess that settled it. He was our cat.

* * *

I sat across from Ethan in the coffee shop, feeling hopeless. "I'm getting tired of it, Ethan," I blurted out. "Everything I do now she twists into something that I'm doing for 'us.'" I made quote marks in the air.

"What are you complaining about? My wife spends ninety percent of her time telling me how much of a screw-up I am. At least Sarah praises you."

"But how does buying a cat collar equate to settling down? I didn't even put her cell phone number on the tag. In fact, I went to buy the collar to stop thinking about our situation."

"What do you mean?"

"I was driving myself crazy, sitting at home thinking about how I can no longer call my apartment my apartment anymore, and then Hank dashed out onto the deck." I explained my fears that I would never find Hank if he escaped and how I had wondered whose cat he was.

"Maybe Hank wanted to go to Taco Bell."

I paused, but didn't ask what he meant. "Everything I do, she sees as me settling into our relationship."

Ethan tugged at the corner of his moustache and considered my words.

"If I go to the grocery store and pick up food she likes, I am shopping for us. If I pick up food on the way home, I am providing for us. I feel so trapped."

"She isn't trapping you—you are."

I ignored his comment. "She's even thrilled with our sex life. Lately, I've only put out for quickies, but she saw this expert on a morning talk show who said quickies are good for a relationship. So, once again, she thinks I'm a hero."

"I need a refill. Do you want another chai?" He gestured to my empty cup.

I nodded.

Ethan made his way to the counter while I stared at the foothills of the Rocky Mountains in the distance. How could I feel so trapped when there was so much space out there? I needed to move. I needed to move far away.

He handed me my chai and took his seat again. "So, how's the hero?"

"I'm not a hero. I'm a cad. No ... wait ... I am a piece of shit."

"I don't think you are."

"Seriously, Ethan. Is this all life has to offer? Do all of us settle down just because we are too scared, or too tired, to go after what we want? Do we buy a house, buy a car, and get a pet?"

"And what do you want?"

"Not to be a piece of shit, I guess. Hey, do you think Starbucks sells courage? I could use a few shots in my chai."

"Can I ask you a question?"

I nodded.

"Is being with Sarah so bad? What is it you dislike so much?"

"She likes me, and I don't deserve it." I shrugged. "I'm not used to being liked. What do you dislike so much about your marriage?"

"I can't provide everything she needs and wants from me."

Both of us fell silent and sipped our drinks.

Then I smiled. "Why did you have to bring up Taco Bell? Now I'm craving a bean burrito."

"You better not cave in. You might fart more than normal in your sleep."

I laughed. "Don't be a jerk. Can I tempt you with a taco? It's right across the street. My treat."

"Sure, why not? I don't have to worry about farting in bed; I *want* to turn her off."

Sitting down at a table with our burritos, I asked Ethan, "What did you mean, about Hank wanting to go to Taco Bell?"

"It's a song." He bit into his burrito and cheese oozed

onto his hand.

"There's a song about a cat going to Taco Bell?"

"No. A beaver."

I whipped my head up to meet his eyes. "A beaver!"

He laughed and dabbed his hand with a paper napkin. "The song is called 'Wynona's Big Brown Beaver.'"

Shaking my head, I said, "Seriously, Ethan. You listen to weird shit."

"Oh, don't be so uptight all of the time. I'll bring the CD in next week. You might like it."

"Okay, I'll give it a listen ... would you mind if I ripped it?" I removed my second bean burrito from its wrapper and doused it with hot sauce.

Ethan placed his hand on my shoulder. "Look at you tossing around new lingo! I've never been prouder."

I threw a hot sauce packet at him.

Chapter Twenty-Four

"On your right, you'll see the new high school. This is a great neighbourhood for kids."

"Oh, that's great. I teach high school English. Wouldn't it be wonderful to get a job across the street from home?" Sarah turned to me and smiled.

Sarah's real estate agent prattled on about the neighbourhood. I sat silently in the backseat of the agent's car as we drove from one house to the next. Sarah and the woman chatted incessantly about this and that. I stared out the window, pretending to care about the surrounding neighborhood. Inside, I was fuming that we were looking at houses on a Friday night, but I would smile and nod occasionally when Sarah turned to look in my direction.

When we wandered around the houses, I feigned interest. Sometimes, I asked questions, but I mostly just kept a huge fake smile plastered across my face.

Afterwards, I took Sarah out to dinner to her favorite Vietnamese restaurant. She was glowing, immensely happy, but I was suffocating inside. I kept pouring Sriracha hot chili sauce into my noodle bowl. Each time, Sarah would laugh at me, because I was already in tears, my mouth was on fire, and my nose kept running. The more she laughed, the less we talked about finding a place together, so the indigestion would be well worth it, I figured.

The next morning, I rolled out of bed early for what turned out to be an extremely cold bike ride. I stayed out long enough to avoid Sarah until she left to go shopping with her mom. Rose's car pulled out of the parking lot just as I was carrying my bike upstairs. She honked, smiled, and waved. I waved back.

I stripped down and stood under the hot shower for as long as I could stand it, stepping out only once my entire body was parboiled and red.

Dressing in sweats and a sweatshirt, I then went into the front room. Despite the hot shower, I still felt chilled to the bone, so I sat in front of the fireplace with my laptop. CNN was on, but I had it muted. Sometimes I preferred reading the scrolling news at the bottom of the screen.

Sarah had asked me to look up some properties online while she and her mom shopped. I was not sure why, since we were working with a real estate agent anyway, but I'd said I would. Instead, I found myself surfing random sites—reading about cities on the East Coast. I had always considered moving out east, which had so much more to offer history lovers. Fort Collins was not a place in which I wanted to settle. Colorado was steeped in Western history and Native American history, but neither of those fields floated my boat.

By the time Sarah arrived home, I hadn't completed anything for her; in fact, I didn't even hear her enter.

"Don't you look studious over there." Her smile was wide, sincere.

"I'm sorry, honey. I didn't hear you come in." I slammed the laptop shut and rose to help her with her bags. "Wow, did you guys leave anything in the stores?" I gave her a peck on the cheek.

I grabbed all of the bags and carried them into the

bedroom. After poking around in the bags a little bit, I returned to the front room—and stopped in my tracks. Sarah was looking at my laptop.

I had slammed it shut without closing the window I was looking at, but I still decided to act quickly. "Hey there, you snoop, what are you up to?" I sat on the ground behind her and put my legs around her.

"I wanted to check my email. Are you going on a trip or something?" Her voice quivered.

I wrapped my arms around her tighter. "Kinda."

"Oh. What do you mean 'kinda'?"

I paused, and then took the plunge. "You've always mentioned going out of town for a long weekend. Valentine's Day is on a Thursday this year. I thought we could go out to New York, or Boston or something. I'm leaning towards New York, since you love to shop." I gave her a squeeze.

Sarah just sat there, silent. I couldn't tell if she bought the act or not.

"It was just a thought. We don't have to."

"What? Are you kidding? Of course I want to go. I just didn't expect this." She turned around and kissed me.

"Can you take that Friday off? I'm sure my kids wouldn't mind not going to class that day. I'll tell them I'm going to a conference. I thought we could fly in late on Thursday night. That would give us two full days. Then we can come back on Sunday."

"We should start planning. It's only a couple of months away." She grabbed the laptop and her smile conveyed a sense of urgency.

Before I knew what was happening, I was handing over my credit card to pay for airfare and hotel charges. I had never been to New York City. First time for everything, I guess.

* * *

"I think I'm going to move to Boston."

Ethan stirred his coffee well, and then responded, "Have

you told Sarah yet?"

I glanced out the window and tried to spy the mountains through the falling snow.

"No, I haven't. She may have suspected the other day, but I think I got around it." I told him about the impending trip to New York City. The entire time I was talking, he stared at me directly but never said a word or showed any emotion.

"Why New York in February?" he finally asked.

"Unfortunately, I was looking at cities out east. I couldn't say 'Let's go to Mexico.' She wouldn't buy that. Besides, it has Broadway and lots of shopping for her."

"So why are you going to New York if you want to move to Boston?"

"I don't want her to know anything about Boston."

"It is a secret location that not many know of ..." he remarked dryly. "So are you going to disappear one day? Will you tell me, so I don't have to sit around wasting a day waiting for you?" Something in his tone dripped with anger, or was it jealousy?

"Well, smartass, I haven't thought about all of the details yet. But I'll be sure to send you a memo."

He put his hands up, palms out. "Don't get mad at me. You're the one being a coward. You're willing to uproot your life and move 2,000 miles away rather than break it off. It's pathetic."

I felt my temperature rise. "For your information, I'm looking into colleges out there. There're more teaching opportunities in Boston. I plan on finishing my dissertation within a year, and I'd like to get some connections out there. I've already been talking with some professors I met at conferences."

"That's right, Lizzie, keep telling yourself that. Soon enough you'll believe it."

"At least I'm not scared to chase my dreams. How's your dissertation going? Oh wait, you quit your program and you are teaching high school English. You're a babysitter." I tucked some loose strands of hair behind my ear and glowered at him. Surely, my comment would get a rise out of him.

"Because teaching freshmen in college is a huge difference. People in glass houses, Lizzie."

"I wish I had a glass house. I would throw the biggest rock through it and smash it all to pieces."

"You already have a rock, you idiot. You are just too scared to heave the damn thing."

"What are you talking about?" I pulled my jacket tighter around me to combat the chill in the air.

"Tell her the truth. Are you really *this* stupid?"

"What should I tell her? 'Hey, I really like you, but I'm not sure about this long-term thing. In fact, it scares the crap out of me.'"

He rubbed his chin, and studied my face intently. "If that's how you feel, then yes."

"But I would miss her." I could tell that my words shocked both of us.

"Would you miss *her*, or would you miss having someone there?"

"How do you know the difference?"

He shook his head. "Only you can answer that question."

I've always hated that response.

Later that night, I considered asking Sarah to move with me. What if she said yes? Wouldn't that bind me even more? True, we wouldn't have a mortgage together, but would I feel even more obliged to stay in the relationship, no matter what. If she moved, she would have to change her life completely. We would both be more dependent on each other. Dependent. I hated that word.

If she would agree to a long-distance relationship, that would be ideal. There would be an adjustment period when I moved to Boston, sure, but I thought it would work. Of course, convincing her might take some time.

Chapter Twenty-Five

Snow fluttered outside the window. There was not enough on the ground to stick, so once the flakes hit the wet cement, they blended into the sidewalk.

"Are you guys sticking around for Christmas this year?" Ethan causally glanced in my direction and then watched the snow falling again. "We're going to my parents' house. Are you guys going to Sarah's mom's house?"

I shook my head. "No, we're going to Peter's." I never referred to the house as Maddie's. The house was definitely Peter's. It was large, over-bearing, and in poor taste; I couldn't associate Maddie with those qualities.

"My, my, my, you're spending a lot more quality time with your brother." He gave me a knowing smile.

"Don't you insinuate anything. Sarah's mom is taking another cruise with friends, and Sarah insisted on accepting the invitation. Apparently, she prefers spending the holidays with any family, instead of just with me. I'm not sure whether to be insulted or not. I suggested spending the week in Breckenridge."

He stirred his coffee. "What, you don't want to go?" he

said mockingly.

"I'm dreading it more than ever this year."

"Why's that? Did you and Maddie have a fight or something?" He chuckled.

"No. It's nothing like that. I just don't want to go."

"Spill it, Lizzie." Ethan set his cell phone on the table, accidentally bumping his coffee. He reached for my napkin to wipe up the splotches.

How could I tell him what I was afraid of? I was too old to be worrying about such silly things. Ethan's eyes bored through me.

I pointed to my bracelet.

Ethan shook his head. "I'm not following you."

"Come on. She gave me a bracelet right away. What kind of gift will she give me for Christmas? What will Sarah think? And what if Sarah finds out about the bracelet? She'll catch me in a lie. Then our relationship really would be over."

Ethan shook his head. He sauntered back to the counter, refilled his cup, and then came and sat back down. "I wish I had your problems."

"Why is that?"

"Seriously, Lizzie! Do you think Maddie is that stupid? And so what if Sarah finds out? All along, you've wanted to find a way out. I don't understand why you fight so hard to stay in a relationship you don't even want! I wish I had your problems—because they're all imaginary." He pushed his chair away from the table, causing me to wince as the chair legs scraped along the floor.

"What problems do you have that are real?" My voice quivered with anger.

"She wants to adopt a child. We've started the process. Soon, I may be a daddy."

For an expectant father, he didn't look too happy about it. He looked so unhappy that I didn't even try to joke that at least he wouldn't have to sleep with her to father the child.

"Does she know you hate kids?"

"I don't hate them." He sighed. "I just don't want any. They poop and piss in their diapers. And they cry. They smell. And we don't make a lot of money. Not all of us have a trust fund and can go to Breckenridge for the holidays."

Ethan had always struggled with bodily functions, I knew. Piss, poop, and sweat grossed him out. All sexual acts repulsed him. There were times when I thought his wife must have loved him more than any woman had ever loved a man, history or no history. How could she be with a man who was repulsed by not only her secretions, but also his own? To my knowledge, Ethan never masturbated, let alone fucked. Kissing was probably out of the question as well. I imagined oral sex certainly wouldn't be an option. It was as if he and his wife would live like siblings for the rest of their lives. No wonder she was desperate for a child.

I let the trust fund comment slide. I've lived with that stigma all of my life, and while I resented people thinking I was a typical trust fund baby, few people knew I received a scholarship for my studies. Also, instead of asking for money, I worked my way through my undergrad years. But I also knew that I couldn't pursue a degree in history without a trust fund. Not many people get rich by studying history. It helped that Sarah also came from money. One of us could always suggest an expensive dinner or a weekend away without making the other feel bad. If Sarah had been a boy, my mother would have been so proud of me; she could have bragged to her friends at the club about me dating someone of "our" status.

"What are you going to do?" My instinct was to offer Ethan money. I always had that instinct. I hated watching people suffer because they didn't have what I had too much of. But experience has taught me that people don't like to be reminded they are struggling and I am rich—and not rich from my own endeavors, but rich because my parents are rich. People really hated that.

"I can't really refuse her now, can I? She's been making

all of the sacrifices, and I think I owe her."

I stared at a table of high school students. They were trying to act dignified, drinking lattes and discussing a movie they had seen the night before.

After a pause, I asked Ethan, "Do you think that's fair?"

"Fair to whom? My wife? Yes. Me? No. And the child? Well, it's not fair to the child at all. But then again, how many fathers really want their children?"

His coldness was a cover; I could tell by his eyes that the prospect weighed on him. Ethan never wanted to hurt a soul. He was tormented enough about ruining his wife's life, which was why he would never leave her. She never had to worry about him cheating on her. And now he would have to account for another life. It was too early to know if that life would be ruined, but it didn't look good. It definitely didn't look good.

Chapter Twenty-Six

Christmas Eve arrived much faster than I wanted it to. Sarah and I were expected at Peter's for dinner, and since my parents would be at the house on Christmas morning, Sarah and I decided to exchange our gifts on the morning of Christmas Eve.

We had decorated a small tree, which pleased us both; our mothers had always gone crazy with Christmas opulence during our childhoods—all white lights and sophisticated ornaments. I had always loved the simplicity of bubble lights and could stare at them for hours and be completely at peace, but they were never deemed dignified enough for my mother. Sarah had chosen our ornaments, cute little decorations from all of her favorite childhood Christmas shows—the kind her mother despised. Sarah loved the *Mickey Mouse Christmas Carol* the most, and you could tell by looking at our tree.

The tree made me smile. I wish I liked my mother enough to invite her over and rub her face in it; her disdain would be priceless.

Sarah and I had also agreed on a budget for gifts. We were not allowed to spend more than three hundred dollars on each other. But while shopping for my mother's gift in Tiffany's, I found a stunning amethyst ring. As soon as I saw it, I knew Sarah would love it. I bought it for her without thinking. With one purchase, I had blown the budget out of the water. Not wanting to let on, I purchased other gifts, too, and wrapped them separately.

As we unwrapped our gifts, I kept the Tiffany's box in my pocket. Sarah had already started to get up to clear away the wrapping paper when I handed her the box.

Her eyes lit up and then she slapped my arm playfully. "I can't believe you! We had a deal—no more than three hundred dollars." She slowly opened up the box. "Wow. It's beautiful. You even remembered my birthstone." Sarah hugged me and then slid the ring onto her finger. She kept admiring the amethyst, smiling, for the rest of the day.

* * *

Both of us sighed when we pulled out of the parking lot and hit the road for Peter's house. For so many years, I had avoided the family on holidays or had made only the quickest of appearances. I never understood the incessant need to be with family on special days. All families did was fight, bicker, belittle, and abuse each other.

Yet that year, Sarah and I had agreed to spend several days at Peter's. Sarah didn't have any siblings or other close family, apart from Rose, so when Maddie invited us, Sarah had jumped at the chance. It seemed her desire to be with family—even one as dysfunctional as mine—overcame her desire for a peaceful holiday. I said yes only because Maddie asked, and to make Sarah happy. But once we started heading to the house, both of us had reservations.

No one should make plans for Christmas months ahead of time, I thought. *Or even weeks ahead.* Christmas always seems so far off when you agree to attend, but when the day arrives, it's as if you'd rather be kneecapped than go. Sometimes, I wished I were an orphan like Hank.

One solace was that Maddie had insisted Hank come too. He sat in his carrier in the backseat and meowed, or "talked" as Sarah called it, the entire car ride. I had become unashamedly, if not surprisingly, attached to the little guy.

We arrived before my parents, so at first the evening was relaxed. Peter seemed at ease. Maddie had a cheese and sausage platter out, and all of us sat around nibbling and chatting. In the background, *It's a Wonderful Life* was on TV. All in all, it wasn't a bad night.

When I slipped into the kitchen to get another cocktail, Maddie followed.

As soon as we were out of earshot, she slapped me on the back. "Why didn't you tell me you got Sarah a ring for Christmas?"

I filled my glass with some vodka and mixed it with cranberry juice. "You never asked."

"I can't believe you didn't spill. It's a huge deal. And nice job with the ring. It's beautiful." Maddie grinned.

It struck me that her smile was too wide. She looked too happy. I had hoped that she wouldn't notice the ring at all. "Thanks," I said, feeling suddenly awkward. "It's her birthstone. Why is it a big deal, though? It's not a diamond."

"It's a piece of jewelry. Women love jewelry. And it's a ring. She put it on her ring finger. Seriously, how do you not know this?" Maddie crossed her arms, waiting for me to respond.

I gulped my Cape Cod and stared at her. The bracelet Maddie had given me jangled on my wrist as I took another gulp. "She didn't say much when she opened it. She just gave me a hug."

"Have you noticed she keeps staring at it? She never even told me you got it for her. I could tell by the way she looked at it, and then at you."

I made another Cape Cod. Why did some women have to make such a big deal about things? I had seen the ring and thought she would like it, end of story. But no, Maddie and

Sarah had to ponder the meaning. What did the ring signify? What were my intentions? It was a gift—that was the intention. Why can't people just give a gift? When Maddie had given me the bracelet, I hardly knew her. But I had been with Sarah for more than a year. I bought her gifts all the time. It was just a gift. She should know it was just a gift. Plus, it matched the necklace I got her for our anniversary.

My racing thoughts were interrupted by the doorbell. Maddie's face paled and my stomach flipped. Enter The Scotch-lady.

"Well, I guess the fun is over." I made another drink for myself and one for Sarah, even if having another drink was probably a mistake.

I walked into the front room, still carrying the drinks, to see Peter fawning over my mother's new outfit—yet another navy blue power skirt and blazer. Her white shirt looked so crisp it might crack in half. I shook my head. *No one wanted to see that*, I thought. Her hair was pulled back too tight in a bun. I wondered if she'd recently had work done.

"Oh great, you brought the cat."

Hank took one look at the brittle Scotch-lady and jumped into Sarah's lap.

I walked over to them and handed Sarah her drink before taking a seat on the armrest of her chair. Hank purred as I scratched his head. I still hadn't said hello to my parents, and I wondered if I should even bother.

My father sat down on the couch and opened a magazine. Peter chatted to Mom. Maddie, sitting near us, said nothing.

Yes, I loved the holidays. The tension was so worth it. I tried not to remember that I could have been sitting in front of a roaring fire in a cabin in the mountains instead, absorbed in a good book, a drizzle of snow covering the ground. *Stop it, Lizzie. You're only torturing yourself.*

After dinner, my parents stayed longer than was normal. I kept staring at my watch. When my mother left the room, I got up to get some quiet time in the kitchen. Maddie and Sarah were deep in conversation, so I didn't think anyone would miss my company.

I stared out the window. The house was on a hill, overlooking Denver. Beyond, the city lights twinkled in the cold, cloudless night.

I heard the pad of feet entering the room, but ignored the intrusion. The person opened the back door of the kitchen. While trying to stay focused on the lights, I heard a weird *shooshsing* sound.

Turning, I saw my mother trying to push Hank out the door.

"What are you doing?" I rushed over and scooped the kitten up.

"I just thought he would like some fresh air."

"Bullshit!"

Her eyes glistened with hatred.

"Hank is an indoor cat. There are coyotes and foxes everywhere out there."

"What, you don't want your precious child to make new friends?"

"He's part of the family now. We don't associate with those beneath us remember? You taught me that?"

She sniffed. "Well, he certainly didn't learn that from you."

"Meaning?"

"You know perfectly well what I mean. You're always throwing it in my face." She moved closer to me. "It's because of you we can't have bigger functions this time of year."

"By all means, throw bigger functions. I don't give a fuck if I don't associate with you or your friends."

"Come now, you two, play nice." Maddie entered the room, hands on hips. Her voice was firm. Sarah was right behind her.

I glared at my mother for a second longer. Then I said, "Thank you Maddie, for the reminder. I wasn't taught that by my parents." I turned my back on Mom and prepared to leave the room.

My mother retorted, "I don't even understand half of the stuff you say. If you want to say it, say it. Don't hide behind snide remarks."

I whirled to face her. Her words were bursting in my mind like bubbles. Bitch, coward, liar, cunt, two-faced whore—I wanted to shout. How I despised her. How I hated being related to her. How I wished she would—

Sarah took Hank from me, and I melted at her sorrowful eyes. No. It wasn't the right time. I stalked out of the room and headed upstairs.

No one spoke. I heard the footsteps of their dispersal. A few minutes later, Sarah came upstairs and we went to bed.

Sarah's final words for the night were, "Gotta love family time."

I buried my head in the pillow. Hank jumped off the bed and hid in the closet, curled on a pile of clothes.

Surprisingly, the next morning went well. The four of us exchanged gifts. Peter and Maddie had opened their gifts for each other the day before as well.

I was surprised by the thoughtfulness of the gift Sarah had purchased for Maddie and Peter—a personalized basket that included wine, cheese, crackers, and other delicacies. She had also included a day spa voucher for the two of them. It was to the new, trendy spa that was all the rage. Even I had read about it in the paper, and I remembered Sarah and her mom talking about it at one of our dinners at Jay's Bistro. I made a mental note to send Sarah and her mother to the spa for a day.

Maddie handed us our gift with a smile and said, "I guess we had similar ideas."

Disappointed, I let Sarah open the gift. I didn't want to go to a dreadful spa. Sarah took the lid off the box and squealed.

Dammit! I was sure we were going to the spa.

Sarah pulled a piece of paper out of the box and waved it at me. It wasn't a spa. The gift certificate was for a weekend for two at Vail.

"I thought, since the two of you are out of school right now, you could use some time together." Maddie smiled.

I was relieved. Getting a pedicure before sitting in a sauna did not appeal to me. And what's up with drinking weird fruit, veggie, bee pollen, and wheat germ concoctions. No thanks!

"This is great! I can't wait to get Lizzie on a pair of skis," exclaimed Sarah.

Peter laughed. "She's never skied in her life."

"It's true," I told Sarah. "I haven't. Can we snowshoe instead?"

"You'll fall down no matter what, Elizabeth. You might as well go skiing and not be a pussy."

I glared at Peter.

Sarah's lips brushed my cheek and then she left the room with Maddie. Peter and I just glanced at each other, neither of us saying anything. My brother went into his office and I followed Sarah and Maddie into the kitchen to help them finish preparing dinner—prime rib, Peter's favorite.

The three of us chatted, whiling away time.

"Maddie, I hope you don't mind, but I brought Lizzie's favorite." Sarah went to the fridge and pulled out a bag. Then she plopped the parsnips onto the counter.

"She won't go skiing, doesn't listen to music, but she loves parsnips. You got yourself a weird one, Sarah."

"Oh, I'm sure she has some positives. I keep hoping I see them some day." She smiled at me.

"Really? I know she's a workaholic, absorbed in her research ninety percent of the time."

"That's true. And the other ten percent she's asleep. But I have to admit, she does clean Hank's litter box every day."

"Well, I'm obviously not appreciated here." I interrupted. "If you'll excuse my workaholic-self-absorbed ass, I'm going to hang with my cat and read about the Hitler Youth."

Maddie called out after me as I left the room, "You can both be pussies together."

I heard Sarah laugh. "And don't forget to clean his box."

Those two becoming closer made me uncomfortable. They seemed like old friends.

Chapter Twenty-Seven

The two of us sat by the fireplace in our room in Vail. Maddie had splurged on a really nice condo in the heart of the town. Blanketed with fresh snow, Vail reminded me of a quaint, Dickensian village. Everyone was merry and enjoying themselves. The town bustled with activity, people running to and fro to the slopes, shops, and restaurants.

Everyone except us.

"Will you stop giggling?" I squirmed in my chair, trying to get comfortable. The fire was raging, but I was still freezing. "Can I take the ice bag off? I'm chilled to the bone."

Sarah came over and took the ice from my elbow. "Wait until Peter hears about this." She laughed again.

"Sarah! You better not tell Peter."

"Don't you think he'll find out?" Her words had the whiff of betrayal. "We're going to their house on New Year's. It's only a few days away."

"I don't have a cast. I can put the brace on my arm and cover it with a thick sweater. I don't use my left arm all that much."

"Lizzie, you grimace every time you move it."

I looked at my elbow. When we had arrived, Sarah immediately wanted to go to town for lunch. Famished, I readily agreed. My mistake; I have never been known for my grace and adding ice to the mix made for a potentially dangerous situation. People in my family should only be around ice in cocktails. We were not athletes.

As we had hurried out of the condo after unpacking the car, I hadn't even noticed the ice on the steps. My feet flew out from beneath me and my body flipped into the air. Hanging in midair for a second, I grabbed the handrail with my right arm, which caused me to come crashing down on my left side, or, to be more exact, my left elbow. Pain stabbed through my arm as soon as I hit the ground, but extremely embarrassed, and knowing several people were around, I had instantly popped up off the ground and brushed myself off. After reassuring Sarah I was fine, we had gone to lunch.

We spent the afternoon shopping, and I hadn't even let on to Sarah that I was in pain. In one store, I secretly bought some Advil and took it when she wasn't looking.

Later that evening, when I was changing for dinner, Sarah had seen it.

"Lizzie!" she had exclaimed, hurrying over to look at my arm. A bruise was already forming, and it was quite swollen.

Instead of going to dinner, we went to Urgent Care. I refused to go to the emergency room. For some reason, Urgent Care was less damaging to my wounded ego. Only pussies went to the ER.

After several hours and some X-rays, the doctor determined I had a hairline fracture. Not even a real break—a wimpy hairline fracture. Just like my wimpy illness.

Fortunately, they didn't cast for such injuries; instead, I had a lightweight brace that slipped on my arm under my clothes, and I was ordered to rest my arm and ice it. The good news was that I didn't have to get up on skis. Another winter and I still hadn't skied—that was quite a feat for a Coloradoan. I'm still not sure why I was so proud about that.

* * *

"What's wrong with your arm?"

"Nothing. Why?"

Ethan stirred his coffee. "You're holding it funny. Usually, you have your arms on the table, and you gesticulate when you talk. But today, you have it in your lap, and you keep rubbing it with your other hand."

"Hmmm … that is odd. I didn't know that I was doing that." I left my arm in my lap but held onto my cup with my good arm. "So how was your Christmas?"

"Oh, the usual. The parents kept hinting they're ready for grandkids. Kept making comments like, 'Wouldn't today be great if there was a little one to spoil.' Between them and my wife, I was going crazy."

"How's the adoption process going?"

"To tell the truth, I'm staying out of it. She's taking care of it. She likes to keep me informed, but I tune her out."

I chuckled. "We are two peas in the same pod."

Ethan nodded. "So seriously, what's wrong with your arm? Are you wearing a brace under your shirt?" He reached over, but I swatted his hand away.

I looked down at my arm, but I still didn't move it. Sarah had promised me she couldn't see the brace. I would have to wear an extremely thick sweater so people couldn't see it. I told Ethan the whole story.

"You are the only person I know who goes to the ER so much."

"It was Urgent Care."

"Oh, sorry, Urgent Care. And who breaks their elbow? Forget about living in a cold climate. You need to live in a desert. Do you remember when you broke your knee? Hobbled to your classes on crutches for weeks, looking pathetic. They even had a service that would have escorted you to all of your classes on a golf cart, but no, not Lizzie; you had to act tough. You've broken two bones that are almost impossible to break. How in the world did you break your elbow?"

"It's a talent of mine. Falling is easy. Landing—now that is the key part."

"Maybe you should take ballet classes, football players do it to learn how to fall, so they don't get injured."

"Are you serious? Or do you just want to see me in traction?"

"Actually, I would love to see you in a tutu." Ethan giggled.

I grimaced at the thought.

"Why didn't you just tell me, instead of trying to hide it?"

"Oh, I don't know. I had hoped people wouldn't notice it. It was embarrassing enough. I don't want to relive it each time someone sees me."

"Maybe you shouldn't wear the brace."

"I've tried. Sarah forces me to."

"Forces you to! For such an independent person, I find it funny you're scared of her."

"I wouldn't say I'm scared of her. I just don't want to listen to her jibber jabber about it. It's easier to wear the brace."

"She's not here now. Why don't you take it off?" His smiled was designed to coax me.

"I tried that, but she found out." I rubbed my elbow. The chill in the store made it ache.

"How in the hell did she find out?"

"I forgot to put it back on. And I had to hear about it the rest of the night."

"What's with our women? They always find out what's going on." He laughed. "So does it hurt?"

"Not too bad. It's a small fracture. Mostly it just aches. But if I bump it on something, that's when it feels broken."

"How long do you have to stay off the bike?" He stuck his stir stick in his mouth.

"A few weeks. The doctor said it would heal pretty quickly." Fortunately, I was ahead of schedule. I only needed

300 more miles to finish my challenge.

"How about your ego?"

"Luckily, only Sarah and you know about it. And you two already know I'm a fucking moron."

"True."

We both raised our drinks. "Cheers."

Chapter Twenty-Eight

The good news about New Year's Eve at Peter's was that our parents had other obligations. My father always spent New Year's Eve with all of the top brass of his company. That year, the president was hosting one of those Murder Mystery Who Done It parties. All of the participants had to dress up as if they were in the roaring twenties. I would love to see my mother dressed as a flapper. Peter said Dad had to dress as a baseball player. Oh, to be a fly on that wall. I wondered if they gave Dad that role because he didn't talk. He would just have to carry a bat around and look stupid: not much of a stretch for him.

The bad news was that we were spending New Year's Eve at Peter's house with his friends. But Maddie's parents were coming as well and I was curious to see Peter around his future in-laws.

The afternoon started off okay. Maddie and Peter were frantically getting everything ready, so Sarah and I offered to help.

"Take it easy," Sarah whispered in my ear.

Peter had other ideas in mind. Before I knew it, I was

helping him transport tables and chairs from the basement.

Sarah looked horrified, but said nothing. She and Maddie disappeared into the kitchen. Several minutes later, they returned and Maddie started helping with the lifting. I was hustled into the kitchen where Sarah placed a frozen bag of peas on my elbow. No words were spoken. I helped Sarah prepare some appetizers with my good arm.

When Sarah and I went to our room to shower and dress for dinner, Hank was curled up on the bed. I spread out next to him.

"Don't be mad, but Maddie knows about your arm." Sarah joined us.

"I figured."

"She promised not to say anything."

"Yeah, I don't think she will tell him." She was good at keeping things from him. "To be honest, I don't care who knows, except Peter and my mother." I paused. Here I was, late in my twenties and I still felt the need to hide any weakness from my childhood tormentors. "I'm tired of them not being nice to me."

Sarah rolled over onto her side to face me. I was still on my back, unable to roll over and prop on my elbow.

"You know, that's the first time you ever said anything about the way they treat you."

"I don't like to think about it much. I thought about it too much in my younger days."

"What were they like?" She brushed some wisps of hair out of my eyes, letting her fingers linger on my cheek.

"Pretty much how they are now. The only difference is that I used to get really upset all of the time. What you saw last week was a cakewalk to the way it used to be. I would either get so angry that I'd rant and rave, or I would storm out and cry. I learned to turn my emotions off."

She stared at me. Hank rolled onto his back and stretched, and I smiled. "You're really lucky, Sarah."

"What do you mean?"

"You love your mom. I don't even like mine. I'm envious of how you guys get along. I try not to interfere too much with you two."

"What do you mean by that? I thought you didn't want to spend time with us."

"Why would you think that? What you have with your mom is special. I didn't want to intrude."

"You wouldn't be an intrusion. In fact, I know Mom would love to have you hang out more. She always wanted more daughters."

I thought about it. How was it possible that Rose wanted more daughters when my mom hadn't wanted me at all? Maybe Mom just would have liked a different daughter?

"How did she take it when you told her you were gay?" I asked.

"My mom? I didn't tell her. She told me."

"What?"

"She sat me down one day and said it was okay to be gay. She knew I was, and I guess I wasn't dealing with it well. I would date guys, but I hated it. Is that why your mom doesn't like you?"

"I don't think that's the only reason. It's a big part, but I think mostly my mother thinks I'm weak. I never had a hard exterior as a child. I cared about animals, the environment, people … you name it. And I didn't go into business. I studied history. For her, liberal arts mean I'm extreme liberal. In her mind, I am an intense flower child, which makes me weak *and* an embarrassment."

* * *

Maddie's parents arrived early for dinner, before the other guests arrived. Peter seemed somewhat anxious, puffing his chest out more than normal until he resembled a small bird roosting to stay warm on a chilly winter day. I thought I even saw a trickle of sweat on his brow.

The six of us sat in the living room, and during a lull in

the conversation, I studied Maddie's parents. They did not surprise me at all. From the beginning, I could tell they were kind, loving people.

"So, Peter, how are the Broncos doing this season?" asked her father.

"Uh …" my brother looked flushed. Our family did not follow any sports, and neither of us played team sports. Peter had played tennis, but quit when he determined he wasn't the best player. Lately, he had started to play golf, but only in an attempt to further his career, not because he loved the sport.

"Well, Tom, from all of the grumbling I hear around the watercooler I'd say they aren't doing all that well," Peter responded. "But you know the Broncos." He chuckled meekly.

Tom laughed. "Yeah they have a way of starting off so good and then crumbling right before the playoffs. Fortunately for us, the Chargers are peaking at the right time." He sipped his beer. "Who's your pick for winning the Super Bowl?"

I couldn't tell whether Maddie's father knew Peter was faking it, or whether he was trying to have a father–son moment with his future son-in-law, but out of the corner of my eye I could see that Maddie was enjoying this football grilling just as much as I was. She had to know Peter knew nothing about the sport, let alone the names of the other teams.

"It looks like a tough field right now …" Peter's voice trailed off and he took a sip of his bourbon.

None of us knew what he meant by that; the season was almost over and the teams were narrowing down quickly. Tom shook it off and tried a different approach. "Now, this is a good beer." He held it up and looked at the label. "Fat Tire, huh? Is it a local beer?"

I waited for Peter to implode. He was a bourbon man, probably because he thought it was a more manly drink. In family and his business circles, at least, it was a more manly drink. This conversation was fast demonstrating that he couldn't talk to Maddie's father about simple "man subjects"—football and beer. Even I could bluff on those topics, but not Peter.

"Fat Tire is from our hometown, Tom. They brew it in Fort Collins," Sarah jumped in breezily, unwilling to watch Peter suffer anymore.

I chuckled to myself in the knowledge that Peter had to be rescued by a girl. Tom looked at the beer label again and then took another swig.

Maddie's mom saw a break in the conversation and turned to me. "We have heard so much about you. How long have you two been dating?"

I stared in disbelief. Never had a parent asked me how long I had been with anyone. On most family occasions, I was completely ignored. And Sarah was sitting right next to me, so it was clear she knew I was dating a woman. Several seconds rushed by before I composed myself enough to smile. I answered, "Over a year now." I looked at Sarah, who smiled back at me. *At least I got that answer correct*, I thought.

"I think the Giants have a good shot this season, Dad. Eli wants to prove he's better than Peyton." Maddie looked smugly at Peter—a look that said, "Fuck off," or was I imagining that?

Tom turned in his chair to face his daughter. "Well, the Colts are out of it completely this year, with Peyton's injury."

While Maddie chatted with her dad about sports, her mom asked Sarah and me about living in Fort Collins. Peter sulked in his chair. Normally, he dictated the conversation.

* * *

Even though I had dreaded attending a party with Peter's friends, the evening turned out to be less painful than I thought it would be. For the most part, Peter stayed with his friends, and Sarah, Maddie, and I hung out with Maddie's parents. The conversation flowed easily, and the love and attention they showed their daughter surprised me. It shouldn't have, since Sarah had a loving relationship with her mother, too, but I had always thought Sarah was the exception.

I assumed everyone interacted with their parents like I did with mine. After interacting with Sarah's mom, and now Maddie's parents, I was starting to wonder if only a few people hated their families.

While I pondered this, Peter and one of his buddies crashed our inner circle, standing there clutching their bourbons, awaiting a break in the conversation.

When he sensed a pause, Peter pounced. "Lizzie, how was the skiing in Vail?"

I paused to think up a believable story, and Maddie interjected, "Peter, why don't you introduce your friend?"

Peter looked flustered. Regaining his composure, he said, "My apologies. Samuel, I would like to introduce you to my sister Lizzie, Sarah, and Maddie's parents, Tom and Joan."

Samuel smiled, or at least I think he did. His lips moved for a second.

"So, Lizzie, how was the skiing? Samuel has a holiday home in Vail. He's heading up there tomorrow and would like a ski update. Did you get your pussy ass up on skis?" My brother laughed maliciously.

Sarah came to my rescue. "Actually, we decided to rent some snowboards. By the end of the weekend, Lizzie could have given people lessons."

Maddie seemed to glow with happiness.

Peter stammered, "I-I don't believe it. You don't seem like the snowboarding type."

"Snowboarding, huh? I guess that is good and all," Samuel chimed in, "but I prefer skiing. If it was good enough for my ancestors, it's good enough for me."

None of us knew what in the hell he meant by that, except Peter.

"I concur, Samuel," said Peter. "Snowboarding is for

hooligans. Lizzie … I guess … well, I guess I'm not that surprised by such behavior considering …"

Sarah muffled a laugh.

Was he implying that because I was gay I was also a snowboarding hooligan?

"I tried snowboarding a few years ago." Maddie's dad joined the fray. "I couldn't stay up on the damn thing. Not only that, but by the end of the day, my armpits were on fire from pushing myself up off the ground every few seconds." He turned to me. "Bravo, Lizzie, for trying." He raised his beer glass in my direction. I used my good arm to raise my cocktail.

Out of the corner of my eye, I saw Maddie rise and whisper in Peter's ear. Blushing, he abruptly left the group.

Samuel stood there briefly before excusing himself. Before he left, he did that weird lip thing again. Another attempt to smile?

"What did you tell him?" Sarah turned to Maddie as soon as Peter had left.

"I told him he had a bat in the cave," said Maddie, her words drowned out by Sarah's snort of laughter.

Sarah quickly covered her mouth and Maddie's parents chuckled and politely veered the conversation in another direction.

Casually, I pulled my phone out of my pocket and texted Ethan, asking what Maddie meant.

He replied: *LOL … Lizzie, it means you have a booger in your nose. Happy New Year.*

I glanced at Maddie and then at Peter, who had just returned. He threw Maddie a look I knew was designed to be intimidating, but she kept smiling anyway. It took everything I had not to laugh. My esteem for her skyrocketed.

Peter approached our group slowly. His fake smile alerted me that he was ready to attack.

"I do love your sense of humor, Maddie." His voice was strained.

"I don't know what you're talking about." She gave him a peck on the cheek.

I knew this wouldn't appease him. Peter never could take a joke.

He turned to me, nudged my arm, and started to say something. He stopped. I felt him tug at the brace.

"What are you wearing? A brace!" He laughed. "What'd you do, hit a tree while snowboarding?" Merriment danced in his eyes.

I was a deer in the headlights. If he found out now, I knew he would take all of his aggression out on me.

Sarah laughed. "You won't believe this, Peter. After amazing me with her snowboarding skills, on our last run, an out-of-control skier took her out at the bottom of the slope."

Maddie's smile bolstered Sarah's bravado.

Sarah continued. "It was quite terrifying, actually. This poor chap ended up seriously injuring himself when he finally collided with a building. But before he stopped, he mowed down three people that I saw." She took a sip of her beer. "Who knows how many more he hurt. Lizzie saw him coming and ran to push a child out of the way. In the process, Lizzie got creamed. The mother was so appreciative. She wanted to give your sister an award!" Sarah turned to me and added, "But you know Lizzie, she didn't want to be in the limelight."

"I didn't know we were in the presence of a hero." Tom raised his glass to toast me yet again.

Peter seethed.

Maddie glowed.

Sarah smiled at me. A sense of relief flooded through me and I kissed Sarah in front of all of Peter's guests. I don't know who was more surprised by that, me or Peter. At that moment, she was my hero.

Chapter Twenty-Nine

On the third Thursday in January, I finished my bike challenge. It was a cold but tolerable day for riding. Sarah and I had quarrelled about me getting back on my bike just two weeks after falling on my elbow, but I was undeterred. Eventually, she had given in. I think she saw it was a battle she would lose. And really, how much more damage could I do to my elbow?

Still, I didn't want to rub her face in it, so I rode when she was at work. She must have suspected it, but I never confirmed her suspicions.

On that particular Thursday, I had hopped on my bike around noon and made my way from campus to my favorite bike trail. It was fitting to finish my challenge on the same trail I had started riding during my illness. The trail felt like a close friend who had helped me through the challenge of getting back in shape. No matter what, it was always waiting for me; actually, it beckoned me.

Mile 3000 came and I paused for a moment on the trail, a smile creeping across my face. I had an urge to drink a glass of champagne; instead, I peddled on.

Once I got back in my office, I changed my clothes and rushed home to shower. Instead of celebrating alone, I drove to Sarah's school, parked next to her car, and waited.

When she spotted me, a radiant smile lit up her face.

I rolled my window down. "Can I take you to dinner?"

She looked curious, and then glanced over at her own car.

"Never mind about your car," I said. "I have time to drive you to work in the morning."

I had never seen her look so surprised, so happy.

"Where are you taking me?"

"I was thinking of this tapas place in Boulder."

She opened the car door and climbed in. "I like where this evening is heading."

"What can I say, Sarah? I heart you." A thought flashed through my mind. "How would you like to stay in a hotel tonight? We can check into a nice hotel, have a fancy dinner, and neither one of us will have to drive home."

She leaned against the car door to look at me. "Lizzie, are you trying to sweep me off my feet?"

"I haven't before now?" I teased.

"It's coming more naturally for you these days." She rubbed my thigh. "I like it."

After dinner, Sarah and I returned to our hotel. Fortunately, the tourist season was over so we were able to check into a posh room. The view of the Rocky Mountains made the cost of the suite well worth it.

I had arranged for the hotel to chill a bottle of champagne for us. I wasn't a big fan, but Sarah loved the stuff. We sipped our champagne while partaking in a bubble bath. The bear-claw tub fitted both of us with plenty of room to spare. Leaning against Sarah, I played with the bubbles on her leg.

"What are we celebrating tonight?" asked Sarah.

"Why do you think we're celebrating anything? Maybe I felt spontaneous." I squeezed her thigh.

She tipped some of her drink on my head. "Spill it, Lizzie."

"Hey, now!" I laughed. "If you dump it all on me, I won't give you anymore."

I ducked my head under the water. As soon as I surfaced, she wrapped her arms around me. I felt her hard nipples press against my back.

"Come on. I want to know."

I glanced over my shoulder to study her face. "Okay, if you must know, and kill the romance, I reached a personal goal today."

"Which was … ?" her voice trailed off.

"I—"

"What?" she shouted, splashing water on me.

"It's silly, that's all. I'm embarrassed to tell you."

"Lizzie, you fart in your sleep. How can you be embarrassed to tell me anything?" She joked.

I slapped her leg gently, causing a spray of bubbles. "Careful now! Or I'll fart in the tub."

"You better not!" Sarah laughed.

I flipped around to kiss her. Then I settled my back on the opposite side of the tub so I could watch her face.

"I set a goal, about six months ago, to ride my bike 3,000 miles. Today, I reached it." I shrugged.

She giggled.

I reddened.

"What's embarrassing about that?" She looked bewildered.

I ducked my head under the water again. Popping back up, I wiped the water out of my eyes. "Oh, I don't know … it seems kinda childish."

"I wouldn't say that. To be honest, I'm not surprised at all. You love to challenge yourself." She sat up, exposing her exquisite breasts. "I'm proud of you."

I looked away.

She turned my face and stared into my eyes. "Seriously.

When we first met, you were still struggling with your illness. Remember the first time you took me hiking?" I tried to turn away, but she tightened her grip. "You could barely hike a mile. Your heart raced, your legs almost gave out, and you huffed and puffed. Now, you've ridden your bike 3,000 miles. Sometimes you amaze me. I love the fight in you."

I didn't know what to say.

"Now it's time for me to confess." She wiped some bubbles off my nose. "I thought you'd been offered a teaching position today, and you were going to tell me we had to move."

My muscles tensed, and I couldn't draw a breath.

She continued. "I know that we may have to move, but …" She looked out the window at the mountains. Only a faint outline against the purple-black sky was visible. "It'll be hard."

I felt a window of opportunity. Maybe now was the time to suggest a long-distance relationship.

I started to speak, but she interrupted. "But I'd rather move with you, than be away from you." She leaned in and kissed me. "We should start celebrating things more. I like your style."

A devilish look came across her face, and then she dumped her entire glass of champagne over my head. Before I could react, she hurtled out of the tub, sprinting towards the bed. I chased her, sloshing water all over the bathroom floor. We landed on the bed together, laughing.

She pinned me on my back and looked around. "We've made a mess of this comforter. It's all wet."

"I'm hoping to make an even bigger mess." I attempted to prop myself up, but she held me.

"Patience, Lizzie." Her eyes wandered all over my body. "Yes, all of the bike riding has been good for you."

"Has it now?"

She licked her lips. "Very much so." Her eyes continued to devour me.

"I'm glad I can still turn you on."

"Maybe if you paid more attention to people, you'd notice how often people check you out."

"Oh, please!" I waved away the idea to the best of my ability, since she had my wrists pinned.

"Maybe it's a good thing that you don't notice."

"Trust me, I notice all of the people who check you out." I gave her a knowing look.

"Good." She flashed a sexy smile.

"Good? What's that supposed to mean?" I tried to wiggle free.

"It means good." Slowly, she bent down and took my nipple in her mouth, sucking it, occasionally biting it. I ran my fingers through her short, wet hair. After visiting my other nipple, she moved lower—kissing and licking my stomach on her way down. Her hands gently ran along my body, her fingertips soft and graceful. Down she went.

My eyes closed and my back arched slightly when I felt her tongue on my clit. I loved that first touch every time. It sent a rush of excitement pulsing through my body. No one had ever made love to me like Sarah did.

I let out a small gasp.

Sarah heard me and moved further down to my thighs, teasing me. Pleasurable teasing. And excruciating. Minutes passed. My hips moved more urgently.

"What's the matter, Lizzie? Is there something you want?" Her tone was seductive.

I pulled her head back to where I wanted her, and her tongue darted inside me. Searching. Tasting. Flittering in and out.

She moved back to my clit and took my swollen lips into her mouth. Slowly, she slid a finger inside me. Then two. I wanted it. I wanted her. More. Harder.

Sarah relished being inside me. Leaving her fingers inside, her body moved up. Her lips found my mouth. I tasted me on her tongue as her fingers continued to move in and out of me, frantically.

My fingers dug into her back. My back arched further. I started to see flashes of light behind my eyelids.

"Harder." I whispered in her ear. "*Harder*!"

I felt all of her fingers inside now.

Again, I felt her tongue on my clit.

Oh, my fucking God!

I moaned, much louder. Sarah held my hip down with her free hand.

Bright flashes of light burst in my eyes, causing them to roll back.

My entire body tensed, and then trembled.

Sarah stopped her lapping tongue and held it in place.

A second wave hit me.

Then my body relaxed.

She laid her head on my stomach, both of us sweaty and content. Not content—blissful.

At that moment, I never wanted to lose her. Life without Sarah … I couldn't imagine it right then.

My body shivered again.

"Aftershocks." She giggled.

"Come here." I pulled her up into my arms. "I love you, Sarah."

"Good."

I laughed. *God! What a woman!*

Chapter Thirty

On the last day of January, I was sitting in my apartment when I heard the squeal of tires spinning in the parking lot. It had been snowing nonstop for a couple of days, so the parking lot was one huge ice-skating rink and tenants were struggling to pull in and out of their parking spots. Ignoring the screeching tires, I turned back to my reading, only to be interrupted by the phone ringing.

Irritated by all the distractions, I glanced at the caller ID: Maddie.

"Hello."

"Hi. What are you up to?" She sounded overly perky.

"Not much. Just reading a fascinating article on wanderlust. What's up with you?"

"What the hell is wanderlust?"

"It means a desire to wander. It was part of the back to nature movement. Youths wanted to leave the cities behind and wander around in nature."

"Oh. Who would have thunk it? Speaking of nature ... how about all this snow?"

"I know. It's been crazy. It hasn't snowed like this in

years. We've been stuck in the house all weekend. Are you and Peter surviving?"

"I'm not too sure about Peter. He's on a business trip, and he can't make it home. And I got cabin fever, so I decided to visit. Can you help me get my car unstuck?"

I paused and stepped out on my balcony. Sure enough, Maddie was sitting in her car, which was wedged on top of an ice chunk.

She smiled and waved at me.

With a sigh, I went downstairs to help.

Maddie rolled down the window and said, "I thought if I gunned it, I could force the car into the spot."

"How did it work out for you?"

"Great—if you don't count getting stuck." She laughed.

I called Sarah on her cell, for help. After twenty minutes of trying to push and rock Maddie's car into a parking spot, our neighbor Evan appeared, tied a chain to her car, and used his F250 to pull her car off the iceberg.

"I'm starving!" Maddie exclaimed as the three of us walked upstairs. "It took me more than four hours to get here."

When we entered the apartment, Sarah offered her a hot drink and I was put in charge of ordering enough Chinese food to last three people a few days. I cringed at the thought of some poor kid delivering the take-out in this weather, but Sarah and I had not planned for the storm and our cupboards and fridge were empty.

The food wouldn't arrive for an hour, so Maddie, still tense from her drive, opted for a hot bath and a glass of wine.

While Sarah and I scrounged in our closet for some warmer clothes for our guest, I pondered why Maddie had risked her life to come to Fort Collins wearing nothing but a dress. No coat. Nothing. In the middle of a blizzard! Was she insane?

"I think she's terribly lonely," Sarah whispered.

"How long has Peter been out of town?" I asked.

Sarah looked at me, her head cocked. "That's not what I meant, exactly."

We didn't have a chance to finish our conversation.

Maddie burst into the room. "This is great. I haven't had a sleepover in years." She was wearing Sarah's bathrobe and I suspected she didn't have anything on underneath.

Maddie didn't appear flustered at all. And Sarah beamed with happiness. I felt like vomiting.

* * *

The following Saturday, I met Ethan for coffee and told him all about Maddie's visit and her car.

"How in the world did she get her car on top of an iceberg?"

"Beats me. Seriously, Californians should not drive in the snow. I'm surprised she wasn't killed." I set my cell phone down on the table. Ethan eyed it and sniggered. "I know. It's ancient."

As he grabbed my phone to get a closer look, he steered us back to our conversation. "Lucky that guy was there."

"Yeah, if it hadn't been for Evan, her car would still be there in April."

"Thank heaven for Evan." Ethan chuckled.

"You're such a nerd."

"You should talk. This coming from someone wearing a shirt with actual portraits of all of the Presidents of the United States on it, and not even the band—the actual politicians."

"There's a band called the Presidents of the United States?"

"Yeah they sing that 'Peaches' song."

"Oh. I like peaches."

"So, you've heard the song?"

"What? No." I shook my head.

Ethan rolled his eyes. "Why do I even try?"

"They sing a song about peaches?" My voice filled with disbelief.

"Yes. It's about how much they like them."

"You listen to strange crap." I leaned back in my chair and stretched my legs out under the table.

"Because a biography on Alexander Hamilton is much more thrilling."

"He wasn't even a president, so there." I stuck my tongue out.

"Yeah, I know. I went to elementary school, remember."

I looked down at his shirt. "Whatever. You have a *The Great Gatsby* shirt on." I noticed, with some surprise, that it had a small stain near the collar.

"Let's agree that we are both nerdy. But I'd rather be a nerd than a dork."

"What's the difference?"

"Literally, a dork is a whale's penis. Figuratively, it's a geeky person who is socially awkward."

"And a nerd?"

"I feel a nerd is just someone who is passionate about his or her subject, or something, like you are passionate about history. Every day you have some nerdy history T-shirt on. Even when you're teaching, your undershirt says something or has a historical quote."

I shook this off. "Sarah made a comment that I didn't understand," I told him.

"Was it a three-syllable word?" He smiled.

"Oh, Ethan, you're on a roll today. Anyhoos, as I was saying, she said she thinks Maddie is lonely and unhappy."

"Uh-huh."

"Well, do you think it's true?"

"Lizzie, please tell me you aren't *still* trying to steal your brother's fiancée."

Was I? If I was, I wasn't doing a splendid job. Something was holding me back. *What?*

Ethan studied my face. "Let's face it: your brother is an asshole. He works all the time. He dotes on your crazy mother, and he thinks your father is a banking god. That would be a difficult household for anyone to live in."

"But she always seems so happy ... well, most of the time. And she's pretty funny."

"You crack me up. Funny people can be sad. A lot of funny people hide their sadness behind their humor. Think about it, Lizzie. She's never home. She practically lives up here. For someone who is about to get married, she spends very little time with her soon-to-be husband."

This bothered me. Yes, it would be incredible to hook-up with Maddie. She was the whole package. Beautiful. Smart. Sexy. Confident. But she was more than that. Maddie wasn't the type to be put on a pedestal to admire. She demanded respect. Was that holding me back from trying to seduce her? Would she want a relationship and not a casual fling?

Chapter Thirty-One

"Are you getting excited about your trip?" Ethan immediately ignored my answer and instead looked at his phone, reading the latest text message from his wife.

"I guess so," I told him. "I've never been to New York. I want to see all the historical stuff, and Sarah is excited about seeing a show."

"Why are you going to New York again?" He glanced up at me.

"Because I want to live in Boston." His questioning annoyed me. Surely, I had already explained this to him! Was he actively trying to annoy me?

"So why not go to Boston? I bet you'd love all the tea party history and all that jazz."

"I didn't want Sarah to find out I want to live in Boston."

Was I sure I wanted to live there?

"Does she know you want to move at all?"

"She knows it's my last year at CSU. And she knows I will have to move when I find a job."

"Are you looking for a job?" Ethan glanced sidelong at

his phone again.

"No. I've decided to take some time off and finish my dissertation. I'm thinking of writing a book. I don't know if working a regular job is my thing."

"And you want to live in Boston to do this? Why can't you do it here?"

"I think a change of pace will help me concentrate more." I was making crap up as I went along.

"Have you ever been to Boston?"

"Nope." I was tiring of his interrogation.

"But you want to live there?"

I knew what he was doing. Ethan always lectured me about running away from my problems. What did he know? He quit his program early.

The move to Boston may be perceived as rash to outsiders, but I felt that I needed to do it. Life was getting too comfortable. Too predictable. Stifling, in fact. What would become of me if I stayed?

"I'm not being a coward?"

"Would I say such a thing?" Ethan raised his eyebrows in mock amazement.

"I know what you're trying to do, Ethan."

"And what's that, Lizzie?" he asked, searching my face.

"I'm not running away."

"Of course not. You are just picking up and going to a city where you know no one, you don't have any job prospects, and you don't have a place to live. It all sounds perfectly reasonable to me."

I mulled this over. *No prospects. No, don't listen to him, Lizzie.*

Stay strong.
Do not let yourself get tied down.

* * *

Fuck."

I rolled over in bed. "What's wrong?"

"I think something bit me."

I fumbled for the light switch on the hotel nightstand. Our flight to New York had been delayed, so we hadn't settled down into our room until well after one in the morning.

"Let me see."

Sarah held out her hand and pointed to her ring finger. I could see a slight red mark. That didn't concern me as much as the fact that her finger was swelling. When I tried to remove the ring, she winced in pain.

"Here, let me try." Sarah yanked on the ring, but it wouldn't budge.

I called the front desk for a cab to the hospital.

"What are you doing?"

"Honey, we have to get that ring off your finger. I didn't know you were allergic to insect bites." I rushed around getting dressed and threw a pair of jeans and a sweater for Sarah to put on.

"I didn't either. Will they have to cut the ring off?" She sounded deflated and tenderly rubbed the ring I had bought her for Christmas.

"I don't know, baby. Let's get you to the hospital, okay? We'll see what can be done." I kissed her forehead and whisked her downstairs to the waiting cab.

When the receptionist in the crowded ER department saw Sarah's finger, a doctor was called immediately. Within one minute, she was receiving treatment. No rooms were available, so they led her to a gurney in the hallway. As she was being seated, a nurse jabbed a needle into her arm. Sarah hadn't even seen it coming. She jumped about a foot and cursed, but the nurse was too busy to apologize. The doctor explained he would have to cut the ring off. He was holding something I assumed was a ring cutter.

Tears filled Sarah's eyes. "Don't let them cut the ring off." She pulled her hand away from the nurse.

"We have to get this ring off." The doctor eyeballed me

like it was my responsibility.

"It's okay, honey," I coaxed. "We can get this ring fixed or we can get you a new one. But look at your finger; it's turning blue."

"But you gave me this ring."

"And I can get you a new one. A better ring. Just let the doctor take care of your finger."

"What's wrong with this ring? Why would I need a better ring?"

I was astonished that she chose this moment to quibble about my word choice.

"There's nothing wrong with this ring, but I don't want you to lose your finger! All you have to do is tell me whether you want it fixed or whether you want a new one, and I'll make it happen."

"When can we replace it?" She looked up at me, tears streamed down her face.

The nurse looked at me like I was an idiot, and her eyes screamed, *Hurry things up!*

"We can go shopping first thing tomorrow. I promise." I placed my hand on her shoulder tenderly.

Sarah let them cut the ring off.

After several hours of observation, she was released from the hospital. I wrapped her up in my coat and took her back to the hotel. I had requested that the bedding be changed completely, but the hotel staff felt so bad they had upgraded our room. We now had a fantastic view of Times Square, and an extra night if we wanted. Sarah fell asleep at seven in the morning. I noticed the swelling on her finger had finally subsided, and I fiddled with the damaged ring in my pocket. Exhausted, I leaned against the wall and watched her for some time before I joined her in bed and closed my eyes.

* * *

You did what?" Ethan exclaimed.

"I bought her a ring."

"No … No! Wait." He shook his head. "You bought her a diamond ring?"

"I know. I know. But what was I supposed to do? Her finger was turning blue, and I promised I would buy her a new ring. Ethan, her finger was blue … and the nurse—she looked like Nurse Ratched, by the way—was staring at me with a look that said I needed to act fast. So I acted: I promised her a new ring."

As soon as Sarah had woken up after sleeping off all the medication they gave her at the hospital, she had asked when we were going shopping. Before I knew it, we were at Tiffany & Co.

"How big is it?" Ethan was clearly baffled.

"It's not that big. It's only two carats."

"Two carats!" He slammed his cup down on the table. His high, falsetto voice rattled me.

"Is that big?" I felt helpless and stupid when it came to these things.

"I got my wife a one-carat, and I thought that was nice. How much did it cost?"

"Let's just say it was a lot more than the amethyst one."

"I bet." He shook his head. "Did it come in a blue box?"

"What?"

"My wife told me that if the ring wasn't in a blue box, it wouldn't be good enough."

"Did you have to buy a blue box?" I saw a silver lining. I didn't buy one.

Ethan laughed. "Boy, you are a moron when it comes to this stuff. Tiffany & Co. has blue boxes. All women want their engagement rings from Tiffany's."

"Engagement ring? What the fuck are you talking about?" After purchasing the ring, I had done my best to banish this thought from my mind.

He stirred his coffee, smirking. "Did you buy the ring from Tiffany's?"

"Yes."

"It's a diamond ring?" He examined me over the rim of his glasses.

"Yes."

"What finger is she wearing it on?"

"Her ring finger." I whispered, deflated.

"Yep, you're engaged." He got up for a refill.

I pondered the new pickle I was in. When he came back I said, "But I didn't ask her to marry me. Don't I have to ask?" I was grasping for straws.

"I seriously doubt she's taking that technicality into consideration." He laughed. "Can I be your best man?"

"But we can't get married! It's not legal here, thank God." I was suddenly flooded with relief.

"It's legal in Massachusetts, and you are thinking of moving there. It will be a legal marriage if you get married there." His expression told me that he relished my situation.

"But she doesn't know that."

"You better tell her. If you pick up and leave, that will be considered abandonment." He laughed some more. "You know, for someone who doesn't want to commit, you sure know how to tie yourself down. A mortgage, a cat, and now marriage—a legal marriage, I might add. What's next, a kid? I know a good adoption agency." He winked at me.

So much for not getting tied down. I pulled my sweater off.

"What's the matter? Is it getting too hot for you?" He howled with laughter.

"Oh, you're so funny." I rubbed my face.

It was getting hot. I groaned.

Chapter Thirty-Two

Ethan was running late, so I sat at a table and listened to my new iPod. When he walked in he started to laugh.

"What?" I pulled the headphones from my ears.

"You were actually rocking out. I didn't know you could do that."

"You didn't know I could bob my head?"

"Nope. I didn't think you had any sense of rhythm."

"Well, show me your moves." I wiggled my butt in my chair in an attempt to dance—a pathetic attempt, because I nearly toppled over.

"No way. The only time I showed my moves was on my wedding day. Never again. And I wouldn't suggest using that move you just did." He shook his head gravely. "By the way, has Sarah picked the song yet for your first dance as a married couple?"

"What are you talking about?" I asked, startled.

"You are a relationship idiot. Don't you know you'll have to dance at your reception?" He waggled his finger in my face.

"Reception? Dance? What are you talking about? This isn't what you call a traditional wedding."

"For some reason, I don't think Sarah will see it that way. I think she'll want the whole nine yards. I'm going to grab some coffee. Do you need anything?"

I stared out the window. "What? Uh? No, thanks."

When he returned, I asked, "So you think I will have to help pick out a cake, china patterns, a dress, and all that shit?"

"Yes, you knucklehead. You're getting married. What did you think? You could just stand under the stars and make a promise. Weddings are a lot of planning and work. Who put the music on your iPod? I have a feeling it wasn't you." He pushed his glasses higher on his nose.

"Sarah gave it to me as a gift. It's great. She put music and audiobooks on it. And she even put the 'Monster Mash' on it. I love it."

"The 'Monster Mash'?" He stared at me as if termites were swarming out of my skull. "You know that's a Halloween song, right? When was the last time you dressed up on Halloween? Did you even go trick-or-treating as a child?"

"Yes, you numbskull. I know it's a Halloween song and I think I went trick-or-treating once or twice in my life. I like the song. Why does everyone question why I like the song? It's fun, light-hearted."

"Okay, besides the 'Monster Mash,'" he shook his head in disbelief and curled up the corner of his moustache. "Have you listened to all of the music?"

"No. There are hundreds of songs on it."

Ethan picked my iPod up and started to scroll through playlists and artists. I sipped my chai and tried to fathom the mess I was in. A wedding?

He chuckled. Then he placed the iPod on the aluminum-topped table in front of me. I looked at the screen, at a mix labeled "Our love songs."

"How did you find that?"

"I've been married a lot longer than you, Lizzie. I know how love-starved women act. I bet those are the songs she's considering for the big day."

I was flabbergasted. "But we haven't even set a date yet."

"Doesn't matter."

I sighed, rose, and went into the bathroom. Staring at the mirror, I splashed cold water on my face. Then I went out and sat down again.

"Feel better?"

"No."

"Oh, you got your shirt all wet." He indicated my collar. "I haven't seen you this messed up since you started grad school. You going to be okay?" Ethan's face wore his "Cheer up, tiger" look, but I could tell he was enjoying my misery.

I shrugged.

"Do you think she wants kids?"

"Oh, God." I put my head in my hands. "I think I'm going to puke."

"Do you remember when you puked minutes before your orals after your first year of grad school?"

I could tell Ethan was really enjoying himself now.

"I bet you puke before you walk down the aisle. Or better yet, I hope you puke right when they ask you to say your vows. Will she make you write your own vows? I bet she does."

I pushed back my chair with a screech and ran to the bathroom. When I returned, a bottle of Sprite sat bubbling away on the table. I sipped it slowly, the bubbles and sugar nice and sweet in my mouth. "Thanks."

"Anytime, puker. So when should we start writing your vows? I wrote mine. Maybe you could just borrow mine but change the name."

I ran back to the bathroom again to the sound of Ethan's chuckling.

* * *

By the time Sarah had returned from her shopping excursion, I was recovering on the couch and watching a Cary Grant movie. I had vomited non-stop for several hours and I was struggling to keep my eyes open, let alone to follow what was going on. Hank was curled up next to me.

"Hi, honey. I thought for sure you would be riding your bike. It's such a beautiful spring day." Sarah bubbled with perkiness. She pulled a candle out of one of the bags and placed it on the coffee table.

I grunted.

"Uh-oh … is someone crabby today." She sat down next to me. The movement of the couch made me ill.

I bolted to the bathroom, and Sarah followed.

"Jesus, I'm so sorry. I didn't know you were sick."

When I finished vomiting, I leaned against the bathroom wall while Sarah wiped my pale face with a wet cloth. I closed my eyes to stop from puking again.

She sat with me for several minutes. Finally, she said, "You ready for bed?" Her voice was so sweet. I wanted to crawl into her arms, but I was too weak.

"Yes. Thanks."

She helped me out of my clothes and tucked me in. Then she went into the front room, where I heard her rustling through bags. She returned to set a new clock on the nightstand.

"I got us an iHome, so we can listen to your iPod at night. What do you want to listen to?"

"You decide, honey. I'll fall asleep pretty quickly."

I prayed she wouldn't play the love songs. Luckily, she chose jazz. Then she crawled into bed with me until I fell asleep.

Chapter Thirty-Three

As soon as I heard the familiar "ping" on my computer, I knew Maddie couldn't sleep as well. It was well past midnight, and Sarah had gone to bed hours ago. After she had fallen asleep, I had crawled out of bed in an attempt to get some work done. Instead, I ended up surfing the web, looking for places in Boston. Pipe dream or not, I still looked. It relaxed me.

I opened up the email and read: *Congratulations, you rat! I ran into Sarah and saw the rock! Nice job with the ring. I guess you decided to take the plunge after all. Why didn't you tell me?!*

I sighed. I couldn't write back that it was all a horrible misunderstanding. What kind of impression would that make? I was positive Sarah hadn't disclosed all of the details as to why the ring had been purchased. I wrote back: *Howdy, my fellow night owl. To be honest, I can't take much credit for the ring. Sarah picked it out. What's new with you?*

She fired a response right back: *Don't try to change the subject. Seriously, we need to have a party to celebrate your engagement. We can call it the "Plunge Party" and everyone can bring you a plunger.*

I tried to think of a stalling tactic, and wrote: *Hey now, you have enough on your plate. We can think of a party after your wedding. Besides, Sarah and I haven't worked out all of the details.*

Her response: *Details … what do you mean details? You're getting married, right?*

Goddammit! Why did she insist on cornering me on the subject? I replied: *I guess I mean we haven't set up a timeline for the event.*

I felt better writing "event" than wedding; it seemed like that gave me a way out.

Several minutes passed before I received her response: *LOL … timeline … you are such a historian. I'm off to bed. I'll discuss the party with Sarah the next time I see her. Sweet dreams!*

I shut down my computer and went into the bedroom. Sarah had kicked off all of the covers. My eyes lingered on her naked body for several minutes.

Was our relationship what she wanted? Was it satisfying for her? Was it what she dreamed of when she started falling in love with me? Did reality ever fulfill our dreams? Or do dreams just continually set us up for failure and disappointment?

Our engagement was clumsy at best. I hadn't really whisked her off to New York City to propose. In fact, I still wasn't convinced our engagement was even official. Sure, a ring was exchanged, but is that all it takes to seal the deal?

I heard a mournful train whistle off in the distance.

Finally, I got undressed, crawled into bed with her, and embraced her. She smelled of lavender, sweet lavender. I never liked the smell until I smelled it on her. I kissed the back of her head and drifted off to sleep.

* * *

"What if she thinks you're having an affair with Maddie, or with anyone else for that matter?" Ethan rubbed the stubble on his chin.

"Wouldn't that be a good thing?"

"How in the world would that be a good thing?"

"Wouldn't it be better for her to despise me? I'm no good for her. I can't be what she wants me to be."

"And what does she want you to be?"

"Oh, I don't know ... a character in a Jane Austen novel, or something."

Ethan frowned. "I seriously doubt Sarah wants you to be like Mr. Darcy. She doesn't seem to be putting that pressure on you. I think, my friend, you are putting that pressure on yourself. Stop watching Hugh Grant films. They aren't real. And when have you read any Austen?"

"All I'm trying to say is that I don't think I am good enough for her. I'm not romantic. I don't rush home every day with flowers and such. I like to work long hours. I like being by myself."

"Name any couple you know who does that—and Valentine's Day doesn't count."

"Not my parents, that's for sure."

"So, because your parents have a bad relationship, you are doomed, as well. That's a good theory to live by. That way you never have to try and you avoid any type of failure. Have your history studies warped your personal life that much? Let me guess: if you don't know your past, you're doomed to repeat it. So, since Lizzie's parents have a bad marriage, Lizzie should avoid marriage or it will be a horrible union that will ruin everyone. Grow up, Lizzie, and take responsibility for your own life."

"Ethan, there are days when I think I should fake depression. Just imagine. I could mope around all of the time and she'd be too afraid to press me on the house thing, or anything for that matter."

He fidgeted in his chair. "Wow. I thought I was an asshole, but you take the cake on this one. That plan sounds awful."

"I didn't say I was going to do it. Sometimes I just think about it, that's all."

"Lizzie, you're right. It would be much better to fake

suicidal thoughts and torture the poor girl over a long period of time instead of just being honest with her."

"Why can't she be the one who leaves?"

"Are you serious? God, you are the most self-indulgent person I've ever met. We meet here every week and all we do is talk about your problems. Every fucking week. Oh, every once in a while, you poke fun at my life, but you don't really care. Not everything is about you, Lizzie."

"Me? I've been talking about Sarah this whole time." I barked.

"No you haven't. You've been talking about you disappointing Sarah. She loves you—you moron. Love isn't perfect. You have to accept that. Or you'll have a miserable life. A fucking, miserable, lonely life."

* * *

Sarah crashed into the apartment, rushed up to me, and kissed me passionately. She was holding a paper bag, which crushed up against my chest when she leaned in. Then she said breathlessly, "Hi beautiful!"

"Well, hello. Boy, you look happy."

A grin split her face and her eyes danced merrily.

"I am happy."

"Okay, happy girl, can I pour you a glass of wine?"

"Sounds perfect. I picked up some Chinese for us. Would you like to have a picnic with me in front of the fireplace?"

"I was going to grade some papers tonight," I said in a teasing voice.

She set the bag on the kitchen counter. Then she took her shirt off and started to kiss me. She smelled wonderful. Orange blossoms? Was that the scent?

"Oh, all right ... I guess my students can wait."

"There's one rule for this picnic."

"Really? And what's that?"

She smiled as she pulled off her bra. "No clothes

allowed." Her fingers flew to the zipper on her jeans. Then, changing her mind, she started to unbutton my shirt instead. As she reached around to undo my bra, I returned her kiss. Sarah tugged at my shirt with urgency, keen to get me in front of the fireplace. Even though she rushed the act, it was not a quick fuck. We went at it repeatedly for several hours; by the time we finished, and lay in front of the fire picking at the Chinese food and sipping wine, I was exhausted. Neither of us spoke. I placed my head on her stomach and she ran her fingers through my hair.

"Come on, Lizzie, dance naked with me."

"What?" There was no way I was going to dance naked.

Sarah popped up from the carpet and tugged on my arms. "Come on, grandma! Loosen up a little." Her eyes sparkled; she looked radiant. I couldn't refuse.

Afterwards, we settled back down on the floor, Sarah said, "Oh I forgot to tell you, Maddie called me today."

I tried not to react. "Oh, really. How is the troublemaker?"

"She sounded good. She mentioned you two talked a few nights ago about an engagement party. She's so sweet."

"She's very thoughtful." My heart started to race. So that was why Sarah had planned this romantic fuckfest.

"Oh, she said you were quite formal." Sarah paused and then put on a southern accent, "We don't have a timeline yet." She laughed and continued to run her fingers through my hair.

I didn't respond, still hoping the whole thing would go away.

"I told her we could wait until after her wedding. There's enough family drama right now ... well, on your side. My mom wants to take us to dinner."

I licked her nipple, not lingering long; I inched my way down toward her navel. Her soft skin and scent beckoned me. I worked my way down. Down. Down. I didn't stop until she came again.

Chapter Thirty-Four

It took all of my energy to open the door to the coffee shop. I wasn't sure if Ethan would be waiting inside. I thought back to our last meeting and couldn't help feeling that our friendship was teetering on a precipice. Would it survive? Should it?

"Well, look what the cat dragged in?"

"Sorry, Ethan. I was running late." I fell into the chair opposite him.

"Geez Louise! You look beat."

I nodded slowly.

"What the hell happened to you? Did someone slip you some Special K or something?"

I laughed mirthlessly. "No, I've been burning the candle at both ends. Between teaching and Sarah, I'm exhausted."

"Okay, I'm following the teaching part. How does Sarah fit in?"

"Ever since New York City she has been a fuck machine. I mean, she wants sex all night, and then again before work. Man, I'm beat."

"You mean ever since you gave her the ring?" he teased.

"Yeah. And she's much more assertive about it. Passionate even. It's pretty hot, but I am tired. I could probably curl up on the floor right here and go to sleep." I gazed down at the filthy floor. Even that wouldn't have deterred me right then.

"Oh man, that's too bad, Lizzie. You sit right there and I'll get your chai." He stood up.

"Thanks."

He paused. "You really are tired. No comeback whatsoever. And you said thanks." Ethan wandered to the counter and then returned with my chai.

I took a gulp, which burned all the way down.

"So, my tired friend, are you going to go through with this marriage?"

"I don't see a way out of it." I fidgeted with my earring.

"Are you serious?" He sounded flabbergasted.

"What can I do now?"

In a firm voice he said, "Tell her the truth."

"And what do you propose I say? 'Hey, I said I would buy you a ring because I was scared of the nurse and I panicked to save your finger.'" I paused. "Maybe I could throw in, 'and I like what you can do with your finger.'"

"Is that the truth?" He stared through me. What did he see? Himself?

"Sort of."

"What do you mean 'sort of?'" Ethan crossed his arms and tilted his head.

"Let's face it, Ethan, I am a relationship idiot. I don't know what I feel or what I want. Right now, I can barely remember my name."

"Poor little Lizzie. She's been cornered into marriage. Everything is out of her hands." He frowned with melodrama and his moustache drooped. I noticed it was smeared with cappuccino froth.

"I think I will put that on my tombstone." I smiled.

"You are an idiot. And not just with relationships."

"How's the adoption process going?"

He sighed. "It's out of my hands."

Both of us burst out laughing.

"No seriously, Ethan. How's it going?"

Ethan discussed his trials and tribulations for once while I downed three chais.

* * *

When I got back to the apartment, Sarah was already home.

"Hi, honey. I wasn't expecting you to be here." I sat next to her on the couch, slouching against the cushions.

"Yeah, I told Mom I wanted to take a nap. I'm beat." She rested her head on my chest.

"Tell me about it. I just drank three chais."

"That explains why you look so flushed. And your heart is racing."

"I'm shocked. You didn't shop at all?"

"Oh, we did for a couple of hours. I bought a new painting to hang over the couch, but I was too tired to hang it." She gestured to the painting that leaned against the far wall.

I didn't say anything.

She kissed my forehead. "Do you want to take a nap with me?"

"Sweetheart, I would love to."

We crawled into bed, naked, and she held me while we slept for hours. I awoke feeling wonderful. Sarah also woke up refreshed—so refreshed that we went at it again.

* * *

"You have to go to the office?" Sarah looked hurt.

"I know. I know I installed the Internet so I would be home more, but I have a lot of grading to do, and I have to enter information at work," I told her, lying my ass off. I didn't even think my story made sense. I just wanted some alone time. "I'll come home as soon as I can. I'll be counting the seconds until I get back."

"Until you'll be back with me, you mean." She wrapped her arms around me and began to lay delicate kisses up my neck—my major weakness. She knew that if she kissed my neck just right, I would be hers for the night.

"I better go, sweetheart, so I can get back as soon as possible."

She pulled me toward her and slid her hand down my pants. I felt the feather-light brush of her fingertips, then the grasping hardness of them as she fingered me briefly, her eyes hard on mine. She pulled her hand out and sensuously licked her finger. "Hurry back. I heart you."

"I promise." I kissed her goodbye. I briefly considered staying. Then I saw the painting against the wall. No. I needed space.

I didn't go to the office. In truth, I'd never had any intention of going. Instead, I texted Maddie, hoping she would be in town. She was staying at the hotel near Coopersmith's and agreed to meet me for a late lunch.

When I walked into the restaurant, I saw her sitting at the bar chatting with two guys. Two good-looking guys. Jealousy burned inside me. I approached with every intention of whisking her away.

"Hey!" Maddie jumped off her barstool and hugged me tightly. "You got here fast." She held my hand and turned me towards the two men. "I would like you to meet my friends, Joseph and David. They just adopted their first child." She turned to me and announced, "Lizzie and her girlfriend recently got engaged." She let go of my hand. "You should see the rock Lizzie sprung for. Wheweee! I was jealous when I laid my eyes on it for the first time." Maddie nudged me with her arm.

Joseph and David congratulated me and I reciprocated, feeling silly that I thought they were putting the moves on Maddie. Sarah has always teased me about not having any gaydar.

Their buzzer trilled and they excused themselves, leaving the two of us alone at the bar.

"Can I tempt you with a drink? Will Sarah pick you up if I get you drunk?" Maddie didn't wait for an answer and motioned to the bartender.

Ignoring the Sarah part, I responded, "I could really use a drink."

Maddie ordered a rum and Coke for me and another merlot for herself. The drinks arrived promptly, and Maddie raised her glass. I sipped my drink—no, I inhaled half of my drink.

"Everything okay, Lizzie?"

"Y-yeah," I spluttered. I knew my face and my voice betrayed me. Try as I might, I could not fake a smile.

"Come on, there's a table in the back. Let's talk." Placing her arm around my waist, she guided us to a dark corner.

She smelled of peaches. I envisioned running my hands over her body, tasting her sweet nectar, exploring every inch of her with my tongue.

"Do you want to tell me what's bugging you?"

Her voice shattered my fantasy. I sighed. I didn't know where to begin. So, I didn't.

"Did you and Sarah fight?" She queried.

"N-no." Why couldn't I talk to her? Openly.

"Hey, you texted me, remember?" She joked. "Come on! Tell me what's going on." She placed her hand on my leg and gave me an encouraging squeeze. The warmth spread, igniting a tingling sensation that delighted and frustrated me.

How could I be happy with Sarah and still lust after Maddie?

"Oh, I don't know." I tugged at my Northface vest. "I'm feeling ... stifled."

Maddie laughed. "Let's get you out of your vest. You must be roasting." She helped me undress.

"I remember when your brother and I got engaged. For weeks, I couldn't breathe," she babbled. "I think what you're feeling is normal."

What I was feeling was not normal! I wanted to fuck her right then and there.

"Trust me," she continued. "It gets easier. This is a big change for you. All your life, you've been independent. You never were close to your family. Now, you're asking Sarah to spend the rest of her life with you. That's a *big* deal. No wonder you're flustered. You have no experience of letting someone in." She put her hand back on my leg, higher up this time.

I chuckled. Maddie was trying so hard to put me at ease, yet I felt myself getting hotter, more desperate. Frantic. I wanted to taste her. To feel her legs wrapped around me. Be inside her. Feel her body convulse after experiencing an exhilarating orgasm. God, I wanted her.

"Have you talked to Sarah about this?"

"No!" I didn't mean to shout, but for a moment, I thought Maddie knew what thoughts I was entertaining.

She put her fingers to her lips. "No reason to shout. I wasn't going to tattle on you. You can trust me with your secrets. I've trusted you with mine."

I wondered if it were possible to have an orgasm from her touch alone. *What if my eyes suddenly roll back into my head? Will she think I'm having a seizure? Will she call 911?* The thought made me smile. It emboldened me.

"How do you do it?" I asked.

Confused, she replied, "Do what?"

What did I mean? I had to say something. "Act happy."

"Trust me, I have my dark days." She pulled away from me and sat back in her chair.

"Like in Estes."

She nodded.

I wanted her to elaborate. I needed to hear her thoughts. I needed a signal to pursue her.

Maddie gave me nothing to go on.

We sat there in silence.

Flustered, I offered to buy her another glass of wine. She accepted. When I returned to our table, I noticed her happy demeanor had returned. As I handed Maddie her glass, our fingers touched, and I saw a sparkle in her eye.

"Drink up, Lizzie. I feel like dancing."

"Dancing? Where?" My eyes scanned Coops for a new dance floor.

"Not here, you idiot. Around the corner, there's a new gay club." She downed her wine.

Unable to resist her allure, I drained my glass as well.

Sure enough, there was a new gay club right around the corner. Not that I would have gone on my own. Only Maddie could get me there.

Inside, Maddie bought another round of drinks. At first, she danced with some gay boys. It looked like they all knew each other.

Maddie disappeared for a few minutes, and I leaned against the wall, focusing on the handful of people dancing. My drinks were going straight to my head.

Maddie popped up before me. "It took some doing, but you have to dance with me during the next song."

I set my drink down. "And why is that?"

"Just wait." She cocked her head, waiting to hear the music.

That's when I heard it: the 'Monster Mash.'

"Are you serious? How does one dance to this?" I asked, but I didn't wait for an answer, just followed her to the dance floor.

The drinks worked their magic. Or Maddie did. She twirled around me and made me look halfway decent. Afterwards, we danced to several more songs until a slow song came on and Maddie maneuvered me off the dance floor.

My entire body felt relaxed. "Would you like something to eat?"

She nodded, thinking. "But not at Coops. I can't handle

another meal there. I dine there more than I do in my own home."

"Shall we go to your room and order in?" I looked hopeful.

"Yes! Let's get pizza." She bounced in her seat like a child.

Her excitement set all of my nerve endings afire.

We didn't finish our drinks. Both of us wanted to leave—and fast.

When we entered Maddie's hotel room, my bravado started to falter. I excused myself and hid in the bathroom. While dousing my face with cold water, I heard Maddie on the phone, placing our order. I thought briefly of Sarah. *Stop!*

"Hope you don't mind, I went ahead and ordered." She flashed me her confident smile.

"Not at all." I walked to the window. "This is quite the view. You can even see the gap from here."

She got off the bed and joined me, standing close. "What gap?"

"Horsetooth." I gestured to the hills, but I could tell she didn't see it. Pulling her in front of me, I placed my arms around her but didn't hold her; instead, I pointed to the gap. "You see that part of the foothills that looks like a horse's tooth?"

She nodded.

I took in her scent.

"That's why half this town is called Horsetooth."

She rested her head against me. "I had no idea!"

My arms enveloped her. She didn't resist. Finally, the moment I had longed for had arrived. Not wanting to waste a second, I leaned down and kissed her neck.

It was pure ecstasy. Her salty but alluring skin electrified my tongue. A fire burned inside me. My face felt hot. My cheek stung like a bee sting. Several seconds passed before I realized that Maddie had whipped around and smacked me across the face. Hard!

"What the hell do you think you're doing?" she shouted.

Dazed, I asked, "Why did you hit me?"

"Why did I hit you?" She pushed me away. "Why in the fuck did you kiss my neck?"

"What?" I rubbed my cheek, pondering. "Why did you invite me to your room?"

"Invite you? You invited yourself, remember." She glared at me. "I thought you needed a friend."

Her comment smarted. A friend—that's all I was.

"I know you aren't yourself today, but this—" She started to hyperventilate. "Th-this is unacceptable!"

I went to her, to comfort her.

She slapped me again.

"Stop hitting me!" I staggered back against the window.

"Stop coming onto me!"

"Isn't this what you wanted?" I screamed.

"Are you insane, Lizzie? Why would I want Peter's sister to kiss me? I thought we were friends. My one ally in the family. And now I find out you want to get into my pants. Lizzie, you may distance yourself from your family, thinking you're better than them, but you are just like them!"

Stunned, I said nothing.

"Don't just stand there looking stupid. Get the fuck out of my room!" She threw my vest at me and then shoved me out the door.

"Maddie—"

She slammed the door in my face.

A couple walked by in the hallway. Pulling my shirt collar up, I scurried to the staircase. The elevator seemed too slow, too confining. I wanted outside, and quick.

As soon as my feet hit the asphalt of the parking lot, I received a text: *If you don't tell Sarah, I will!*

I threw my phone down. It didn't shatter completely. Exasperated, I stomped on in it until it was unrecognizable.

Seriously, Lizzie. You thought Maddie tried to seduce you by playing the "Monster Mash." Are you that much of an idiot?

Chapter Thirty-Five

Even if it was just weeks before Peter's wedding, I decided I better tell Sarah. I took a long bike ride first, to clear my head, and then came home and showered quickly. I wanted to talk to her before I lost my nerve.

"Hi," I said, walking into the front room and looking her directly in the eyes.

"Hi," she replied, looking puzzled.

Already, my nerves had started to falter. I could feel my heartbeat in the hollow of my throat, right where I imagined Sarah's hands would be when she heard the news. Fighting the instinct to run to the bathroom and vomit, I settled beside her on the couch and fumbled with the drawstrings on my pajama bottoms. Then I mumbled, "Can we talk?" I pulled the drawstrings tight, watching the thread slip in and out of my fingers.

"Honey, what's wrong?" Sarah put her arm around my shoulder and I rested my head on her arm.

"I …"

How could I say that I tried to fuck Maddie?

I nuzzled closer to her and she kissed the top of my head

and held me tight. It felt good, which made me feel worse.

"What's wrong? You're starting to scare me."

"I don't know how to tell you."

She squeezed me tighter.

Sitting up, I looked her in the eyes. "I'm not sure I want to buy a house."

Sarah took a deep breath. "All right. We can talk about that." She straightened on the couch and looked me in the eyes.

"I just don't know if I am ready for such a huge step. And now that I'm taking a year off to finish my dissertation, I don't think staying in Fort Collins is my best option."

She continued to stare at me. I could see her mind grappling with what I had said.

"Are you saying you want to move from Fort Collins to finish your dissertation?"

"Yes, but—"

"But what?" She pulled away from me.

"There's something else. Something you should know." I braced myself.

She crossed her arms. "I'm waiting."

Oh, shit! What have I done? I looked into her eyes, which welled with tears. *Why have I hurt the one person I love?*

Yes, I was in love with Sarah.

Finally, I was at peace with that—just when it was ending.

"I—"

"You what?"

"I may have …" I couldn't get the words out. I swallowed. Then I blurted out, "I made a pass at Maddie."

"You what!"

"I—"

"You fucking asshole!" She sprinted off the couch.

I bowed my head. "If you knew how sorry I am."

"What? Is that supposed to make me feel better, Lizzie? You know what makes me feel better." She yanked her ring off and chucked it at me. I ducked and it slammed into the wall. "Fuck you and your ring, Lizzie."

"Sarah, please, let me explain." I moved towards her.

Her eyes showed no love. All I saw was coldness. Icy anger.

"You asshole! You fucking asshole!"

She drew nearer to me. I had my back against the wall, trapped. Sarah balled her hands into fists. Preparing for a one-two strike, I turned my head and closed my eyes. She fell against me, fists first, into my chest. All of her strength dissipated. Her shoulders heaved and I felt the wetness of her tears on my neck. As I tried to embrace her, she quickly shoved away from me, staggering back.

"You asshole," she whispered.

I stood motionless. My heart shrieked inside my chest, telling me to make it better. My head knew better. I couldn't fix this.

She charged past me to the front door. "I'm going to my mother's!"

She slammed the door as she left.

I stared after her until all I could see was the closed door.

* * *

Several tense days passed before I received an email from Sarah.

Please let me know when you won't be in the apartment so I can pick up my stuff. I have thought long and hard, and I don't want to see you. Please respect my decision and don't try to contact me, other than letting me know when I can come by.

She didn't sign the email. I'm pretty sure she wanted to tell me to fuck off. Maybe her mom helped compose the email to rid it of all vitriol. But I knew Sarah. She was not calm about the situation. If she had the chance, she would throttle me. I also knew that I deserved it. God, I was a fuck-up.

I sat on the couch all night and watched old movies,

Hank curled in the crook of one arm. I didn't cry—I was numb. No thoughts, feelings, or anything else, pulsed through me that night. Occasionally, I would flip the channel, but the rest of the time I just petted Hank—until he bit my hand. He didn't leave my lap, but even he didn't want me to touch him.

Finally, my eyes closed, but as my thoughts drifted off, the sudden realization hit me: Sarah was gone. Forever. I had done it. I had pushed her away.

I was a fucking idiot!

Chapter Thirty-Six

"What do you mean you don't want to be without her?" Ethan's coffee cup was reflected in his thick glasses as he stared owlishly at me over the cup's rim.

"Just that ... I don't want to be without her, Ethan. I think I screwed up big-time." I did the best I could to fight back tears, but I felt them forming anyway.

"You have been trying to brush her off for almost a year now. Please help me understand this." He sounded angry, and a little baffled.

"Really, I don't know how to explain it. I'm just as shocked as you. But I want her back." I gripped my cup of chai tightly.

We sat in silence and watched a toddler throw a tantrum because her mother did not want to buy a Starbucks bear that was dressed up in Fourth of July clothes. The child screeched non-stop for more than a minute. Finally, the mother relented, beaten. She purchased the bear before pulling the tear-streaked child out of the store by one arm while the brat waved the bear victoriously with the other.

"So why did you do it?" He stroked his chin, musing.

"What?"

"Why did you break up with her?"

"I didn't. She broke up with me."

He laughed, but it sounded hollow. "Yeah, that's right. You only tried to sleep with Maddie. What did you think? You could keep Sarah and have Maddie on the side. The best of both worlds. Or did you purposefully sabotage and now regret your idiocy?"

I chuckled and wiped away some tears. "Well, I've never claimed to be the brightest."

His eyes softened. "Seriously, though. Why did you do it? Was all the talk just bluster, so I wouldn't know you cared for her—that you care for her, I mean? You cared for her the whole time. Are you that caught up on being the tough guy that you pushed the right one away?"

"I screwed up." I shivered.

"Yes, you did."

I put my head in my hands. "Do you think I can make it better?"

"Sweetheart"—Ethan put a hand on my arm, gave it a little squeeze—"I have no idea. A lot of damage has been done."

"What would you do?" I looked hopeful.

"For one thing, I wouldn't have tried to fuck Maddie."

I laughed. "No shit, Sherlock. Is there anyone you would willingly sleep with?"

He squirmed in his chair and said emphatically, "No!"

"I wish I felt the same way."

"Trust me, it adds different complications." He looked away.

"I'm sorry, Ethan. That was insensitive."

He waved my words away and said with his southern accent, "Miss Lizzie, I'm not the one you should be apologizing to. You need to come up with a plan."

"A plan." I nodded my head. I loved plans. Challenges.

He leaned across the table and placed his slender fingers

on mine. "If you love her as much as I think you do, fight for her, Lizzie. Fight!" He then slapped my hand. "If you don't, you'll never forgive yourself."

Chapter Thirty-Seven

I had no idea where to begin to make things right with Sarah. And I also knew I had to talk to Maddie. The wedding wasn't too far off. I couldn't delay talking to her. Using the text function on my new cell phone, which had all the bells and whistles, I informed Maddie that I had told Sarah. It was a gutless way of communicating, but I still didn't tell her that Sarah had left me. I didn't see a need.

Not a minute passed before I received a reply: *Thank you. Can we talk?*

I groaned. How much crow did I have to eat? Of course, I couldn't say no; she was going to be my sister-in-law. I asked where and when.

To my surprise, she wanted to meet in my apartment in ten minutes. Quick—like a Band-Aid.

Ten minutes had never felt longer. I waited in my front room, like a child waiting to get immunized. Full of dread.

There was a knock on the door. For a second I considered jumping off my balcony and running for the hills. Who would really miss me?

Get it together, Lizzie. You did this to yourself.

I stood, swaying a bit, and answered the door.

"How's my future sister-in-law?" Maddie set the tone right away.

What could I say? I just stared, mutely.

"Are you going to let me in?"

"Are you going to slap me again?"

"Are you going to try to kiss me?"

"Never. Never again." I rubbed my cheek. My jaw was sore.

"Good. I'm glad we cleared this up." She pushed her way into my apartment.

I turned. "Is that it?"

"What? Did you want to talk about it *ad nauseam*? That doesn't seem like you." Her tone was accusatory.

"Seriously, I tried seducing you and you don't want to rip my head off?" I was bamboozled.

"Lizzie, you aren't the first person to make a pass at me. You aren't the first to misread my friendliness. My friends and family always tell me I'm too footloose and fancy free." She paused. "However, I didn't expect it from you."

"Not the first nitwit—"

"Goodness, no!" she interrupted. "But I had thought that since we are going to be family, I would be safe around you." She laughed. "A gay guy even made a pass at me once. And nitwit? Seriously."

"Maddie, I'm so sorry … not about the gay guy … you know what I mean. I—"

"You better be. And don't worry, I won't tell Peter."

I pushed my hands deep into my pockets. "Thanks." I knew she couldn't.

Maddie's face softened. "How did Sarah take it?"

My instinct was to shout, "How the fuck do you think she took it?" Instead, I shrugged. "Not too good. She left."

"Is she coming back?" she asked, and I detected a spark of hope in her voice.

I shook my head. "I don't think so." Tears formed.

Maddie looked torn. Was she afraid that if she hugged me I might kiss her again?

"Lizzie, I'm so sorry."

I stifled a sigh. "It's all my fault."

She laughed. "I wish I could tell you you're wrong."

"Oh, don't worry. I've sat around for hours ruminating on my actions."

Maddie chortled. "Ruminating! Lizzie, get off your high horse. Maybe if you spent less time ruminating and more time living, you wouldn't be in this situation. What's with you Petries? Why can't you act like normal people?"

I started to answer, but she shushed me.

"What's your plan?"

"My plan?" My voice sounded hollow, even to me.

"To win Sarah back?"

"She's asked me not to contact her. She wants me out of the apartment so she can pack up her stuff. In fact, I'm leaving tonight. I'll be gone for at least a week. I don't want her to feel rushed." I motioned to my suitcase in the corner. "I'm taking off for Jackson Hole."

Hank came crashing into the room, upsetting my books on the coffee table.

"Who's watching him?" Maddie gestured to the rambunctious kitty.

"I'm dropping him off at a kennel. Sarah's mom is allergic, so he can't stay there."

"A kennel!"

For an instant, I thought she was going to whack me again.

"Hank, pack your bags. You're coming home with me."

Hank darted out of the room.

"Maddie, that's kind of you—"

"Lizzie, we're family. He's coming with me, and if you try to stop me ..." She made a fist.

"Okay." I backed away. "Thank you."

I waited a few minutes after our farewells, and when I

felt certain Maddie had left, I went back inside, grabbed the photo of Sarah and my bags, and skedaddled.

It had been some time since I had been on a highway that didn't involve traveling to a family member's house. I felt free, exhilarated. There was an endless road before me, and I wanted to conquer it. The sky was brilliant blue and the horizon beckoned to me.

Six hours later, my body started to revolt. My eyes wanted to shut and my back and legs screamed. I couldn't remember getting much sleep lately, and I had been on my bike at six that morning.

When I spotted a hotel with a vacancy, I pulled into the parking lot. After settling into my room, I went to the diner and silently jumped for joy when I saw they served breakfast day and night. I ordered hash browns and a mound of greasy bacon and relished the junk heading right into my belly. Still hungry, I followed it by polishing off four large pancakes.

Afterwards, I wandered around outside, but there wasn't much to see. No matter. I would be in Jackson Hole the next day.

* * *

The next morning, my eyes popped open at four. I knew immediately that I would not be able to fall back asleep. The only good thing about these highway hotels was that the restaurants were always open. Once again, I gorged myself on pancakes, hash browns, and bacon. Then I packed up my meager belongings and hit the road. Thank God Sarah bought me a GPS unit or I would have been hesitant to hit the road in total darkness.

"You couldn't find your way out of a paper bag," she had told me when she gave it to me. It was a little harsh, but not too far off the mark. My sense of direction was severely lacking. I should always go the exact opposite of my gut feeling; however, I was too stubborn to ignore my intuition.

I wanted to be as far away as possible, and the car could

not take me fast enough; yet, a part of me didn't want to be gone. I listened to the playlists Sarah had compiled for me on my iPod. Maddie would have been proud—I didn't listen to a single audio book. For hours I held off, but I finally listened to the love mix Ethan said included the songs Sarah must have been considering for our wedding. I listened to all of them—several times—to see if I could pinpoint which one she might have chosen for our first dance.

But I was at a loss. Most of the songs sounded the same. Anyway, I told myself, there was no need to concern myself with that anymore. I sighed. God, I was turning into a mushy sap. *Snap out of it, Lizzie.* I glanced down at Sarah's picture by the odometer.

* * *

After locating a hotel that had a vacancy for at least a week, I checked into my room, showered, and dressed. Soon, I was wandering around the city square. The quaintness of the Old West made me smile. For an hour I wandered around staring at cute shops, the antler arch over the street, and the stagecoach in the street, until some of my loneliness left me. I found a spot in the tiny park in the centre of the square and watched the locals and tourists pass back and forth.

When my insatiable appetite overwhelmed me, I found a cafe with patio seating so I could continue people watching. Once again, I was gluttonous. I inhaled a massive bacon cheeseburger with fries and a chocolate malt. I longed to hop on my bike afterwards, but I had left it at home. I hit the shops instead, wandering in and out, checking out all the trinkets and novelties for tourists.

It didn't take too long to purchase a couple of T-shirts, fudge, and chocolate. It also didn't take long to notice that most of the shops were the same. Not wanting to look at T-shirts anymore, I changed tactics and wandered into a jewelry store. That was my mistake.

As soon as I started peering into the glass cases, I could

not stop thinking of Sarah—thinking that she would have liked this bracelet or that a certain necklace would look incredible on her. The thoughts invaded my mind. I started envisioning her wearing them. *God, what was I thinking in chasing her away? What a fool.* Sarah was perfect for me in every way— pretty, smart, funny, caring, and most of all, she let me be me. I could work late hours and go for long bike rides. She rarely bugged me about spending more time with her.

Get a grip, Lizzie, I told myself. *Concentrate. You are here to forget, not to beat yourself up. Pull it together.*

I made a break for the exit, confusing the poor salesperson who had pulled out all the merchandise for me. I felt like an ass. But how could I explain? I knew I had acted like a jerk, and that I was wrong. I didn't need a stranger to tell me that too.

How could I say sorry? How could I take back my actions over the past year? Just telling her I loved her wouldn't cut it. You can't put a Band-Aid on a gaping wound. Attempting to change her mind with nothing more than words, or hugs and kisses, seemed impossible. I had to demonstrate that I loved her. And that meant owning up to my feelings and my failings—I was never good at that either. Plus, there wasn't evidence any of my attempts would work. I usually only set goals I knew I could attain. Buying jewelry wasn't going to help me.

I needed to find something to occupy my mind, but it was too late in the day to hike. Instead, I found a used bookstore. That was it: I would buy an enormous book and focus on the words. Force my mind to wrap itself around something else. I didn't want to think about my life. And I certainly didn't want to think about Sarah.

I considered buying a thick book on economics, something that would require all my brainpower to understand, but I knew that wouldn't work. My mind would inevitably wander.

Instead, I headed for the fiction section. I wandered up

and down the aisle until I spied a copy of *The Thorn Birds*, and I chuckled, remembering Maddie reading the book in Estes. But I didn't want a book about a forbidden love affair. I continued scanning the shelves and found a fantastic old copy of *David Copperfield*. From the wear and tear the book had endured, I knew it had entertained many people. It was perfect. I also glanced at a copy of *The Witching Hour*, another monster of a book. I purchased both. Who knew how quickly I would read them? There were too many hours in one day. I needed to keep my mind off my regrets. Hiking would occupy part of the day, but what would I do at night?

My next stop was the liquor store. I would need plenty of gin and tonic, my new favorite vice. Too much rum and Coke gave me the jitters. Back in my hotel room, I filled the ice bucket to chill the tonic water. Sipping a gin and tonic, I opened to the first page of the Dickens book, looking forward to the suffering—the orphan boy tossed out into the world. Please Charles, give me some solace. I needed an old friend to spend time with, a friend who wouldn't judge, talk, or look at me like I was a fool.

Several hours later, I could no longer ignore my grumbling stomach. I tucked Sarah's photograph into the book to keep my place, found another greasy spoon restaurant, and ate until I thought my stomach would burst. Then I returned to my room, curled up on the bed with my book, and drank.

The next morning, I woke up early once again. I did not remember falling asleep, but then again, I did not remember much of the night before. I had plans to hike all day, so I found an early-bird restaurant, an easy thing to do in an outdoorsy town, and wolfed down a hearty meal. The place was kind enough to pack me a couple of sandwiches and apples for lunch.

I purchased a yearlong pass to the park, and at that moment, I never wanted to return to Fort Collins at all. Everything I knew and loved was over. Maybe I would buy a place here and live in hiking, biking bliss. I made a mental note to check out available real estate. Part of me felt foolish, thinking like that. How could a reasonable adult run away? The other part of me thought: *Why the fuck not? What was keeping me in Fort Collins, or Colorado for that matter?*

It was beautiful, but it did not compare to the beauty of northern Wyoming. Would Boston be better? Did I care about teaching that much? I was an outdoor girl. I loved research. I loved quiet and being left alone. Being alone in a city would not be hard, but it wasn't the type of alone time I wanted.

The thought of leaving Colorado energized me. I couldn't wait to get to the trail and explore. I had decided to hike around String Lake, so I wore my bathing suit underneath my clothes. I wanted to test how chilly the water would be in June. Usually, I came to these parts during late July or August.

Just being on the trail, surrounded by nature, eased the tension from my body. I sucked in the fresh air, heard the rustle of the breeze through the treetops, like the whisper of Nature itself.

It didn't take long to work up a sweat, and I started to peel off some of my layers. By ten in the morning, I was famished again. I stopped and unhitched my rucksack to eat one of my sandwiches. Turkey and cheese, stacked high on fresh-baked bread—the type of sandwich I imagined loving mothers made for their children each day before sending them off to school. I sat down on a log and watched the chipmunks grow braver and braver. I knew I shouldn't feed them; nevertheless, I enjoyed watching them.

The buzzing sounds of insects invaded my ears. I couldn't see them, but occasionally one whirred near my ear. Swatting at the invisible assailants, I wished I had remembered to pack bug repellent. Sarah would have remembered. *Stop it.*

I shut my eyes on Sarah's image and listened to the wind whistling through the leaves. A deep breath reinvigorated me.

I could live here.

Whack!

I sneered at the squashed bug on my arm.

I should have brought some spray. Dammit! A butterfly flitted past me. I gazed at the cerulean sky through squinted eyes. What had Lewis and Clark felt when they first stepped foot here? Did they want to explore? Conquer? Tame?

The possibilities were endless then. Now, tourists crawled over the land, despoiling the sense of freedom. From my vantage point, I spied at least twenty people on the trail below, winding their way to my spot. Their prattle shattered the tranquility.

I shut my eyes again, relishing the sound of the wind, the insects, and the chattering chipmunks.

The sound of something crashing at my feet forced my eyes open.

"I'm sorry," said a man, as he leaned over and picked up his water bottle, which sat near my foot.

I nodded and watched him amble away with his wife. They looked happy. Not alone.

I sighed and scrambled to my feet. I needed to focus on the trail.

* * *

As long as I kept moving, I could keep my mind off Sarah. Physical exertion had always been a way to distract myself from trouble or sadness. I relished pushing my muscles to the point of exhaustion, and the beauty around me made the pain more bearable.

After hiking all day, I made a reservation for dinner at the Jackson Lake Lodge. I was dying for a steak. I requested a table by the window, so I could watch the moose come to drink at the watering hole.

Back at my hotel, I showered before climbing into bed and reading until I fell asleep. My body was so relaxed from all of the exercise that I didn't even bother to make a drink.

I kept this schedule for the next three days: up early and hiking until I could barely walk, and then finishing my day by eating steak while watching the moose at the watering hole. On day five, I woke up early and could barely move my legs. My entire body rebelled against any physical exertion, and a slight limp made me look like I was suffering from hemorrhoids. Hitting the trails alone in that state was not advisable—even my stubborn-ass knew that.

Instead, I wandered the square once more. Again, everything reminded me of Sarah. When I passed a real estate office, I stopped to look at the properties. Maybe Boston was not the right place for me. Maybe I should be in the mountains, isolated, so I could finish my dissertation. And on the days I didn't want to work, I could disappear on the trails. The idea appealed to me. It appealed so much that I made an appointment with an agent.

Afterwards, I wandered about the square again. *Screw it*. I marched into the jewelry store and bought all of the crap I thought Sarah would love. The salesclerk patiently boxed and wrapped each item. Finally, I had some peace of mind. Sarah never said I couldn't send her stuff. She didn't have to know it was from me. I just wanted her to have it.

Chapter Thirty-Eight

As soon as I got back into town, I called Maddie to let her know. I had stayed two days longer than originally planned. Of course, she had said that minding Hank was no problem, but I didn't want to trouble her any further. Besides, I missed the scamp. I'd offered to pick him up, but she had insisted on bringing him to my apartment and planned on dropping him off after work.

My apartment seemed empty. All traces of Sarah were gone, even the candles. The large picture she had bought the day I met Maddie at Coopersmith's no longer leaned against the wall. I had hoped it would still be there, as a sign that things could get back on track. She even took the fancy new margarita blender. I couldn't blame her, but still.

The barren apartment closed in on me. I needed to get out on my bike. After my ride, which helped loosen my taut muscles from hours spent in the car, I unloaded my luggage. I had ended up buying a lot of bric-a-brac for my new place, as well as Sarah's gifts. I stopped unpacking for a moment to look at them, piling the boxes on the table. As soon as I had, Maddie knocked on the door.

I let her into my apartment and freed Hank from his carrier. He immediately disappeared around the corner, into the back of the apartment.

"I guess he didn't miss me all that much," I said, watching his tail vanish around the door.

Maddie was staring at the pile of boxes stacked on the table. "I see Sarah rubbed off on you. It looks as though you hit every store in Jackson."

I reddened.

"Can I see what you bought?" Of course, she didn't wait for an answer. She mumbled to herself as she snapped open the jewelry boxes. "For some reason, I don't see you wearing any of this."

"I thought I would get some Christmas shopping done."

"Of course. You're always thinking ahead." She paused and started to say something, but then didn't.

I changed the subject by asking if she wanted to go to dinner. She accepted, but wanted to change first, so we decided to meet at Beau Jo's Pizza. Coopersmith's was off-limits now.

When she left, I hopped on my bike to ride to Old Town. Being alone in our apartment was not what I needed. The next day, I picked out one of Sarah's necklaces and mailed it to her mother's house. I didn't include a note.

* * *

Ethan sat across from me with his arms folded. "So, did you find any answers while wandering aimlessly in the woods?"

"Yeah, I did, unfortunately."

"What does that mean?" He looked skeptical.

"All this time, I've been trying to prove myself. Trying to be a survivor. I didn't need anyone. No one was going to get in the way of my success." I stirred more sugar into my chai. "I wasn't going to be a waste of space. I was going to push myself and push myself to the top. Fuck Peter and my mom. I would be better than them. They would finally have to admit that I wasn't a loser. But it didn't feel right. Deep down, it didn't feel right."

"What didn't?"

"All along, all these conversations and all those bike rides and hikes, I was searching for answers. What did I want? Why did I feel so lost and trapped? And the entire time, the answer was right there: Sarah was the answer."

"Then why did you push her away?"

"Because. Is the answer that simple?"

"What do you mean?" Ethan cocked his head.

"Is that what life is about? I've worked so hard all of my life. Does anything I've done or accomplished matter? Or am I like everyone else, and all I want is someone to go home to? Someone to love me? What if she decides one day that she doesn't love me anymore? Then what do I have? What if she decides that I wasn't the person she thought I was?"

"Oh, honey. Is that what's been driving you crazy? You don't feel like you matter to the world? You need to stop thinking on such a cosmic level. Fuck the world! You don't need to be a pre-eminent scholar. Just be you. Why do you try so hard to prove yourself? Stop turning your life into a challenge. Sit back and enjoy it. Sarah wasn't going to leave you if you didn't perform on a grand scale."

"She did love me, didn't she?" I felt tears dripping down my cheek and I looked away so he wouldn't notice.

"Yes, Lizzie, she did." He hesitated. "I'm betting that she still does. What are you going to do about it?"

"My head is spinning." I closed my eyes and pictured her naked, dancing with me in front of the fire. I loved her so much.

"Life is so cruel, Ethan. I thought I was fading away or drowning in the relationship, that I was becoming normal. Buying a house. Settling down into a routine. I was afraid my life would become boring, or like my parents' life. But now all I want is to have it all back. Sarah was the only thing that made sense."

I fidgeted in my chair, not sure if I should get up or stay and finish my train of thought.

Stop running.

"Growing up around my mom and Peter taught me that in order to survive I had to be strong and stay one step ahead. I focused so much on that thought, that I didn't realize not everyone is like them." I let my head fall back and stared at the ceiling. "All my life, my family let me down. Then, when I got sick, I felt like my body let me down. I kept waiting for Sarah to let me down. Ironically, I let her down. And I drove her away. Stability scares the hell out of me." I looked at him. "What's wrong with me?"

"You want me to tell you everything? Or just the top three?"

"Can you name the top three right now?" I smiled and wiped a tear off my cheek.

"You're a workaholic. You are self-absorbed. You always think you're right." He checked them off on his long, effeminate fingers, and grinned.

"Huh. You didn't even have to think about it." I stared out the window. "And I wasn't even referring to any of them."

"What were you referring to?" Ethan flashed a smile. Then he sipped his coffee and grimaced. "Jesus!" He sucked his bottom lip a little. "Too hot."

"Why don't I have more people in my life? I can count on this hand, one hand"—I pointed to my left hand, the fingers splayed—"how many people I care about. I see people, and I know people, who have an endless supply of friends and loved ones they care about and who care about them."

"An endless supply. That's funny." He blew into his coffee. "You have an odd view of human beings."

"Seriously, what's wrong with me?"

"Lizzie, ask yourself if these people with an 'endless supply' really care about all the people they know. There is nothing wrong with being independent and not addicted to collecting Facebook friends, but if you are pushing people away ..." his voice trailed off.

"Go ahead, say you told me so." I braced for it.

"I would love to. But I can't. I've been fucking up, myself."

Ethan's furrowed brow spurred me to inquire. "What? Is there something wrong with the adoption? With you and Lisa?"

He sat up straight in his chair. "Actually, it's going well." He ran his fingers through his hair. His nails were meticulous. "While you were gallivanting in the Tetons, I was doing a bit of soul-searching. Oddly, I have *The Little Prince* to thank for that." His eyes sparkled.

"The children's book?"

"Yes. I was preparing a lesson and I pulled my copy off the shelf. When I opened it, I glanced at a note I had written to Lisa years ago when I gave it to her before I left for college." His voice faltered and his eyes glistened.

I felt my eyes moisten, watching him. "This is a fine mess. Both of us are a wreck."

He laughed. Then his face became serious. "We have to stop. I know I can't keep coming here each week, bashing my marriage and Lisa. It's—"

"Not helping either one of us. I know. You told me before that I needed to grow up." I squeezed his hand. "I'll always be here for you, Ethan. But you're right. I need to get my life back together, and you need to focus on Lisa."

"And on the baby."

I stared. Everything went quiet. Then all of a sudden it hit me.

"When?" I asked, feeling a sudden rush of excitement.

"Any day."

Ethan looked giddy. He reminded me of the grad student I had met years ago. Full of life. Love.

"Wow!" I sat back in my chair. "Wow."

"I know … I never thought I could be excited about having a baby." He giggled girlishly.

"Oh, Ethan. I'm at a loss … I really do wish you the best."

He removed his glasses and wiped his tears on his starched shirt. "Thanks, Lizzie."

We stood and made our way to the parking lot. I gave Ethan a hug. He held on tight. I stiffened.

"You hug like a man," he teased.

"You hug like a girl."

"This isn't goodbye, Lizzie." He placed his hand on my shoulder.

"Yes, I know. Until we see each other again." I paused. "Maybe we should meet at the top of the Empire State Building in a year."

He chuckled. "And I thought you couldn't be romantic. Look out, Lizzie. Once you release your inner romantic, there's no stopping it." He looked down, into my eyes. "Don't give up, Lizzie. You love her. For once in your life, do not run away."

* * *

A couple of days later there came a knock on my door. Few people stopped by my apartment without calling first. My heart jumped into my throat, strangling me. Sarah? Had she liked the flowers I'd sent?

I rushed to the door and yanked it open.

My hopes were suddenly squashed.

Maddie stood there, a concerned look on her face.

"Hi," I said, and invited her in.

She surveyed the place with a glance. "Well, this is a little better than I was expecting."

"What?"

"It's a little messy, but I was expecting a total wreck … dishes and dirty clothes from your trip."

The mess consisted mostly of my books and journals

spread all over the coffee table. I was intentionally drowning in work. When work wasn't occupying my mind, it always wandered to thoughts of Sarah. And when I thought about her, it was nearly impossible not to call her.

Maddie walked over to my bike, which leaned against the wall. Since Sarah had left, I had never bothered to hang it up out of the way. Maddie examined the odometer. "You're still riding. That's good news, I guess."

She walked into the kitchen, and I followed. "Have you eaten anything since you got back?" she said as she opened the fridge.

"I've been eating out."

"Where are all of the takeout containers? The leftovers? This kitchen looks like no one has been in it for months. Nothing has been used or is out of place."

I didn't say anything.

"All right, missy, get out of your sweats. We're going to lunch."

I tried to protest, but the fire in her eyes stopped me dead. Quickly, I turned and went to the bedroom to dress.

Within half an hour, Maddie and I were seated at Beau Jo's. Maddie placed our food order and asked for a glass of wine for herself and a rum and Coke for me without even giving me a chance to turn it down. Then she ordered two large pizzas with all the fixings. "You can take the leftovers home."

I sipped my water and avoided eye contact.

"So what are you going to do?"

"What do you mean?"

"Are you going to call her?" Maddie fixed me with a glare.

"She asked me not to."

Her eyes softened. "But you miss her?"

"Of course I do."

"You love her?"

I nodded.

"That is all I needed to know."

I laughed. "Are you gathering intelligence?" I stared out the window at the mountains, so solid, so permanent. I had convinced myself I didn't need that. I was attempting to squeeze out the last drops of my youth. For me, finishing my PhD marked my official entrance into adulthood. I would no longer be sheltered by my student status. It was time to grow up. Happy memories with Sarah slowly flooded my mind.

Maddie put a hand on my arm and I noticed I felt nothing. No frisson of attraction. She was a friend, nothing more. "Stop thinking so much," she told me. "Don't let your brain dictate your life. Open up your heart and chase your dreams. Everybody has dreams, but not everyone has the heart to plunge in headfirst. Take the plunge, Lizzie. You may not always succeed, but you won't die wondering."

Our pizzas arrived. "But don't worry about that right now. I need you to finish your drink so you can have another one."

"Really? Why?"

"You have a wedding to attend, and I'm betting you haven't given a thought to what you'll wear."

"What's wrong with what I'm wearing now?" I smiled.

"That's what I thought." She winked. "After we finish up here, we're going shopping for a dress. If you don't dress appropriately, your mom won't let you in. And you don't want to miss the show."

"The show!"

"Trust me, it won't bore you. Do you think I could get your mom to dance on top of any tables? We could spike her scotch with acid or something."

"My life is bad enough right now. I don't need to be traumatized by a strip show featuring my mother."

"Oh that would never happen. I think she sews those navy suits to her skin." She laughed.

"Can't you just pick out the dress and send it to my place," I whined.

"No! And I don't want to hear any complaints, missy."

"Good luck with that."

"Oh, don't worry. I brought some duct tape. I'll tape your mouth shut. Now I know why Sarah did all of your shopping for you." She passed me a napkin and gestured to the corner of her mouth. "You've got sauce on your chin," she said, smiling as I dabbed at it. After a few quiet moments, she said, "Oh, by the way you have a hair appointment the morning of the wedding. Don't miss it."

She flicked me a card with the appointment date and time. The directions were scrawled on in her long, looping handwriting. I sighed and put it in my back pocket. Then I shoved a piping hot slice of pizza into my mouth.

"Now that's a good girl." Her eyes sparkled. I didn't have to heart to tell her that I had been eating all along, gorging even, and that the reason there were no leftovers in my apartment was because my appetite was out of control. I wanted Maddie to feel she was accomplishing something.

Chapter Thirty-Nine

The day of the wedding finally arrived. Without Sarah as my buffer, I felt more out of place than ever. Full of nervous energy, I stood outside, staring at the flowers that enlivened the grounds of the posh hotel. Peter had rented all of the rooms of the small hotel to accommodate all of the out-of-town guests. It was located just outside of Denver and specialized in weddings. Maddie had insisted the wedding be outside, rain or shine. Mom insisted that the Californian in her made her want to get married outside rather than in a church. According to The Scotch-lady, Californians were barbarians who preferred living in the wild. Fortunately, the weather was beautiful and the summer flowers were in full bloom.

I stood awkwardly off to the side while the other guests trickled in. Not only did I feel out of place standing there, but I also looked stupid. Maddie had chosen my dress, and while it wasn't taffeta, thankfully, dresses never did fit me right. My left shoulder is an inch higher than my right, so the dress hung on my frame at a slant. To make it worse, I kept catching myself slouching to offset the slant. I felt like a hunchback in pink Chiffon and contemplated scratching like a monkey to round out the picture.

"Hello there."

It was a voice I hadn't heard in weeks. And for the first time, it sent shivers down my body. Slowly, I turned around. Sarah.

She stood there wearing an off-white strapless satin dress, stark against her golden brown skin. She had a sassy new haircut, with highlights, and her neck was encircled by one of the necklaces I had sent her.

"Hi." I paused for a moment, not knowing what to say. Not knowing whether to say what I wanted to. I decided to go for it. "You look fantastic. I love your new haircut."

She blushed, and looked down at her feet. I stared at the flowers behind her, feeling like we were on a second date.

Several seconds passed in silence.

"How have you been?" It had only been weeks since she left, but it felt like years.

She smiled and shrugged. Then she started to laugh, which caught me off guard. "Maddie didn't tell you that she called me last week to insist I come?" She shook her head. "You know, Maddie, she has a way."

I laughed with her. "Tell me about it. I'm wearing a pink dress." I held out a part of the chiffon skirt.

It made Sarah laugh even harder. She had never looked more beautiful.

"By the way, how did she convince you to come? She pouted to make me wear this dress. And she got me drunk."

Sarah's eyes softened, and then she looked at the ground again. "She said you would be lost without me, and that you needed me. Don't worry, I know those were her words not yours; you would never say that." She smiled.

"She's right, though," I said quietly. "I am lost without you."

A few people approached and I played the hostess and directed them to the seating area. Sarah never took her eyes off me and I saw they were wide with pure shock. When we were alone again, she asked bluntly, "Did you mean that?"

"Yes." I stared directly into those beautiful brown eyes. "You know that phrase 'You never know what you have until it's gone.' Well, I learned the true meaning of it."

"Please, Lizzie, this is hard enough. The wedding … you … Maddie. Please don't play games with me." Her voice and eyes were pleading with me.

"I know you have no reason to trust me, but I'm not playing games."

Another couple approached. Sarah and I rushed through polite conversation and then I took her arm and directed her away from the wedding area. Screw being nice to my mother's friends, who couldn't even remember my name. Most of them didn't even know I was a member of the family.

When we found a private spot, Sarah pushed my arm away. "I don't understand you at all. If you felt that way, why didn't you try to call me?" The threat of tears choked her angry words.

"Sarah, you asked me not to contact you. I thought that after all I put you through, I could at least respect your last wish."

"I didn't want to talk to you."

I laughed but stopped myself, and looked at her, suddenly panicked that I had blown it again.

But a smile inched across her cheeks. "This is a fine mess. I'm crying, you look miserable, and your brother is getting married in less than an hour."

"True." I felt like we were in a soap opera. I fidgeted and then came to a decision. "How about we just enjoy this day together? You're here because Maddie gave you a guilt trip. I'm here because I have to be. Let's just make the best of it. At least there'll be cake."

Sarah smiled. "I do like cake."

I took her hand and we strolled back to the guests. A few heads turned, and for the first time, I didn't give a shit. I hoped my mother saw us holding hands at my brother's wedding on my birthday.

Sarah made pleasant chitchat with more arriving guests. She could charm the pants off of the pope, I thought, if he wore pants under his robe.

Out of the corner of my eye, I saw Maddie hiding behind a tree, waving for my attention. I whispered in Sarah's ear and gave her a kiss on the cheek. She smiled and continued making small talk with some of Maddie's guests.

Grabbing my arm, Maddie began to pull me frantically into her room. For the sake of tradition, Peter and Maddie had separate rooms the night before the wedding. Before I could say anything, she blurted, "I'm not going through with this."

I smiled briefly. The thought of my brother being stood-up at the altar pleased me.

"Calm down, Maddie." She was pacing back and forth. I thought for sure she would crash right through the wall.

My statement pissed her off. "Calm down …" She turned on me. "Calm down? Why should I calm down? What a fucking asshole. He had the gall to tell me to get used to it. That she wasn't going away." She kicked a trash can across the room. "What a fucking asshole!"

Dumbfounded, I asked her what she was talking about.

"Like you don't know. Everyone knows. He isn't very secretive about it."

"Seriously, what are you talking about?"

Maddie stopped suddenly and looked taken aback. "You really don't know."

I shook my head.

"He's cheating on me."

It all made sense instantly. That was why he was never home. That was why she would get a forlorn, lonely look sometimes. That was why she spent so much time in Fort Collins. How could I be so stupid and insensitive not to notice? In her hotel room, she said I was more like my family than I knew. Now I understood.

"Honestly, Maddie, I didn't know. I'm so sorry."

"I thought for sure you knew but were too nice to mention it." She collapsed into a chair. "He wants everything to be perfect. A perfect career. A perfect wife. Perfect kids. And a perfect mistress. I was just another piece of the perfect puzzle. He needed a beautiful wife to go with his perfect life. No one wants to marry the mistress. But this isn't the 1800s. Wives don't just look the other way anymore. I'm not your mother."

"What?"

"Really, Lizzie? Are you that oblivious to everything? Your father has been having an affair for years. You can't possibly think he works all of the time." She threw her arms up in the air, exasperated.

"I guess I never gave it much thought." I shrugged. The news didn't affect me. I felt no pity for my mother, no anger at my father. I had cut them from my life long ago. Their actions no longer had any impact on me.

"Peter even told me I should learn from his mother. She had everything she wanted: money, houses, rich friends, expensive vacations. But look at her, Lizzie, she's miserable. I don't want to be miserable." Her eyes screamed bloody-murder.

I wished Sarah were here; she would know what to say. I stood awkwardly and offered to tell Peter the wedding was off.

Maddie looked up at me. "No," she said.

"You don't plan on going through with it, do you?"

She laughed. "No, I don't. But I don't plan on telling him that. Let him stand up there and look like a fool. See how he likes it."

The image was delightful. I smiled and nodded.

"I saw Sarah with you."

"Yes, she told me you guilt-tripped her into coming."

"You really are clueless, aren't you?"

Instead of being offended, I answered, "Yes."

"Don't mess this up, Lizzie."

My confused look must have urged her to continue. "Yes. I guilted her, but she came, didn't she? She came. She still cares. Yes, she wants to make you suffer for a while. But she's a woman; that's what we do. Don't mess this up again. Are you ready to take the plunge?" She hit me in the arm.

I couldn't believe that one minute she was telling me she was not going to get married, and the next she was calling me a moron for ruining my relationship with Sarah.

"I hope not to ruin anything. But right now, what are we going to do?"

"I think I am going to leave."

"Where can I take you?"

"Lizzie, if you go with me, I think Peter will figure it out."

"Um, Maddie, I don't know if you noticed, but I'm not particularly close to my brother, or to anyone else in my family. I don't give a fuck what they think."

She threw me a look of relief and said, "Let me change out of this horrible dress." She rushed behind the changing screen.

"Okay, let me go get Sarah."

She popped back into view. "Bravo, Lizzie. You might not fuck this up after all."

"I hope not." I disappeared out of the room.

Sarah was in the same spot, talking to a new couple. I approached quietly, and when there was a break in the conversation, I excused us and directed her to Maddie's room. On the way, I quickly explained we were leaving with Maddie.

Sarah didn't even bat an eye. "Thank God," she said. "Your brother is such an asshole."

I almost said that it runs in the family, but decided against it. How had I been so oblivious to everything? It astounded me. Ethan was dead-on. I was self-absorbed.

By the time we got back, Maddie was ready to go. She had left the dress hanging in the room with a note that read,

"Give it to her."

As the three of us exited the room, The Scotch-lady approached. For once, she didn't have a drink in her hand. She looked naked, vulnerable.

"Going somewhere?" she hissed.

At first, I wanted to tell her to go to hell. Then I looked at her—looked at her properly for probably the first time in years. She looked small. Weak. Sad.

"Mother—" *What to say?* "I didn't know. I'm sorry."

She misunderstood. "Don't apologize. I'm happy to be rid of both of you." She glared at Maddie and then at me. "Really, I thought this would be one of the worst days of my life, but now I've killed two birds with one stone, wouldn't you say?" She cocked one thin eyebrow.

Her ire did not hurt. I felt sorry for her.

I considered giving her a quick hug. Maybe Maddie sensed this, because she yanked my arm away to save me from my mom's reaction if I did.

"That's right, Elizabeth. You better leave with your harem." She clenched her jaw. "It looks like we can have a proper Christmas party this year—just like I've always wanted. With you gone, things can be normal again."

I looked at her and bowed my head. Hopefully, that would make her happy, even if it were a fleeting happiness.

We piled into my car. It was only noon, and it was so nice out that I decided we should go to the mountains. Maddie was wearing jeans and a T-shirt, but Sarah and I were still wearing dresses. Not digging the pink dress, I had packed a bag of clothes to change into at the first opportunity. However, Sarah had planned on heading back to Fort Collins later that night, so had nothing to change into.

I pulled off I-25 at the nearest mall.

"Sarah, I think it's time I bought you clothes for once."

"Why? Where are we going?"

"If it's all right with you two, I thought we could go to Breckenridge for the weekend."

"That sounds fantastic, but I can't use my credit cards, or at least I don't think I can. I'm sure Peter will have them cancelled within minutes of finding the dress." Maddie looked despondent.

"You can count on that. No worries, though. He doesn't have access to mine. And since we are on summer break, Sarah and I don't have any classes on Monday. So we can make it a long weekend."

"I'm supposed to be on my honeymoon, so I don't need to be at work on Monday." Maddie sighed and looked out the window.

When we parked, Sarah hopped out of the car first. Maddie squeezed my arm and gave me an encouraging look. She whispered, "Happy Birthday."

Was my gift Sarah? Or was it Maddie jilting Peter at the altar? Maybe both.

* * *

Later that day, the three of us sat at a restaurant in Breckenridge. It was happy hour at The Whale's Tail, and that included ten-cent shrimp and cheap booze. All of us were gorging ourselves on shrimp and beer while Maddie filled Sarah in on the details. Even on the second hearing, I was kicking myself for being so stupid.

When Maddie had finished, Sarah said, "I suspected he was cheating, but I wasn't sure."

"Really?"

Both of them stared at me as if I were an idiot.

"What? Am I just totally blind or am I a fucking moron?"

"Yes," both of them said in unison and then laughed.

Maddie turned to Sarah and asked, "How's Haley?"

"What's wrong with Haley?" I wasn't sure I wanted to know. What if Sarah said they were dating? How would I handle *that* right then?

Sarah ignored me and answered Maddie's question. "Oh,

you are sweet to ask. She's doing better. And she got the restraining order."

Maddie looked relieved. I stared at her face and then Sarah's. "What's going on? Why did she need a restraining order?"

"Michael beat her up. I knew it was only a matter of time, but I couldn't convince Haley of that." Sarah looked on the verge of tears.

"Jesus ... Sarah, I'm sorry. Are you okay?" I placed my hand on hers.

She flicked a tear off her face. Maddie rubbed her back. How in the world did Maddie know about this when I didn't? Then it hit me: Maddie and Sarah were friends. I mean, they must have met up, like Maddie and I did. And I'm betting Sarah never considered that Maddie was hitting on her. Sarah probably knew that Maddie needed a friend and was there for her, like she was for Haley. When Sarah needed a friend, she turned to Maddie, not to me.

"I'm so sorry ... I didn't know how serious it was. Seriously, I feel like an asshole right now." I squeezed her hand more, hoping she would know how awful I felt.

"You're just extremely self-involved," Sarah said in a loving way, but her voice informed me that it hurt her.

Maddie's cell phone interrupted. She stepped outside to speak to her parents.

When I thought Maddie was out of earshot, I said, "Sarah, you thought Peter was having an affair?"

"Lizzie, how can you be so brilliant and yet so stupid? Of course! It was obvious. You just didn't pay attention. You really should pay more attention to the people around you." She withdrew her hand.

"I don't think I paid enough attention to lots of things I should have. Most importantly: you."

"Wow, you are being honest today, or a sweet talker. Am I a fool to believe anything you say?" She pushed her chair away from the table.

"I've had a lot of time to think." I fidgeted with my beer coaster. "Even Hank doesn't like me right now."

Sarah's eyes filled with tears again. "How is he?"

"He's good. He's been very bitey lately, though. Every time I pet him, he chomps my hand."

"Good! You deserve it." She slapped my shoulder.

Maddie came back to the table. "My parents are going to the house to get all of my stuff."

"Will Peter give them any trouble?" asked Sarah.

Maddie laughed. "Gosh, no. Peter is terrified of my father. He's big in the industry. It's how we met." She paused for a few seconds. "So, does anyone need a roommate, or know anywhere I can stay?"

"Well," I smiled, preparing to divulge my secret. "I'm buying a cabin in Idaho, an hour away from Jackson Hole. You're welcome to stay there for however long you want."

Sarah stared at me. I couldn't believe I'd suddenly blurted this out in front of her. After all the looking at houses we had done together, I went away for a week and bought a place.

Then she surprised me. She laughed. "Hmmm … I guess you are capable of buying a home. Or is it less scary if you call it a cabin?"

"Maybe." I chuckled and met her eyes. "Or maybe I liked that it is just a summer home. I'll have to close it up for the winters."

"Why Idaho?" Maddie asked.

"The area is beautiful. The cabin overlooks a lake. Also, I couldn't justify spending millions of dollars for a place next to the Tetons."

She nodded. "Thanks for the offer, but I still have to work."

Sarah stopped staring at me and said, "You can stay with Mom and me. She has a huge house."

Her response stung. I wanted Sarah back home, but the way she said it made me feel as if staying with her mom was a permanent thing. But I couldn't blame her. A few nice words wouldn't wipe away what I had done. The betrayal. It was going to take more. Much more. And it wouldn't be quick. My plan was to persevere and to take baby steps to show her how much I wanted her in my life.

"If you need a car, you can use mine. I'll ride my bike."

"Thanks, Lizzie, but my car is in my name. I insisted on that. And, Sarah, I'll take you up on that offer. Now, let's not talk about that asshole for the rest of the weekend. I'll have plenty of time after Monday to dwell on this. What did I miss while I was gone?"

I raised my beer and hid behind it while I drank. Sarah answered, "Apparently, every time Lizzie pets Hank he bites her." She couldn't help laughing.

Maddie hit my arm, too. "Good. You deserve it. What's this I hear about you thinking of moving out east and not telling Sarah about it?"

I slouched down low in my seat. "It was just an option I was pondering. And I admit, I was an asshole for not telling Sarah about it right away."

"Damn right you were an asshole. Seriously, Lizzie, that's a move Peter would have made." Maddie looked disappointed.

I started to defend myself but thought better of it. She was right. It was a smarmy move. And I was realizing I was more like my brother than I cared to admit. Neither of them had brought up the elephant in the room. How had Maddie convinced her to come to the wedding? Maddie must be more persuasive than I thought possible. Maybe the enormity of Maddie's decision had pushed aside the event from their minds. I wanted to believe that they would forget it entirely, forever. But life wasn't that easy. I was learning that. And I was learning that Maddie and Sarah were the best of friends. I had hit on Sarah's friend. Jesus, I was an imbecile.

"You were considering?" Sarah asked meekly, bringing me back to the conversation.

"I've decided there are other aspects of my life that I need to concentrate on, besides my research and career. For now, that choice is out of the hat." I answered, looking between the two of them.

"Out of the hat? What the fuck does that mean?" Maddie muttered as she shoved another shrimp smothered in cocktail sauce into her mouth. It was hard to believe she had stood Peter up earlier in the day. *Had she planned on doing it all along?* I wondered. If she had, the plan was brilliant, in a crazy, bitchy way. I remembered her referring to the wedding as a show.

"It means that, right now, I am not considering moving. And now I have a place to get away for weekends and stuff."

"So, down the road you may move?" Sarah stared at me earnestly.

"I don't know, Sarah." Having Maddie there helped me open up. Her candor and point-blank questions made me feel good, for once, about answering Sarah honestly. I was finally tired of hiding behind bravado. My family had hurt me so many times that I had started to lie about my feelings to everyone. To Sarah. To Maddie. To Ethan. And to myself. I was like an iceberg, with ninety percent of my real feelings submerged so no one would know how vulnerable I truly felt. I lied so much, and so often, that even I didn't know my true feelings anymore.

"No I don't plan on moving away." I looked at Sarah. "Who knows what next year will bring? But right now, I want to stay put. I have some shit to work out."

Sarah continued staring into my eyes for what seemed like an eternity. Then the muscles in her face relaxed and she looked at peace. "So, ladies, I am in the mood to shop," she said.

Maddie readily agreed, so I settled the bill and the three of us hit the main street of tourist shops. Most charged exorbitant prices for a Hanes T-shirt with some stupid slogan like "Don't Feed the Bears" and depicting a bear holding the sign with the word "Don't" crossed out, but I didn't even mind.

We wandered from store to store, laughing and giggling the whole time. That evening, we had a fancy dinner and stopped at a candy store on the way to the hotel to splurge on homemade fudge. Sarah picked out five different flavors and five pounds of fudge in total. I also bought her some chocolate-covered strawberries, which she had always liked. I couldn't remember ever having bought her any before.

Then we sat in the hotel room drinking wine and eating fudge until shortly after midnight, when we all collapsed with full bellies.

Maddie slept in a single bed, and Sarah and I shared. We both changed separately in the bathroom and then crawled under the covers, both aware of the excessive space between us in the bed.

I reached out and took Sarah's hand. She didn't pull it away.

That was the best day of my life.

* * *

On Monday afternoon, I drove Sarah and Maddie to Rose's house. Sarah had arranged for Maddie's parents to drop off her stuff and her car, and all the junk that didn't fit was put into a storage unit. I marveled at how wonderful Maddie's parents were. Not only did they not mind helping out, they actually wanted to help.

Her dad was flying out on the red-eye to get back to work, but her mom was going to stay for at least a week. Maddie wanted to have dinner with both of her folks before her dad left town, so she rushed inside to change.

Sarah sat in the car with me for a moment.

"Does she know where she's going in the house?" I asked.

Sarah laughed. "Yes. Mom and I had her over for dinner a few times." She paused. "You aren't the only one who had secrets." Her voice sounded triumphant, cunning even. It was sexy.

I laughed. I wanted to say, "I'll tell you mine if you tell me yours." But I didn't. We said our goodbyes and I watched her saunter into the house. She stopped at the door, turned, and waved goodbye. I waved back and sat in the driveway, staring at the door she had just walked through and envisioning myself running through the door, scooping her up and kissing her. I really wanted to kiss her.

Telling myself not to be stupid, I grabbed my cell phone and dialed her number. She didn't answer. I closed my cell phone. *Don't be stupid, Lizzie.*

I dialed again. Still no answer. I left a voicemail saying I would really like to take her to dinner sometime.

Then I hung up and sat in her driveway, staring at my phone. She didn't call back.

Later that night, I heard my cell phone vibrate on my nightstand. I rolled over in bed and read the message: *I'll think about it.*

Smiling, I rolled onto my back and stared at the ceiling. She'll think about it. I petted Hank and told him the good news. He bit my hand, and I laughed.

"You will believe in me," I said. "I'll make her believe in me again."

* * *

Two weeks passed before I received another text from Sarah. It simply read: *Pick me up Friday night at 7 p.m.*

She didn't ask if I was free. She didn't even ask if I wanted to go. Her boldness turned me on.

I showed up promptly at five minutes to seven and waited in the car with the candy I had picked up for her. At one minute to seven, I got out and walked up the driveway. A slight breeze kicked up some dirt and I watched an empty Coke can blow casually in several different directions.

An urge to run overwhelmed me.

I stopped dead in my tracks.

A car drove by and smashed the Coke can into smithereens.

Chuckling at the timing, I conquered my need to run and continued my journey to the door.

I heard laughter behind the door.

Sarah opened the door. Maddie and Rose stood behind her, laughing.

"We weren't sure you would get out of the car," Maddie exclaimed.

I smiled. Then I handed Sarah the candy. She wore a tight T-shirt and jeans, and her body had never looked so good. She turned to take the candy into the kitchen. While she was gone, her mother said, "Don't make me want to run you over with my car again."

I stood there awkwardly, wanting to explain but not knowing how to, until Sarah came back and we excused ourselves.

"Where are we were going?" Sarah asked as we climbed into the car.

"I thought we would go to dinner in Denver and then catch a late movie. There's a great foreign film theatre near the restaurant. I've heard good things about this French film playing there."

Sarah was fluent in French and loved French films. We never saw them, though, since I didn't like them.

"Really?" I detected excitement in her voice. "I thought for sure we would go to Phoy Doy again."

I guessed she had seen through much of my bullshit in the past, when I had attempted to appease her without really trying.

I smiled at her. "I thought a change would be nice. You might be out late, though. Will your mom send a hit man?"

"Oh, Lizzie, it's not Mom you have to worry about; it's me."

And she was right. It was her. It was finally all about her.

Author's Note

Thank you for reading *A Woman Lost*. If you enjoyed the novel, please consider leaving a review on Goodreads or Amazon. No matter how long or short, I would very much appreciate your feedback. You can follow me, T. B. Markinson, on twitter at @50YearProject or email me at tbmarkinson@gmail.com. I would love to know your thoughts.

Acknowledgments

I would like to thank my editor, Karin Cox. I am extremely grateful for all the hours she spent hunting for all of my mistakes and for her wonderful suggestions on how to improve the final product. Thank you to my beta readers who assisted me in the early stages. Lastly, my sincerest thanks goes to my partner. Without her support and encouragement this novel would not exist. Thank you for believing in me. I don't know where this road will take us, but I'm fortunate to have you by my side.

About the Author

T. B. Markinson is a 39-year old American writer, living in England, who pledged she would publish her first novel before she was 35. Better late than never. When she isn't writing, she's travelling around the world, watching sports on the telly, visiting pubs in England, or taking the dog for a walk. Not necessarily in that order. *A Woman Lost* is her debut novel.

49862701R00158

Made in the USA
Middletown, DE
22 June 2019